THE ~~PERFECT~~ DIVORCE

Jeneva Rose is the *New York Times* bestselling author of several novels, including *The Perfect Divorce*, *The Perfect Marriage* and *You Shouldn't Have Come Here*. She has sold more than four million copies worldwide, and her work has been translated into twenty-eight languages as well as optioned for film and television. She lives in Wisconsin with her husband, Drew, and her stubborn English bulldog, Winston.

BOOKS BY JENEVA ROSE

STANDALONE NOVELS

The ~~Perfect~~ Marriage

The Girl I Was

One of Us Is Dead

You Shouldn't Have Come Here

It's a Date (Again)

#CrimeTime (with Drew Pyne)

Home Is Where the Bodies Are

The ~~Perfect~~ Divorce

THE DETECTIVE KIMBERLEY KING BOOKS

Dead Woman Crossing

Last Day Alive

THE ~~PERFECT~~ DIVORCE

JENEVA ROSE

ORION

First published in the United States of America in 2025 by Blackstone Publishing
First published in Great Britain in 2025 by Orion Fiction,
an imprint of The Orion Publishing Group Ltd.
Carmelite House, 50 Victoria Embankment
London EC4Y 0DZ

An Hachette UK Company

The authorised representative in the EEA is Hachette Ireland, 8 Castlecourt Centre, Dublin 15,
D15 XTP3, Ireland (email: info@hbgi.ie)

3 5 7 9 10 8 6 4

Cover and book design by Sarah Riedlinger

A CIP catalogue record for this book is
available from the British Library.

ISBN (Trade Paperback) 9781 3987 2366 5
ISBN (Ebook) 9781 3987 2364 1
ISBN (Audio) 9781 3987 2365 8

Printed and bound in Great Britain by Clays Ltd, Elcograf S.p.A.

MIX
Paper | Supporting
responsible forestry
FSC® C104740
FSC www.fsc.org

www.orionbooks.co.uk

For my gaggle of geese.
May you fly high and stay silly.

DID HE KILL HER?

DOCUMENTARY TRANSCRIPT
CHANNEL 5 NEWS EXCERPT

The Prince William County Sheriff's Office is investigating the murder of a local woman. Earlier today, deputies were called to a residence on Lake Manassas, where the body of Kelly Summers was discovered brutally stabbed to death. Sources say novelist Adam Morgan, the residence's owner, was brought in for questioning shortly thereafter. The Prince William County Sheriff's Office has refused to offer any additional details as the investigation is ongoing.

INTERVIEWER

On October 15, it'll be eight years since the murder of Kelly Summers and her unborn child occurred. Her body was discovered the following morning in your lake house, specifically in the primary bedroom. Adam, can you tell us what happened the night Kelly was murdered?

ADAM MORGAN

No. I can tell you what happened before she was murdered, and I can tell you what happened after, but I don't know anything about her death.

INTERVIEWER

Then tell us what happened before.

ADAM MORGAN

Kelly came over after work, and we did what we usually did when she came over. We had a few drinks, and we had sex . . . several times.

INTERVIEWER

And what happened after?

ADAM MORGAN

I woke up in the middle of the night. It was pitch-black out. Kelly was still sleeping, or at least, I thought she was. I knew I had to drive back to DC, and I didn't want to wake her, so I kept the lights off while I got ready, and then I took off.

INTERVIEWER

Not before writing a letter to Kelly. Is that right?

ADAM MORGAN

Yeah, that's right. I left it on the kitchen counter for her, not realizing she'd never have the chance to read it.

INTERVIEWER

What was in the letter you wrote to Kelly?

ADAM MORGAN

It doesn't matter anymore . . . She's dead.

INTERVIEWER

When did you learn of her death?

ADAM MORGAN

The following day. Officers from DC Metro and the Prince William County sheriff's department showed up at my house in DC, and even then, I didn't know. It wasn't until I was brought in for questioning that they informed me.

INTERVIEWER

Who was Kelly Summers to you?

ADAM MORGAN

In the simplest terms . . . my mistress.

INTERVIEWER

Some people have speculated that if you're capable of lying about one thing—for example, your affair—you're capable of lying about another.

ADAM MORGAN

That's quite the leap. Lots of people cheat, very few murder.

INTERVIEWER

Are you one of those few people?

ADAM MORGAN

I've already told you I'm not.

INTERVIEWER

A jury found it implausible that you'd be able to sleep soundly beside Kelly while she was stabbed thirty-seven times. They also found it highly unlikely that you'd overlook her mutilated corpse when you left in the middle of the night. What do you say to that?

ADAM MORGAN

Does a patient undergoing surgery in a hospital notice when their stomach has been sliced open? No, they don't, because they're under anesthesia. Kelly and I were drugged that night. I don't know by who, but someone drugged us. And as I said, when I came to, it was still pitch-black out; I couldn't see a thing.

INTERVIEWER

The toxicology report indicated Kelly had GHB in her system, but yours came back clean.

ADAM MORGAN

I'm well aware.

INTERVIEWER

How do you explain that?

ADAM MORGAN

The sheriff's office should be the one answering that question because they conveniently waited until after the window of detection lapsed before testing me.

INTERVIEWER

Are you saying that it was intentional?

ADAM MORGAN

Maybe. Or maybe it was just sloppy police work.

INTERVIEWER

Do you believe you were set up?

ADAM MORGAN

Yes.

INTERVIEWER

By who?

ADAM MORGAN

There are quite a few possibilities. Kelly's husband, Scott, for one. It could be whoever that third set of unknown DNA belongs to, the one found inside of Kelly. There's also Bob Miller, the brother of her first husband. Any one of them could have done it.

INTERVIEWER

But not you?

ADAM MORGAN

No, not me.

INTERVIEWER

Can you tell us what was going through your head when the verdict was read aloud?

ADAM MORGAN

I knew my life was over, and I . . . I couldn't believe it. You hear about these people on the news that were wrongfully convicted. But you never expect to be one of them. I didn't murder Kelly Summers, and I will continue to fight against that lie until my last breath.

INTERVIEWER

The Innocence Project declined to take on your case. Why do you think that is?

ADAM MORGAN

I don't know. You'd have to ask them.

INTERVIEWER

So, Adam, what's your plan B then?

ADAM MORGAN

There is no plan B. I just have to keep fighting, keep appealing, and keep the hope that one day my conviction will be overturned.

INTERVIEWER

You still have hope?

ADAM MORGAN

I do. It's the one thing they can't take away from me.

INTERVIEWER

You were famously defended by your former wife, Sarah Morgan. Does she still have hope?

ADAM MORGAN

Sarah is my wife, not my former wife.

INTERVIEWER

My mistake. Yes, your wife, Sarah. You've been on death row for the past seven years, yet she's remained married to you—why do you think that is?

ADAM MORGAN

Because Sarah loves me, and she knows I'm innocent.

1

SARAH MORGAN

I knew when I married Bob, I would divorce him one day, because men are like lawyers. They can't be trusted. And I would know because I am one . . . and so is he. My husband sits across from me at a conference table made for twenty, but there are only four of us in this room today: myself, Bob, and our respective lawyers. I'm trying not to look at the man I spent the last twelve years with. However, I can feel his dark eyes on me, so I meet his gaze just to make him look away. The top two buttons on his starched white shirt are undone, and his tie hangs loosely around his neck. Despite the cool temperature of the room, droplets of sweat cling to his hairline.

"My client is interested in reconciliation." Brad pushes up the sleeve of his jacket, showing off a solid-gold Rolex Day-Date. It's like he's trying to say, *Look how good of a lawyer I am.* He sports slick blond hair and a clean-shaven face, the complete opposite of my husband's dark locks and five-o'clock shadow. Brad is Bob's lawyer, longtime friend, and full-time slimeball. He's known for cutting corners to get the results he wants, which is fine because so am I.

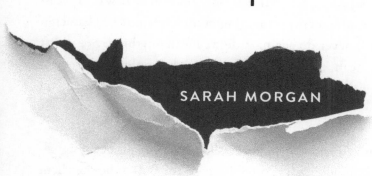

"That's out of the question," Jess says firmly. She cocks her head and sits up a little taller in her chair. Jess is my lawyer, and she does everything by the book. The yin to my yang.

"Sarah, it was one time." Bob clenches his jaw and rubs harshly at his brow as though he's trying to wake himself from a bad dream. But this is our life now, our reality, and he's the one that put us here. "I promise," he adds. "It was just one time."

Isn't that what they all say? It was only one time. It was an accident, an error of judgment, something completely out of character, something they'll never do again. It didn't mean anything. *She* didn't mean anything. Yeah, that is what they all say, but only once they get caught. They're not sorry for what they've done. They're sorry that you know what they've done. And Bob's no different. He's just like the rest of them.

Brad gives him a knowing look and slightly shakes his head, signaling for him to stop talking. I can tell it's hard for Bob to be the client and not the lawyer, but he concedes—letting out a deep sigh as he leans back in his chair and folds his arms over his chest.

"I'd like to reiterate that my client accepts full responsibility for his major error in judgment and has agreed to attend six counseling sessions in order to move forward with reconciliation," Brad says, steepling his hands in front of his face. Streaks of sunlight pierce through the partially open blinds, glinting off his Rolex, making a kaleidoscope of light dance across the wall each time he tilts his wrist.

"Your client should have attended counseling sessions before his infidelity." Jess purses her lips and slowly slides a piece of paper across the table. "These are Ms. Morgan's demands."

Bob uncrosses his arms and leans forward, snapping up the paper before his lawyer can. He narrows his eyes and puckers his forehead as he scans the page. I can tell he's not liking what he's reading, which is exactly the point.

"Absolutely not," Bob scoffs, flinging the paper. Brad catches it as it's still floating in the air and smooths the sheet out on the table.

"We believe it's a fair offer," Jess says.

Brad lifts his head and stares back at her. "My client is not giving up custody of his daughter. He's also not relinquishing his seat on the Morgan Foundation board, nor his stake in the charity."

"I'm not giving up on us . . . period," Bob pleads. He extends his hand toward me, hoping I'll meet him halfway, but I don't reach for it. Instead, I remove my hands from the table and fold them in my lap.

"Sarah, please," he adds.

I bite my tongue to stop myself from responding because I know silence hurts him more than any quip I could ever possibly make. And I want to hurt him as much as he's hurt me.

"My client has no interest in reconciling the marriage," Jess clarifies.

Brad leans over to Bob and speaks in hushed whispers. Bob's face grows more upset with each word. His skin flushes, and his sharp jawline becomes even more prominent as he grinds his teeth.

When they finish with their little chat, Brad clears his throat and straightens in his chair. "Since we don't seem to be making any progress, I think we should reconvene at a later date."

"These meetings are not intended to repair the marriage, nor will they, Brad. The only progress we should be making is coming to an agreement on the division of assets and custody of Summer. I'd like to reiterate that Ms. Morgan requested a clean, quick, and private divorce. We do not wish for this to be dragged out, nor for it to be disputed in court, but we will if we have to," Jess says, her mouth forming into a hard line.

And with that, I stand from my seat, smoothing out my skirt and rebuttoning my blazer.

"Noted," Brad says, packing up his briefcase, an ostentatious and garish orange Hermès piece. "I'll have my assistant reach out to set up another meeting."

Bob rises to his feet and meets my gaze. He's a foot taller than me with wide shoulders and a toned physique. The salt-and-pepper look really works on him, same with the stress wrinkles lightly etched into his forehead. He appears wise and distinguished even though he doesn't act like it.

"I'll give you a call later, Sarah," Jess says as I start toward the door.

I pause and acknowledge her before leaving the room.

"Sarah, wait," Bob calls out, trailing close behind me.

I keep walking, ignoring him entirely—but then, all of a sudden, a hand is on my shoulder, stopping me in my tracks. My heart hammers against my rib cage.

"Please," he adds.

I let out a heavy sigh and turn to face my husband. I can barely even see him standing in front of me because he's already a part of my past. He just doesn't realize it yet, and I don't know how I can make it any clearer.

"What?" I ask.

There's no emotion in my voice because anything I felt for my husband vanished the instant I learned of his infidelity.

"Please don't do this," Bob says in a strained whisper.

His eyes frantically search mine, like they're trying to lock us back in place. But there's no place in the world for us anymore because I can't be married to someone I don't trust. To me trust is like glass. Once you break it, you can't put it back together—and even if you tried, you'd end up cutting yourself in the process. So, you may as well just throw it away.

"You're lucky the worst thing I'm doing to you is divorcing you." My words come out soft, almost soothing.

"Is that a threat?" he asks, his face turning incredulous.

"You know I don't make threats, Bob."

He furrows his brow and starts to puff out his chest, challenging me, but I've seen enough. I shake my head as I turn on my heel and walk toward the elevator. He calls out my name several times, his voice growing quieter as I put more distance between us—or maybe it's just losing its conviction. *Good. I hope that's the case.*

Bob is really testing my patience. All I wanted was a quick and quiet divorce—kind of like his affair, I suppose. But no, he has to fight me every step of the way because he thinks this is something we'll be able to work through. It's not, and deep down, Bob knows that too. I've tried to remain civil; I really have—for the sake of our daughter, who's still blissfully unaware of our imminent divorce. I've put off telling her, wanting to wait until it's a done deal and raw emotions have waned, so the focus can be on her and only her. I seem to be the only one that cares about our daughter's feelings and well-being.

At the elevator, I press the Down button and wait for it to appear. I can still feel Bob's presence, but I don't look back. I truly wish things were different. They were supposed to be different. Parenthood is supposed to make you want to be a better person, or at the very least, make you *think* you're a better person. Motherhood changed me just like I knew it would. But apparently, becoming a father did nothing for Bob. He didn't only cheat on me. He cheated on our family. And he pretended to be something he's not capable of being—decent.

The elevator dings and opens. I step inside, hit the Lobby button, and raise my chin, staring back at Bob. He stands at the end of the hallway, his eyes fixed on mine like we're in the midst of a showdown. His face is a mixture of resentment and sorrow, but there's a glimmer of something else, something I've seen before. I just can't place it. Neither of us breaks eye contact until we're forced to by the closing doors.

The elevator hums as it begins its descent, putting even more distance between us. We've been together for more than a decade but married for a little over a year. Bob's lucky I'm not the same woman I was when I was with Adam, my first husband. If I had had children with Adam, maybe he'd still be around. Because, as I said, becoming a mother changed me, and I know they say people can't change. They can though. At the core, we are who we are—but that doesn't mean parts of us can't soften or harden over time.

2

UNKNOWN

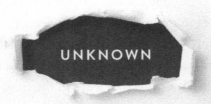

The room is so dark, not even shadows exist here. That's the first thought I have when my body suddenly jerks and my eyes spring open. I blink several times, hoping they'll adjust and find something familiar—but without light, there's nothing. I hold my hand in front of my face, just inches from my nose, but it's barely even visible, a gray figment that my mind hardly recognizes. The air is thick and damp, reeking of mildew and wet socks. I pull myself into a sitting position and press my hands down at my sides, feeling the slight give of a spring mattress. The coils sink under the pressure before rising back into place.

My head throbs, and a harsh wave of dizziness washes over me. I feel sick, like I could throw up at any moment. I rub my fingers against my temples, willing the memories to come back. But they won't. They're gone—maybe for now, maybe forever. *What happened last night? Did I drink too much? Did I get my hands on some LSD or E again?*

"Hello?" I call out into the void as I shift my weight and stand shakily.

The pads of my feet leave the thin mattress and settle onto a cold, hard surface. I take a cautious step forward, and that's when I hear it—the sound of metal dragging across concrete. I try to move farther into the darkness, but my leg is jerked back abruptly. A sharp pain pricks at my ankle, the metal cuff digging into my skin.

"What the fuck?" I reach down and feel the cold shackle. The realization that it's clamped around my ankle, locking me in place, brings on a sudden panic attack. My pulse races and my breaths come out quick and hard. I shiver despite sweat oozing from my pores. "No, no, no . . . HELP! Somebody help! Please!" The tears fall fast, and I scream until my throat is raw and all the air is out of my lungs.

Collapsing onto the mattress, I grab at the chain and yank and tug as hard as I can, shredding the skin on my hands in the process. "Come on, you piece of shit, let me go!" I scream, hoping there's a weak link or that it'll pull free from whatever it's fastened to.

I crawl forward, following the chain to its source—a thick metal pole cemented into the concrete floor. Standing, I run my hands up the pole as high as I can. It must be a support beam that extends to the ceiling because I can't reach the top of it. I return my attention to the chain, feeling my way along the length of it. Tethered like a satellite in orbit, I only have about six feet of slack to move in any direction.

With my hands out in front of me, I start to explore my surroundings. A wall appears, and I place a palm against it, following the coarse concrete until the chain cuffed around my ankle is pulled taut.

"Shit!" I grumble as my shin smacks into something hard. I lean down until the tips of my fingers touch it, feeling a smooth circular rim. It's a bucket, a heavy-duty plastic one you'd pick up at a hardware store. I continue my search. My hands skim across a rough, grainy surface—wood, I think. Something nicks my palm, and I jerk away. Wincing in pain, I bring the wound to my mouth and suck on it until the pain subsides. The tinge of blood leaves a metallic taste in my mouth.

I return to the mattress and pull my knees into my chest and cry, rocking back and forth as I weep. My hand grazes a blanket—no, a sleeping bag. I grab it and cocoon it around my body, shielding me from the dark hell I've woken up in.

3

SARAH MORGAN

My heels click across the tile floor, sending echoes throughout the old building, continuing even after I've left. I pull a pair of sunglasses from my purse and slide them on, shielding my eyes from the climbing sun. My office is just a short walk away in Old Town Manassas. A lot of things in my life have changed, not just me. I'm no longer a named partner at Williamson & Morgan in DC. My choice, not anyone else's. I was tired of having a man's name in front of mine and equally tired of defending depraved individuals with far too much wealth. You can truly get away with anything if you have the means. I'm proof of that, and so are my former clients.

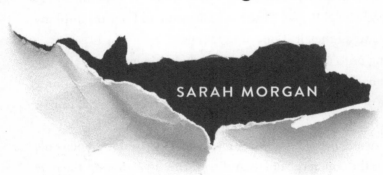

I didn't give up practicing law though. I just gave up who I was practicing it for. My work now is all pro bono—which I prefer because it's more of a challenge. I'm the founder and executive director of a charity called the Morgan Foundation. The words *charity* and *Morgan* in the same sentence must sound odd, an oxymoron of sorts, but they shouldn't. There are a lot of perks in charity work—tax benefits, a polished public image, political influence, and so much more. All of it wrapped up in a sweet bow disguised as goodwill. And the name Morgan? I'm sure you have questions about that. Why keep it? Why name my charity after it? Well, funny enough, Morgan is my maiden name. I never took Adam's, and he never cared. His mother did, but not him. When Adam got his first book deal, he decided to use Morgan as his pseudonym—*Rumple* just didn't have the same air of sophistication. His mother was livid, but what she hated even more was when Adam made it official by legally changing his last name. So, that's why it's called the Morgan Foundation: because *Morgan* is mine, and it always has been.

Bob still works at Williamson & Morgan, except now it's Williamson, Miller & Associates, as he made named partner earlier this year. It took me leaving the firm for him to achieve my position, and even then, it was Williamson & Associates for a long time. It appears that we were never a match to begin with because I outmatched him.

Arriving at a brick building a few blocks away, I take the elevator to the top floor. It opens to a waiting area and a large desk shaped like a crescent moon, where Natalie, the foundation's receptionist, sits. A glass partition wall is positioned behind the desk, separating the atrium from the rest of the office. The foundation's name is etched into the frosted glass, the letters capitalized and bolded.

"Good morning, Sarah," Natalie says, standing from her chair with a smile. She's young and driven, with a can-do attitude and an eagerness to please—ideal traits for someone in her position. Her auburn hair is pulled back in a low bun, and she wears a sleek all-black outfit.

"I set up your nine o'clock in the conference room," she quickly adds.

I furrow my brow and eye my Cartier watch, noting the time. It's twenty past nine. Natalie won't point out that I'm late, but I am late—and that's not like me at all. I respect time more than anything as it's our most valuable resource. Money comes and goes, but time only goes. Not a lot of people realize that. When you give someone your time, what you're really giving them is a piece of you, and that's why you have to be careful with it.

"Alejandro Perez, our fiftieth reformer," Natalie says, thumbing through a stack of papers wedged in a folder before handing it to me.

I scan the pages, familiarizing myself with the content.

"Sarah, I know you have a lot going on." She pauses and gives me a sympathetic look. "So, if you want, I can . . ."

"No, I got it," I say, cutting her off.

"Okay . . . Oh, and your coffee." She plucks a large to-go cup from her desk and extends it to me.

I thank her and round the corner of the glass partition, walking farther into the Morgan Foundation. It's airy with high ceilings, exposed beams, and large arched windows. It's modern meets rustic with a touch of minimalism. There aren't any cubicles because I've never liked them. Who wants to work in a box? That's something we get buried in, not something we should spend our life in.

The floor plan is open concept—save for two corner offices and a large conference room set in between them. The bigger office is mine, and the other one belongs to Anne. Yes, I kept Anne around. She's a great asset because she does what she's told and doesn't ask questions. Plus, it's hard to find someone you can trust these days. Everyone has an angle, something they want and something they're willing to give up to get it. But Anne's not like that. Her role here is much larger than it was at Williamson & Morgan. She's no longer my assistant. She's the office manager and serves on the board of trustees.

Several employees take notice of my presence and pause their work, greeting me with smiles and hellos. I exchange brief pleasantries with each of them. They're proud to work here because we make a difference. I have a staff of twenty, half of which are lawyers and paralegals. The other half supports the reform side of the Morgan Foundation, which is what really put us on the map, and it's why we have so many patrons. Our donors are not just investing in the futures of those selected for the reform program, they're investing in their own futures—because every criminal we reform is one less criminal that's a drain on our system and a detriment to our society. So far, we have a perfect track record, and I hope Alejandro will continue that streak. Through the opaque glass, I can only see the back of his head as he's seated in a conference chair facing the window.

I again flip open the folder to a mug shot of "Case Fifty." He wears no expression, despite sporting a strong jaw and sharp, angled features. His eyes are the color of fresh sage plucked from a garden, a stark contrast to his jet-black hair. A canvas of tattoos adorns his neck, continuing underneath the opening of his shirt. I can't help but wonder how far down they go. In another life, Alejandro could have been a model. Maybe he still can be with the help of my foundation. I skim through the rest of his file, reviewing his criminal record, work history, and application to the program, complete with a written essay.

"Hey, how'd the meeting go?" a voice calls out.

I look up from the folder to find Anne walking toward me. Her shiny bob bounces, and her A-line navy-blue dress sways with each step.

"It went as well as the last one," I say in a hushed voice.

My personal life isn't something I like to talk about with my employees, but Anne's more than an employee. She's a friend, so she knows what's going on with me. I think Natalie does too, but that info was learned from her snooping since I certainly didn't confide in her.

Anne shakes her head in dismay and follows me into my office, which is basically a carbon copy of what I had at my old firm. There's a treadmill in the corner, a plush sitting area off to the side, and an oversized, overfilled bookshelf lining an entire wall. I set my stuff down and pull open a set of blinds. The view is of Baldwin Park and the Manassas Museum, half blocked by a large parking garage. It would have bothered me years ago, but it doesn't anymore. A view is only a view until you stop appreciating it, and eventually, we all do.

"So, what happened?" Anne asks. "Is Bob still groveling?"

I swiftly pull the cord on the last set of blinds, making them snap against the window frame.

"Yeah, and he still thinks we can reconcile," I say, turning to face Anne. "We're making no progress because he's treating these divorce proceedings like they're counseling sessions."

She rolls her eyes. "What is wrong with him?"

"Well, for starters, he's a man."

"True." Anne tilts her head, giving me an amused look. "Why are men?"

I squint, waiting for her to finish.

"That's it. That's the whole question. Why are men?" She chuckles.

I crack a smile and shake my head. My gaze catches Alejandro's folder lying on my desk—a reminder of where I'm supposed to be and what I'm supposed to be doing.

"I've got to go onboard Case Fifty."

"I can take care of that."

"No," I say, retrieving the folder. "You know I like being hands-on. As the founder, it's important that I show how invested we are in each and every case."

"Have you seen him?" Anne takes a step back, leaning her head out my door, pretending to peer in his direction. She pulls her head back in and says, "I'm invested."

"Anne," I warn, half joking, half serious.

"What? I'm kidding . . . mostly. But don't tell Jamie I said that," she says with a laugh, referring to her partner.

"Your secret is safe with me," I say as I exit my office and make for the conference room.

"Let me know if you need any assistance." Anne winks as she splits from me, heading toward her own office.

I pause outside the room where Case Fifty is waiting. My hand rests on the handle for a moment, and I let out a heavy sigh before I enter. Alejandro is on his feet in an instant with his hands clasped together in front of him.

"Sorry to keep you waiting," I say, closing the door behind me.

"Not a problem. I'm used to waiting." He softly smiles.

I don't return it. Instead, I extend my hand out for a shake. I expect his to be firm and hard, but it matches mine. Clearly, he's trying to show me respect.

"I'm Sarah Morgan, founder and executive director of the Morgan Foundation."

"Alejandro Perez, inmate number . . ." He stops himself midsentence, and his cheeks flush. "Sorry, force of habit . . . Umm, it's nice to meet you."

I politely smile to put him at ease. "Well, we're here to kick that habit and ensure you never have to refer to yourself as a number again," I say as I round the table and pull out a chair.

He nods, and I notice he doesn't sit until I'm seated. I lay out his case file as well as a stack of brochures and a large manila envelope before meeting his gaze. The light reflecting through the window catches his eyes, making them appear even brighter than they were in his mug shot.

"First, I want to congratulate you, Alejandro, on being selected for our reform program."

"Thank you. I'm really grateful for this opportunity, and please call me Alex. The only ones that call me Alejandro are the police and my mother."

"I'll keep that in mind, Alejandro."

He tilts his head, squinting for a moment, before relaxing his face into a neutral position. Boundaries are important, especially in cases like this when you're working with people who don't respect boundaries. The law is a boundary, and Alejandro has pushed a lot of them in his life.

"Now, let's review how the program works. Everything you need is in here," I say, sliding the thick manila envelope across the table. "Go ahead and open it."

Alejandro undoes the clasp and slips his hand inside, pulling out a set of keys.

"That goes to your mailbox, apartment, and vehicle, which will be covered by the foundation for the next six months. The apartment comes fully furnished with a washer and dryer in unit, plus a stocked fridge and all your basic necessities to get you started."

His hand disappears into the envelope again, and he pulls out a debit card.

"There's one thousand dollars loaded on there to assist with any additional expenses. It should cover you until you're able to secure employment."

Alejandro nods and flips through the stack of brochures.

"Those are all the resources available to you, as well as information on what's required of you to stay in the program. You must actively look for work. In your file it says you're not a drug user, but you will submit to a drug test every three weeks. If you fail even one test, you're kicked out of the program. If you get into any legal trouble above a simple traffic violation, you're kicked out of the program. You're also required to attend a therapy session every week. Your first one has already been scheduled for you, and it's noted in your agenda."

He retrieves the planner from inside the manila envelope and lays it on the table, examining it.

"Do you have any questions so far?" I ask.

His eyes skim over the keys, agenda, brochures, and debit card, but his expression remains unchanged, like he's not sure what to make of this.

"This is too much," Alejandro says, gesturing to everything on the table. "How can you afford this? And I'm your fiftieth case?" He pulls his head back like he can't believe the good fortune he's just fallen into.

"It's not too much. There are a lot of people in this world that want to help."

"Whose apartment am I staying in, and whose car am I driving?"

"The Morgan Foundation owns a fleet of used vehicles and a large number of properties, so it doesn't belong to a single person. Since our program is six months, we cycle our reformers in and out," I explain.

"Reformers . . ." He smiles. "Makes me think of *Transformers*."

"Yeah, well, that was already trademarked." My mouth starts to curve into a grin, but I quickly extinguish it. As I clear my throat, my gaze falls to his chest and biceps. The tight white T-shirt he's wearing leaves very little to the imagination, and it's obvious he spent his time in prison working out.

"What happens after the six months is up?" he asks.

"You'll be financially responsible for yourself, but the Morgan Foundation's resources will continue to be available to you for as long as you need."

Alejandro tilts his head to the side. "And this is how you fix a bad person?"

His question catches me off guard, and I find myself locking eyes with him again, just for a moment—but in that moment, it feels like we can see into each other's souls. I wonder what he sees in mine.

"No. This is how we give a person who did bad things a second chance to do some good ones."

My cell phone vibrates against the table. *Unknown* is displayed across the caller ID, which is not uncommon in my line of work. A fair number of incoming calls come from prisons, jails, police officers, and burner phones—all of which share the same inviting caller ID.

"I have to take this," I say, picking up my phone and turning my chair slightly away from him. I hit *Accept* on the screen and press it against my ear. "Sarah Morgan speaking."

A heavy breath vibrates through the receiver, and I can almost feel the exhale, as though the person on the other end were in the room with me. Looking over my shoulder at Case Fifty, I notice he hasn't taken his eyes off me.

Turning away, I say, "Hello," into the phone.

"Sarah." A husky voice comes through, one I immediately recognize. It's lost the authority it once held. Life can do that to you. For most, we break down slowly over years and decades—but for some, it happens all at once. He falls into the latter group.

"I need your help," he says.

"With what?"

He exhales noisily. "I don't know exactly, but I've got a gut feeling I'm going to need your legal services."

"Where are you?"

"I'm at the Prince William County Sheriff's Office . . . in their custody."

"I'm on my way," I say, ending the call.

I let out a small sigh as I start to collect my things, pausing only to address Alejandro.

"I'm sorry to cut this short, but I have to go. One of my associates will finish up," I explain as I get to my feet.

"Is everything all right?" he asks.

"No, but it will be."

4

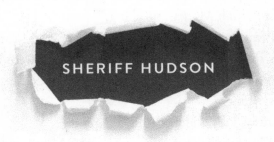

SHERIFF HUDSON

I shake my head at the sight of him standing in front of the inmate calling station with a phone pressed firmly to his ear. He leans against the cinder-block wall to keep himself upright. One of my deputies is positioned off to the side, arms crossed, waiting for the inmate to finish. He was brought in early Tuesday morning. It's Wednesday now, and he's finally woken up from his bender.

My hands ball into fists, but I steal a quick, deep breath and flex my fingers, my knuckles cracking as I bend and straighten them. He's lucky I've got a better handle on my emotions these days. Besides, he's already in a world of hurt, so I don't need to do any further damage, no matter how pissed I am—not only at him but also at myself. If I hadn't given him so many chances, this never would have happened. My deputy makes eye contact with me and stands a little taller, inflating his chest.

"I got it from here," I say, relieving him of his duty.

"Yes, Sheriff." He nods and leaves the room just as the inmate hangs up the phone, his head lolling forward.

I rest my hand on Ryan's shoulder, applying a small amount of pressure. "Let's go, man."

Former sheriff Ryan Stevens lets out a heavy exhale and briefly glances over his shoulder at me. His hair is shaggy and unkempt, going in all directions. Rosacea colors his cheeks, and there's a tinge of yellow to his bloodshot eyes. He drops his gaze, looking down at his feet.

It used to be him giving the commands around here. But not anymore. Things change, and apparently, so do people—for the worse, that is. Ryan *was* slipping for a while there. Then about a year ago, he started spiraling out of control, and it didn't take long for the community to notice their sheriff was a drunk. At first, they took pity on him, but that didn't last long either. There was a petition, a protest, and finally a recall around five months ago. He was out, and shortly thereafter, I was elected as the new sheriff.

I motion for him to walk, and Ryan obliges, barely lifting his feet as he trudges down the hallway. He's quiet other than his labored breaths and his shoes scuffling across the epoxy floor.

When we reach the holding area, he asks, "How long was I out for?"

It's our song and dance, but unfortunately, there's no more music.

"Nearly thirty hours." I unlock the door to his cell; its hinges squeak as I pull it open. Ryan shuffles in, rubbing at his forehead.

"Jesus," he says as he plops onto the two-inch-thick mattress covering the metal bunk. He slumps forward, resting his elbows on his legs.

I widen my stance. "They're gonna bring you in for processing shortly."

Ryan twists his lips, and his brows shove together. "What do you mean 'processing'?"

"You know exactly what I mean."

"I thought you had my back," he says, his head wobbling back and forth.

"Not this time, Ryan."

"Why *not* this time?" His eyes are unsteady, skirting all over the place, like he's realizing this six-by-nine cell could be home for the foreseeable future.

"Because you hit someone with your truck."

His jaw goes lax, and he takes a few beats to speak. "I . . . I don't know what happened."

"I do. You got shit-faced drunk . . . *again*, got behind the wheel, and plowed into a woman out on an early-morning run." My remarks come out louder and harsher than I intended.

"Is she all right?" His voice cracks, signaling his fear.

"No, Ryan . . . she's dead."

He sits motionless as the words hang in the air, swirling over his head. I'm waiting for him to realize the severity of his actions, to understand nothing will ever be the same again. He should be full of shame and guilt and despair because he killed someone, whether he remembers doing it or not.

Finally, his eyes widen as the words worm their way into his brain. "No, that—that can't be true," he stammers.

"It is," I say, shaking my head.

Ryan buries his face into his hands and a cry begins from deep within him.

"I'm sorry," he sobs.

"Yeah, so am I."

If I hadn't kept giving Ryan the benefit of the doubt and letting him off with warnings each time he was picked up for DUI, an innocent woman would still be alive. I'm just as guilty as he is.

Click. Click. Click. Click.

I've heard that sound before.

Click. Click. Click. Click.

It's a woman's heels. Obviously, a lot of women wear heels that make that clicking sound. But this is different. This is slow and methodical. This is a woman walking with purpose. She moves like she has someplace to be, but that place doesn't matter until she occupies it.

I turn to see the figure increasing in size as she comes down the corridor, escorted by a deputy. Her chin is held high. It always is. Her long blond hair slightly curls at the ends, bouncing with each step. She wears clothes perfectly tailored for her body with not a wrinkle in sight.

Sarah Morgan.

"You called Sarah?" I ask, incredulous.

Ryan stares back at me but doesn't say a word. The tears have stopped, and his self-pity is quickly morphing into desperation.

It's been a while since I've occupied the same room as Sarah Morgan. I've seen her in passing, but we haven't really spoken. I know she founded a charity because I've read the puff pieces in the newspaper. I just don't trust her. I never have, and that's why I've kept my distance. Ryan would be wise to do the same.

"Deputy Hudson," Sarah's voice calls over my shoulder. I turn to find her standing in the doorway, her verdant eyes skimming over me in assessment.

"It's *Sheriff* now," I correct.

I'm sure she already knew that, and this is just one of her power plays. She observes the badge pinned to my chest before meeting my gaze. "So it would seem. Congratulations."

I simply nod in return because talking to Sarah is like talking to the police during an interrogation—the less you say, the better.

"But as sheriff," she adds, "you must know that speaking to my client without his attorney present is a violation of his constitutional rights." Her scarlet-painted lips form a hard line.

My chest tightens and the skin beneath my collar starts to perspire. A droplet of sweat trickles down the length of my back, sending a shiver through my spine. "Right. I was just leaving," I say as I step aside and head for the door.

5

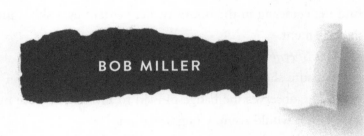

BOB MILLER

"What are my chances of getting full custody of Summer?" I already know the answer, but sometimes you just have to hear it from someone else, like my lawyer, Brad.

We've known each other since we were in law school—where we both did whatever we could to get ahead. It's probably why we're still friends, tethered together by the terrible things we've done.

Brad sits across from me in a café situated in downtown Manassas. He bites into a piece of dry toast, revealing veneers that are a shade too white. Crumbs tumble into his lap, and he quickly brushes them to the floor. My food has gone mostly untouched; I'm still too angry to eat. I can't believe Sarah has the gall to demand full custody, especially given our history. It's an emotional move on her part, completely out of the norm for someone like her.

Brad finishes chewing before he speaks. "Virtually zero," he says, patting his lips with a napkin. "Unless you can prove Sarah is a danger to Summer." He pauses and arches a brow. "Has Sarah ever been violent with Summer?"

The question swirls around my brain, kicking up old memories—well, one, to be exact. It plays out in front of me, as vivid as the day it happened, and I think that's because this was an event that changed the course of my entire life.

Brad and the café fade away, and there I am, standing in front of Sarah Morgan's office, late at night, over a decade ago. Everyone was gone for the evening—even Anne, which was rare because those two were attached at the hip. My knuckles rapped lightly against the door, as I didn't want to appear too eager. I had a plan in mind, and the manila envelope clutched in my hand would set the whole thing in motion.

"Come in," Sarah called from the other side of her office door.

I didn't hesitate to enter, and my presence immediately garnered a look of disappointment. Not surprising, though, because we weren't fond of each other in the slightest.

Her gaze fell to the papers strewn about her desk, signaling she wasn't going to give me her full attention. "What, Bob?"

"I have something for you," I said, crossing the room and placing the envelope right on top of Sarah's case files, my way of showing her that I did, in fact, deserve her full attention.

She paused, eyeing it suspiciously. We were sworn enemies at that point because we were both trying to climb the same corporate ladder. She was ahead of me, having made named partner earlier that year. That promotion wasn't supposed to go to either of us since there were two associates with more seniority—but mysteriously, one was fired for misconduct and the other quit without notice. I always thought she had something to do with them losing their jobs. Partner at thirty-three? Ha! It's only possible if you eliminate the competition, and she was my competition, so I needed to get rid of her.

"What's this?" she asked, trying to act disinterested.

"Just open it."

She hesitated, but then curiosity got the best of Sarah, and her long red nails slipped under the metal clasp, gently bending the prongs back. Opening the flap, she slid her hand into the envelope and pulled out the stack of photographs. I watched her face, studying it, waiting for it to change as she flipped through each one. A trembling lip. A tear forming in the corner of her eye. A furrowed brow. But nothing changed. She was stoic, and it was as though she were reviewing a case rather than intimate photos of her husband with another woman.

"Where did you get these?" she asked, still flipping through them.

"Let's just say . . . I keep close tabs on the woman your husband is having an affair with."

That got her attention, and she met my gaze, slightly narrowing her eyes. "Why?"

"Because she killed my brother."

Sarah lifted a brow and returned the photos to me. "If that's true, why isn't she in prison?"

"Because not everyone pays for their crimes." I cocked my head. "As a lawyer, you, of all people, should know that."

She leaned back in her chair, placing her elbows on the armrests and steepling her hands in front of her face. She was quiet for a moment. I had no idea what she was thinking since her reaction wasn't at all what I'd expected. I thought she'd be inconsolable and destructive, ready to scorch the earth. But no, not Sarah.

"Why'd you tell me this?" she asked.

"I just figured you should know . . . I'm sorry." It took everything in me to offer her my condolences because I didn't mean it. I sealed it with a sympathetic look, hoping she believed it.

"No." She squinted. "I know why you think *you're telling me this, Bob."*

"What?"

"You thought I'd freak out, take a leave of absence, get tied up in some messy divorce, lose my focus. And then what? You'd swoop in and take my partnership."

"Sarah, no. That's not true at all," I lied. She had me pegged, always one step ahead, too smart for her own good.

"It is, and it's exactly why you think you shared this information with me." Sarah leaned forward in her chair, drawing me in with her intense green eyes. I couldn't help but stare back.

"But I know why you actually shared it with me."

I gave her a confused look.

"You want what I want, Bob."

"And what is it you think I want?"

"Revenge." The corners of her lips perked up, forming the most sinister

smile, instantly putting me under her spell. I knew things would be different between us after that. They couldn't not be.

"Bob?" Brad says. He waves a hand in front of my face, forcing the past to melt away and my surroundings to return. "Has Sarah ever been violent with Summer?"

"No." I shake my head. *Not with Summer.* I don't say that part out loud, though, because for now, that's only between me and Sarah.

I sip the mug of lukewarm coffee and pick at my food, selecting a piece of cold bacon.

"What about instances of neglect? Has she ever forgotten to pick Summer up from school? Anything like that?"

I let out a heavy sigh, trying to exhale the guilt and fear that have consumed me ever since I was served with divorce papers. Honestly, I thought Sarah would serve a bullet right through my forehead if she ever found out—so I was shocked that her response to my infidelity wasn't lethal. And that's what I'm holding on to. That's why I think we can find our way back to each other. If she didn't love me, she would have killed me.

"No, Sarah's a wonderful mother," I say.

"Then why do you want full custody, Bob?"

"I don't. I want my family back together."

Brad creases his brow. "I think we're past that. We've already met with her and her lawyer three times now, and she's not budging at all. And have you noticed her list of demands grows longer the more you drag this out? If you continue, eventually, she's going to want everything."

"She's just angry."

"She's not though. She's indifferent, which tells me it's over. The faster you can accept that, the faster you can move on."

I stare at him with unwavering eyes. "I can fix this."

"And if you can't?"

"Then I'll fight like my life depends on it."

Brad cracks a smile. He thinks I'm trying to be funny, but I'm not. I will have to fight like my life depends on it because, with Sarah, I know it does.

6

SARAH MORGAN

“Walk me through what happened,” I say, crossing my legs at the ankles.

Ryan Stevens is seated across the table from me in a private visitation room, unable to hold eye contact.

“I don’t remember anything,” he says, looking down at his lap like he’s searching for the answers he lost at the bottom of a bottle.

“I’m not surprised to hear that, since your BAC level was 0.28 percent. You’re lucky you didn’t die from alcohol poisoning.”

“Wish I would have.” He shrugs.

I narrow my eyes at him. “Don’t go saying that around any of your old buddies. They’re not your friends anymore. They are the law, and you are a criminal. And if they hear you make any threats of self-harm, you’ll be put on suicide watch, which would destroy your chance of making bail.”

“Is that even a possibility?”

I flip through the report, deducing as much as I can. “I haven’t had time to review this in full yet, but from what I gathered, it is a possibility. It’s just not going to be easy.”

“I figured as much,” he says, resting his elbows on the table and propping his head up with his hands. “So, what’s your plan?”

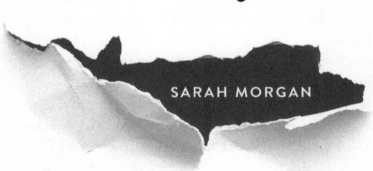

I close the folder and slip it into my bag, giving myself a moment to think. I probably shouldn't be helping him for several reasons. It's not a good look for the foundation, especially considering he's the former sheriff, and more than likely he'll be charged with aggravated involuntary manslaughter. But Stevens and I have history, a bond that tethers us to one another, even if he's not aware of it. So, unfortunately, it is in my best interest to help him.

"The commonwealth is going to paint you as a degenerate drunk who's so reckless with your own life, you've become a danger to society. What I will try to do is paint you as the complete opposite, a storied hero sheriff who slightly lost his way but is deserving of a second chance."

"Is anyone going to buy that?" he scoffs.

"Maybe. Maybe not. But that's the part you let me handle," I say with a nod. "If the autopsy on the victim comes back with any abnormalities that could suggest she was impaired in some way, we might be able to assign her partial fault. However, a jury will most likely check out the minute we try to blame the dead woman. But my team will look for witnesses, review surveillance footage from the area, check road conditions at the time of the accident, and sift through the police report with a fine-tooth comb. If any errors were made during your arrest that could get evidence or even the case thrown out, we'll find them."

"It sounds like the only way I'm getting off is through some lucky break," he says.

I tilt my head, eyeing the sorry sight before me. "That's a fair assessment."

"What do I do now?"

"You sit tight while I go to work. Given your police background and that this is your first serious offense, you do have a good shot at making bail. So, I'll start—"

My phone vibrates against the metal table, slowly dancing itself in a circle. *Jess* lights up across the screen.

"It's my lawyer. I need to take this," I say, gathering my belongings and getting to my feet. I head for the door and knock several times, signaling to the guard that I'm ready to leave.

"You have a lawyer?" Stevens asks. "For what?"

I glance back at him. His brows are shoved together in confusion.

"Divorce."

I click *Accept* and press the phone to my ear. "Sarah Morgan."

"Wait," Ryan calls out.

"One second, Jess." I mute the call before meeting his worried gaze.

"Shoot it to me straight. What are my odds of walking away from this?" He shifts uncomfortably in his chair.

I tilt my head to the side and squint. "Do you remember my former husband's case?"

"Yeah."

"Your odds are worse than his."

7

BOB MILLER

My house doesn't feel like home anymore, and that's probably because I'm not welcome here—even when I come bearing gifts like the bouquet of red roses clenched in my left hand. The seat at the head of the kitchen table as well as the recliner in the living room are no longer inviting. I shake my head in dismay, noticing that Sarah's taken down all the photos I was in, replacing them with ones of Summer or ones with Sarah and Summer together. My footsteps echo like they're taunting me as I walk to the big bay window that overlooks the lake. This view used to bring me peace, but now I don't know what it brings me. With no wind today, the water looks like a sheet of glass, fragile enough to shatter if I just dipped a finger into it. The clouds are dark and heavy, almost ready to fall apart. I could say the same for myself. First, my marriage. Then, these clouds. And then me.

They should be home any minute, and I'm sure my wife won't be pleased to find me here, but my daughter will. Sarah and I agreed to keep up appearances for Summer's sake, at least until everything's settled. For Sarah, that means divorce and going our separate ways—that's what she tells me. For me, that means fighting for our marriage.

A sharp pain radiates in the palm of my hand. I wince, realizing I've clutched the thorny stems too tightly, and switch the flowers to my other hand. A drop of bright-red blood seeps from the wound. Bringing it to my mouth, I suck on it until the bleeding subsides. This is the fourteenth bouquet of roses I've brought Sarah. She does the same thing with them every time, but I hold on to the hope that one of these days she's going to trim the stems and place them in a vase full of water.

The front door opens, and Summer sprints through the house, straight down the hall toward her bedroom, without even noticing me. A moment later, my wife appears, carrying a bag of groceries.

I move quickly, attempting to take the bag, but she refuses, tightening her grip on the handles and jerking away. "I don't need your help, Bob."

Sarah's favorite conflict style is a full-on attack, but her second favorite is obstinance, which I find to be extremely annoying. She thinks if she allows me to help her, then she's caving and her anger is subsiding. So, she won't accept anything from me—not a gift, a helping hand, a compliment, a suggestion, nothing.

Kill her with kindness, I remind myself as I force a smile and extend the flowers to her. "These are for you."

Sarah rolls her eyes and begrudgingly takes them. Maybe this is the day, the day they get fitted for a vase. She sets the groceries and her purse on the counter and moves around the island. I think she's heading for the sink and that they're finally going to get trimmed, watered, and rehomed. But no, she stops right in front of the trash and presses the toe of her stiletto against the garbage can lever. The lid pops open, and she tosses the bouquet into the bin, smashing the flowers down to make a show of it.

I can't help but sigh in frustration as I unpack the groceries. They're mostly ingredients for what I assume will be tonight's family dinner, spaghetti and meatballs, which she knows I hate. And I'm sure that's the exact reason she chose it. Sarah fills a pot with water and places it on the stove, sprinkling a palmful of salt into it.

"Can we talk?" I ask.

"We probably shouldn't without our lawyers present," Sarah says, igniting the burner.

"Don't give me that. We *are* lawyers. They're just there to make sure we don't kill each other."

She swivels her head in my direction, raising a brow at my choice of wording. Other than that, she doesn't react. At the island, Sarah pulls a large kitchen knife from the butcher block. The globe pendant lights above the counter catch the blade, making it gleam.

I exhale, letting the air out of my puffed-up chest, and lower my shoulders to present a calmer demeanor. The macho-tough-guy act has never worked on Sarah. If anything, it only further pisses her off—which is the last thing I need if I'm ever going to make this work.

With a cutting board and knife in hand, Sarah gives an *ahem*—her passive-aggressive method of telling me to get the hell out of her way. I step aside, giving her the space she demands.

"I just want to talk," I say, leaning against the counter opposite her.

She sets an onion on the chopping block and readies her knife. The blade slices through it with ease, thudding against the wood.

"You never even let me explain," I add, trying to get her to talk to me.

Sarah rocks the blade back and forth, quickly dicing the onion. She meets my gaze, wearing an expression so tense, it appears she's made of stone. The knife continues to slap against the cutting board, growing louder as she puts more force behind each chop.

"That's because there's nothing to explain." Her voice is emotionless, like she's reading from a legal document rather than discussing our broken marriage.

"Yes, there is."

"Like what, Bob?" She tilts her head. "Aside from you calling it an 'accident,' what other explanation do you have for fucking some girl in a hotel room?"

I let out a deep sigh and move toward the island so I'm standing straight across from her, staring into her hardened eyes. "It was a mistake, the biggest one I've ever made, and I swear it didn't mean anything. *You* are the only one that matters. It was a big night for me, and I was wasted.

I don't know what happened. One moment, I was giving a speech, and the next, well . . . I don't remember, and I don't remember her either."

"Is your lack of memory supposed to comfort me?" The onion has practically turned to mush due to her incessant hacking, but she keeps going anyway. I'm sure she's picturing me under that knife—or some delicate part of me.

"No, not at all. I'm just saying that it . . . won't ever happen again, *ever*." I lean over the counter, reducing the space between us, hoping my proximity will break through to some small understanding part of the emotionless statue before me.

"You're right about that, Bob, because you can't cheat on an ex-wife."

"Sarah, come on." I reach my hand out for hers, but she jerks away, and the knife slashes across my palm. Blood oozes from the fresh cut, and I clench my fist, yelling, "Jesus, fuck."

"Sorry," she says coolly. "It was an accident." There's no sincerity in her voice, and the faintest smile settles on her face.

She puts the knife down on the cutting board and plucks a hand towel from the drawer beside her, extending it to me. "Make sure you wipe up all your blood."

I hesitate for a moment, my eyes locking on her. They say there's no difference between a scorned woman and the devil himself, and I believe it—because I can't tell which one I'm looking at.

I take it from her and mumble, "Thanks."

"My pleasure," she mocks.

Sarah continues with dinner prep like nothing happened while I wipe up the drops of blood from the counter and tightly wrap the towel around my hand. She grabs a frying pan from the cupboard and places it on the stove, turning on another burner. It clicks several times before an open flame dances beneath the pan, licking at the metal. I need to keep her talking because if we talk, maybe we can find our way back to one another.

"Please don't be so rash. When you found out what . . . happened, you didn't even confront me. You didn't question me. You didn't yell at me. We didn't have a single conversation about it. You just quietly filed for divorce. Come on! Who does that?"

"I do," she says, adding a drizzle of olive oil to the pan, followed by the mushy onions.

"We have a daughter. I know you're pissed at me but think about Summer."

Sarah sifts through the spice cabinet, collecting an array of seasonings. "That's exactly who I am thinking about and why I filed for divorce rather than taking some other course of action."

My wife only has two forms of aggression—passive and completely and utterly destructive. I guess I should feel lucky that she's chosen to use the former since she can't stop reminding me of that. Her reflection in the microwave mounted above the stovetop is a warped version of the woman I know. Maybe it's who she's always been, but I just can't believe that.

"I'm not giving up that easily," I say, squaring my shoulders and lifting my chin to convey my fortitude.

Sarah sprinkles thyme onto the simmering onions, then turns to face me. She angles her head in a condescending manner. "Eventually, you will."

"Mom, Dad!" Summer calls out as she barrels into the kitchen, dressed in a one-piece swimsuit and a pair of shorts. She's slender with long blond hair and bright-green eyes, and she looks more and more like her mother every day. I just hope her appearance is the only attribute she takes after Sarah.

Our attention goes to our nine-year-old daughter, the one thing tethering Sarah and me to each other. And perhaps the only reason my wife slashed me with the knife instead of completely gutting me.

"Can I please, please, please go swimming?" she begs.

The water boils over, hissing and simmering against the hot stovetop.

"Shit," Sarah groans. She quickly tends to it, reducing the heat on the burner and laying a wooden spoon across the pot to dispel the rising foam.

"That's a bad word, Mom," Summer teases. "You're not supposed to say bad words."

"I know, sweetie. Sometimes adults *accidentally* do things they're not supposed to do," she says, briefly glaring at me. "Dinner will be ready soon, and your father hurt himself, so why don't you help him set the table."

Summer gives me a sad look when she sees the bloody towel wrapped around my hand. "Dad, you're bleeding. What happened?"

"I slipped up," I say, my eyes darting between my wife and my daughter.

Sarah pays me no mind, busying herself with dinner prep, while Summer tries to get a better look at my injury. I unwrap the towel, revealing the bloody slash across my palm, two or so inches in length.

"That's gnarly, Dad," she says with a mix of intrigue and disgust. "You need a Band-Aid. No, more like five of them. I'll get the first aid kit." Before she even finishes her sentence, Summer's already bolting toward the hall.

"At least someone in this house still loves me," I say, hoping my wife will admit that she still cares about me, but she doesn't. Sarah adds premade meatballs one at a time to the frying pan, pretending like I'm not even in the room.

8

SARAH MORGAN

The dishes clang against the metal basin as I drop a handful of dirty plates and silverware into it. Bob offered to help me clean up, but I sent him outside to keep an eye on Summer. I just didn't want him around me anymore, and there's only so much groveling I can take. I squirt dish soap into the sink and turn on the faucet. The looming storm has held off for now, but from the kitchen window, I see the sky has darkened to the shade of coal, and the wind is starting to pick up. It'll be here in no time because a storm this big rarely passes.

While waiting for the sink to fill with water, I walk into the living room and flick on the news. It's a welcome background noise to keep me up to date. I assume Ryan's arrest will have leaked by now. Given the seriousness of his crime and that he's the former sheriff, some local station will be clamoring to report on it first. Death and scandal always sell, and in a town of fewer than fifty thousand, their value is even higher. Returning to the sink, I begin handwashing the plates first. We have a dishwasher, but I don't trust it to do a good enough job. Most things you just have to clean up yourself.

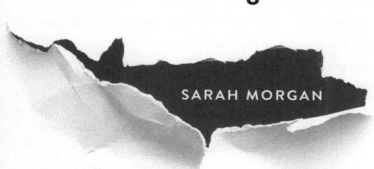

The back deck door slides open, and Summer dashes in, wrapped in an oversized towel, leaving behind a trail of wet footprints as she beelines out of sight and down the hall.

"Careful, Summer!" Bob calls out. "And make sure you hang your swimsuit over the shower rod," he says, closing the glass door behind him.

"I will, Dad!" Summer's muffled voice reverberates from the other end of the house.

I look to Bob, my expression asking, *What happened to swimming?* Without me needing to speak, he explains, "The wind picked up and the lake was colder than someone expected."

I return my attention to the sink, glancing out the window above it. A fissure of lightning flashes across the sky, followed by a crack of thunder seconds later. Rain bursts from the clouds all at once, hammering down with no mercy. Neither of us reacts to the storm outside because there's already a much more powerful one brewing in here.

"A few boards on the back deck need to be replaced." Bob slips his hands into the pockets of his slacks and rocks back on his heels. "Actually, the whole thing should be replaced. I don't want Summer getting hurt, so I'll work on that."

He's clearly looking for an excuse to spend more time here.

"Bob, you don't even own a drill," I quip.

"I meant I would hire someone to fix it."

"It's fine." I blow a piece of loose hair out of my face. "I'll take care of it."

He presses his lips firmly together and takes a small step into the kitchen. "Can I help with anything?"

I shake my head and scrub harshly at a pan coated with oil.

"How about a glass of wine?" he asks.

I want a glass of wine, but I don't want one from him. I don't want anything from him, except his signature on a set of divorce papers. "No, I'm fine."

Bob lets out a tired sigh, lingering between the dining area and the living room. I can feel his eyes, begging me to meet his gaze. They're practically burning a hole in my skin, but I don't look. I just keep scrubbing.

He finally gives up, and his feet pad against the floor, growing a tiny bit quieter as they reach the rug in the living room. My eyes briefly land on him as he plops down on the couch. The back of his head blocks out a chunk of the TV screen, and I wonder if he sat there just to annoy me, but I don't say anything. You have to pick your battles, and he and I are already at war.

A pretty news anchor appears on the screen with a graphic over her right shoulder that I can't fully see because of Bob's big head. I rinse off a pan, set it in the drying rack, and fish out another dirty dish from the sink.

"Breaking news out of Prince William County," the anchor announces. "Former sheriff Ryan Stevens has been arrested on suspicion of DUI and vehicular manslaughter . . . but that's not even the worst of it. Channel 5's Gretchen Waters is live outside the sheriff's office with the latest."

Just as I expected. The news finally hit, although I'm assuming Sheriff Hudson kept it buttoned up as long as he possibly could.

The screen cuts to a young reporter with glossy brown hair and a bold lip, standing in front of the Prince William County Sheriff's Office. The reporter presses a finger to her ear, waiting for her cue to start. There's clearly a slight delay. When the signal comes through, she drops her hand, positions her mic a few inches from her mouth, and puts on her most serious reporting face.

"I'm standing outside the Prince William County Sheriff's Office, where longtime former sheriff Ryan Stevens was taken into custody early Tuesday morning on suspected DUI and vehicular manslaughter charges. According to the police report, Stevens was heavily intoxicated when he ran a red light, striking and killing local forty-four-year-old woman Jackie Clarke, who was out on an early-morning run. We send our deepest condolences to the friends and family of Jackie Clarke."

I return my attention to the sink and continue washing a dish, my hand moving the wet sponge in slow, soapy circles.

"About an hour ago, we received an anonymous tip pertaining to the arrest of former sheriff Ryan Stevens," the reporter continues. "According to our source, Stevens's DNA profile was entered into the Combined

DNA Index System to establish if it was a match to evidence collected from a hit-and-run accident occurring late last summer, which took the life of fifty-seven-year-old Tim Redding. No link was found, and that case remains open. However, in a bizarre turn of events, Stevens's DNA profile matched evidence connected to a double homicide case that happened more than a decade ago."

The dinner plate slips from my hand, shattering against a pot soaking in the sink.

"Turn that up," I yell.

Bob frantically reaches for the remote and increases the volume.

"Twelve years ago, the murder of Kelly Summers and her unborn child rocked this small community for its brutality and highly publicized trial proceedings."

My eyes widen as I dry my hands with a dish towel and slowly walk toward the television—where the past is rearing its ugly head. This is what I was afraid of. I could kill Stevens right now. I probably should have years ago. He was always a slippery loose end.

"Former sheriff Ryan Stevens led and oversaw the Summers homicide investigation and quickly zeroed in on literary author Adam Morgan, who had been having an affair with the victim. Her body was found in his home, and he was the last one to see her alive," the reporter continues. "Adam was famously defended by his wife, Sarah Morgan, a high-profile DC attorney, but was found guilty and ultimately received a death sentence. The case was further publicized after Netflix released the docuseries *Did He Kill Her?*—which detailed the events surrounding the murder of Kelly Summers and the trial that followed.

"A little over a year ago, Adam Morgan was executed by lethal injection. The discovery that former sheriff Stevens's DNA profile matches evidence collected from the victim's body calls into question the validity of the case against Adam Morgan. So the question now is, was the wrong man put to death? We'll have more on this story as it develops. I'm Gretchen Waters with Channel 5 News."

Bob turns slowly in his seat, his mouth parted and his skin ashen. My hands start to tremble. This is the last thing I need right now . . .

another problem. I take a couple of deep breaths, trying to calm myself so I can think.

"Sarah." Bob's voice shakes. "We should talk about this?" It comes out as both a question and a statement.

"No, we shouldn't," I say because I already know he can't be trusted.

9

SHERIFF HUDSON

"Who the fuck leaked this to the media?" I yell to the room full of my subordinates. Clutched in my hand are the results of the DNA analysis that links Stevens to the Summers case, the same one Channel 5 News reported on last night. The papers flap against one another as I hold them up, shaking them. The bullpen is dead quiet, save for phones ringing off the hook. Each call goes unanswered, though, because everyone is frozen in place, scared to make the first move and attract unwanted attention. Their eyes dart, never landing on me. Even Chief Deputy Olson stands quietly off to the side, looking down at her boots, her hands clasped together. She's the one that keeps me calm, but right now, she's giving me the space to vent. Olson knows we're in deep shit too, but she doesn't know just how deep that shit is—because she wasn't around when all this happened.

I always knew there was something off with the Kelly Summers case. Nothing about it ever felt right. I had my theories. This wasn't one of them though. Back then, I tried to dig into it, but I didn't get far. I was too green, too low on the totem pole. And Stevens kept me at a distance, under the guise of there being a potential conflict of interest, given my friendship with Kelly's husband, Scott, who was chief deputy at the time. I know now that was all a load of bullshit.

"Someone better speak up now!" I yell, my heart hammering in my chest. It feels like it's constricting with each passing second. The more my thoughts race, the more my chest seems to tighten. I feel like I'm losing control of my station and maybe even myself.

"We're a team," I say, my voice harsh and firm. "We're a unified front. We plan out what information we share and how we share it. What we don't do is leak things outside of this station. Why?"

I walk to the windows and turn to face my full shift of officers before tugging the blinds open. Six news vans are parked outside, and I'm sure there are more on the way. Broadcast cameras are in position, and reporters armed with microphones are standing at the ready. We're in the center of a media circus, rather than in front of it, thanks to some jackoff who decided to take matters into their own hands.

"That's why!"

Several officers jump at the sound of my knuckles cracking against the glass. It *is* the public's right to know this type of information, but there's a reason we have procedures. This should've been shared via a press conference, not a segment on the nightly news.

I toggle the cord, and the blinds drop, snapping against the windowsill. "Who leaked it? Who!? I wanna know right goddamn now!" I pace back and forth in front of my team, waiting for one of them to step forward.

"Sir," a meek voice calls from somewhere in the back. It's one of my rookies, a thin little thing but reliable. He slowly rises from his desk, stammering a bit.

"Spit it out, Deputy Lane. I don't have time for this."

Lane clears his throat and cautiously glances around the room at the other officers. It's obvious from the look on his face he's already regretting speaking up. "We received the CODIS results after the news segment aired, so the leak had to have come from the lab."

Lieutenant Nagel takes a step forward, lifting his chin. He towers above everyone and sports a strong jaw and an even stronger work ethic.

"Lane's right, Sheriff Hudson. The results were delivered to us after it hit the news."

I squint and move my mouth side to side, stealing a quick glimpse at the lab report clenched in my hand. The delivery timestamp reads 9:42 p.m., and the news segment aired just a few minutes after nine. *They're right.* The leak must have come from the lab, not here. Someone over there probably thought we were gonna cover it up to protect one of our own—so they took matters into their own hands. I could put an officer on finding the person responsible, but from an optics standpoint, leading a witch hunt wouldn't make our department look good, and we already don't look good as it is.

I pull my lips in and nod at Deputy Lane and then Lieutenant Nagel. The deputy retakes his seat, and Nagel falls back in line with the group.

Drawing in a deep breath, I hold it for a few seconds before exhaling. Some of the tension in my shoulders dissipates, just enough to stop me from continuing to use my team as a punching bag. They didn't cause this massive screwup. Most of them weren't even old enough to drive when Kelly Summers was murdered. Shit, it's been over twelve years now.

"All right," I say, my voice calmer this time. "We need to get ahead of this, so the Summers investigation will be reopened in its entirety, and I'll need all hands on deck. If you didn't work here when it happened, get up to speed. If you did, refresh your memory. I want everything from that case pulled, and I mean *everything*. Witness statements, trial notes, testimonies, police reports, every single shred of evidence. Understood?"

"Yes, Sheriff," the room says in unison.

I stand there for a moment, my eyes flicking to each person to ensure the seriousness of my words will sink in. "Good. Now, get to work."

My team wastes no time because we've got no time to waste, immediately scattering in all directions. I head for my office and slam the door closed behind me.

"What the hell did you do, Ryan?" I question the empty room, shaking my head to punctuate my frustration. Even if Stevens were here right now, he'd give me some bullshit answer.

I toss the lab report on my desk and collapse into my chair, staring at the fissured ceiling tiles, wondering how this all happened. Stevens spiraled horribly in the last year or so—but was he ever good? I can't understand how he could have had an affair with his chief deputy's wife. You don't do that to a fellow badge. And what would Scott Summers think of this? Has he heard the news that his former boss betrayed him and may have even had something to do with his wife's death? Actually, is he even still alive? He quit the force and left town shortly after the trial. I never heard from him again.

I walk to one of the filing cabinets lined up against the wall and pull open a metal drawer, thumbing through the folders until I land on the one I'm looking for. I graze a finger over her last and first name printed on the tab of the case file. *Poor Kelly.* I thought maybe we got it right, that we got justice for her, but honestly, the whole investigation never sat right with me. It was too easy. And then there was that mess of a trial. I don't know much about the court side of the law, but Sarah Morgan acting as her husband's defense attorney in a homicide case was clearly a conflict of interest, and the commonwealth never even challenged it. Maybe that was because the evidence was stacked against Adam, and the case seemed open and shut, or maybe it was Stevens pushing it through. Who knows? It was a quick trial too, one of the quickest I've ever seen. Most homicide cases take years to build before court proceedings even begin. But not with the Summers case.

I take a seat at my desk again and splay the folder out in front of me. It's not the complete file, just key details. The fact that we'll have to go through this entire case again—word for word, every piece of evidence, every transcript, every police report and testimonial—is overwhelming, to say the least. Plus, reinterviewing witnesses and suspects will be nearly impossible considering how long ago this happened. It's going to be a lot of tedious work for this office, and more than likely, it'll all be for nothing.

I lift my head, looking at the half dozen filing cabinets along the wall. There are dozens more in the archive room. Once this swells in the media and lawyers smell blood in the water, every single investigation that has Ryan Stevens's signature on it, hundreds upon hundreds, could be up for appeal—depending on what other bullshit he pulled throughout his tenure.

Two knocks on the door save me from my spiraling thoughts.

"Come in," I say.

The door partially opens and my admin, Marcy, pokes her head in.

"Sheriff Hudson, we've got reporters in the lobby demanding you come out and make a statement. I've told them you're busy, but I don't know how much longer I'll be able to keep them at bay."

I let out a heavy sigh and say, "It's fine, Marcy. I'll give them a statement."

She delivers a sympathetic smile. I get to my feet and follow her out of my office, through the bullpen, and down a long corridor leading to the front of the station. My hands ball up into tight fists, so taut it feels like my knuckles could tear right through the skin, revealing white snowcapped mountains. I stop in my tracks. There's no way I can give a statement right now, not without doing something else first. Shaking out my hands, I break away from Marcy.

"Sheriff, the media's out front. Where are you going?" Marcy calls, noticing I've veered off.

"To talk to Stevens," I say, and I hope that's the only thing I'll do to him.

10

BOB MILLER

"Damn!" Brad says.

I take a seat in the chair in front of his oversized desk. I know he bought this thing to make himself look bigger, but it has the opposite effect as he appears minuscule sitting behind it. He's spared no expense decorating his office. The lighting is dim, producing more of a warm glow. His degrees are in gold frames hung prominently behind him, UW–Madison undergrad and University of Chicago Law School. A bar cart in the shape of a globe is within his reach. It sits open, revealing an assortment of expensive scotches and a set of crystal glasses. Floor-to-ceiling bookshelves fill an entire wall, lined with leather-bound spines twinkling with gold foil lettering, all the legal texts one could ever need.

Brad looks up from his phone screen. "This is going to be messy, and it could result in a huge settlement. Is that why you're telling me? Are you trying to delay the divorce to collect on a potential wrongful death suit?"

I give him an incredulous look and lean forward in my chair.

"No, Brad. You know I don't want a divorce at all, so it isn't about money. But this"—I gesture to the news article detailing Ryan Stevens's connection to the Kelly Summers case pulled up on his phone—"is a problem."

He notices the bandage wrapped around my hand and eyes it suspiciously. "What happened there?"

"It was an accident. I cut myself," I lie, letting my arm fall to my side. I don't even know why I'm lying or why I'm still protecting Sarah. I mean, after the news broke, she practically threw me out. She seemed scared—no, terrified. Her brain was working overtime like cogs in a machine being pushed to their limits. I tried to tell her that we'd be stronger as a team. But Sarah didn't want to hear it. She said she needed time to think and told me to leave, so I did.

"Okay . . ." Brad says. "But how is the Kelly Summers case a problem?"

I blink several times, trying to decide how much I can reveal to him. I'm not sure how to play this because I don't know what Sarah is going to do or if she'll do anything at all. Will she wise up and be a unified front with me, like we always said we'd be? Or will it be every person for themselves? Together, we'd be unstoppable, but apart, I don't know what we'd be.

"It's just . . . the timing of all of this is a problem. Sarah and I going through a divorce, and then this leaks. Plus, at one point, I was a suspect."

"But you were obviously cleared," he says.

"Yeah, in that investigation, which was led by a sheriff who was screwing the victim. Kelly and I had history too, and I'm sure that's going to get brought up again." I rub my brow.

"What do you mean you two 'had history'?" Brad careens his head, confused at this new information.

Brad's in the dark about that time in my life. He was living in another state when this all happened, and we'd lost touch. When he moved to the DC area around five years ago, we reconnected, but I never mentioned any of it to him. Why would I? It was in the past and it was supposed to stay there.

"Her real name wasn't Kelly Summers." I pause, knowing the impact this is going to have once it leaves my mouth. "It was Jenna Way."

His eyes go wide. "Get the fuck outta here!"

"I'm serious."

"Jenna Way? That bitch that killed your brother?" Brad shakes his head, leaning back in his chair. "Talk about karma."

I nod, even though I know karma had nothing to do with her demise. It's not always the universe that ensures what goes around comes around.

"Your history with Kelly—or Jenna—is circumstantial at best. It's not enough to pin anything on you, especially if there's no other evidence tying you to her murder."

"I know, and I was in Wisconsin, nine hundred miles away, when she was killed, so it'd be hard for them to tie me to it because I can't be in two places at once."

He raises a brow and taps his pointer finger against his chin. "Unless, of course, you hired someone to kill her?"

I tighten my eyes and rise from my seat. "Are you working for me, Brad, or trying to build a case against me?"

He leans forward, propping his elbows on the desk, while I pace across his lush Persian rug.

"I'm trying to work with you, Bob. *You* asked me to represent you in your divorce, but you've been dragging your heels this whole time. You're not letting me do my job as it is, and now you're bringing up a case that has nothing to do with your separation . . . So you tell me, *what is it* that you want?" Brad's friendly demeanor has faded, replaced with the abrasive, no-nonsense persona he's known for.

I let out a heavy sigh and continue pacing, mulling it over. I don't know what to do. In my heart, I want to fight for Sarah. I want to win her back. But in my gut, I feel like shit's about to hit the fan, and if I don't start thinking clearly, I'm going to get plastered with it. I know I've lost my focus. I've got tunnel vision. Sarah and I have been together for over a decade, and that's not something I can just walk away from unless I know I have no other choice. I *do* have eyes on her, so I know she's not up to anything nefarious, at least not yet. Well, aside from slicing my hand open. I look down at the white bandage, rubbing my thumb over the soft cotton. It was more like a love tap, though, because I know what she can really do with a knife.

"Bob," Brad snaps, indicating his patience has worn thin. "What do you want?"

"I don't know," I say. "I need a little more time to figure that out."

"Fine, but you also need to decide what you want in the divorce."

I shoot him a glare.

"*In case* you're not able to convince Sarah to stay with you," he adds. "And in the last meeting, she said she wants full custody of Summer. That's clearly going to be a battle, so you'll need ammo if you want to ensure that doesn't happen."

"She wasn't being serious," I say.

"She seemed pretty serious to me. Is Sarah one to bluff?"

I stare back at Brad, pondering, thinking of my beloved wife—with her blond hair, green eyes, sculpted cheekbones, and slender frame, she could be confused for an angel. But that's only if you don't know her.

I shake my head. "No, she's not one to bluff."

"Then you'll need ammo."

"I already have it."

He smiles at me, pleased with this information.

I knew from the very beginning I had to have an insurance policy with Sarah, something to guarantee she could never do to me what she did to her first husband, Adam. Right now, I'm glad I have it, but I still hope I don't have to use it. There's no going back if I do.

11

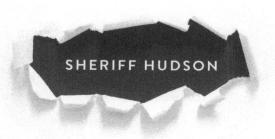

SHERIFF HUDSON

I have to look Stevens in the eye when I confront him about Kelly. I'll know right away if he was involved in her murder because he's never been a good liar. I also have to be sure there isn't anything else he hid from the Summers investigation, or from any other investigation he oversaw, for that matter. The last thing I need right now is any more goddamn surprises.

I wave my badge in front of the reader and pull open the door, entering the intake area. It's quiet in here, empty aside from Officer Clark, who's seated behind the control desk.

"Morning, Sheriff Hudson." Clark's a heavyset man with a bad leg, which is why he's on desk duty.

"How's Stevens doing?"

He looks at his watch. "As of twenty minutes ago, he was asleep, so I'd say he's doing just fine."

"I wanna see him."

"Sure thing, Sheriff," Officer Clark says as he slowly gets to his feet. Pulling the set of keys from his belt, he ambles a few steps and unlocks the steel door leading to the back, where the holding cells are.

I extend my hand out to the corrections officer, palm face up. "I'll take it from here."

He nods and relinquishes the keys to me.

"Does Stevens know anything about the media leak?"

Officer Clark shakes his head. "I don't believe so. I mean, he hasn't had any visitors or made any phone calls since before the news broke."

"Good," I say, knowing it's better if I catch him off guard so he won't have a chance to start spinning stories.

My tactical boots clunk against the concrete floor, echoing off the hallway's walls. For Ryan's own safety, he's being held in a private cell, separate from the rest of the inmates, since criminals don't take kindly to cops or former cops. I have half a mind to put him with the others after what he's done, but that seems more like something Stevens would do, not me.

I reach the last security door to the private holding area where two cells sit side by side. These ones rarely get used as most intakes don't require added security. I scan my badge. The reader beeps, and the door buzzes. I grab the handle and pull it open.

"Stevens, you really—" I start to say, but stop suddenly when my gaze lands on him. My eyes widen in disbelief, and my stomach plummets like I'm on a roller coaster, cresting over the peak of the first drop.

"Medic. We need a medic!" I yell at the top of my lungs, bolting toward Stevens's cell. My throat burns as my vocal cords are pushed to their limits, the muscles in my neck straining to the point of wanting to tear through the flesh holding them back. The keys slip from my hand, dropping to the floor with a resounding *clang*. I quickly pick them up, scrambling to locate the one that opens his cell door.

"Stevens!" I shout.

I try several keys, each with no success.

Realizing no one can hear me through the thick steel doors, I press the call button on my radio. "I need paramedics in the private holding cells now!" I say while trying another key.

The lock clicks, and I throw open the door, sprinting to Ryan. The heavy metal bangs against the wall like a thick gong. His body is lax, slumped forward, lifeless. A belt is looped around his neck, pulled taut, the other end tied to the top bunk. His eyes are wide open, the whites completely replaced with red as the blood vessels have burst under the strain and lack of oxygen. I just hope I'm not too late.

"Hold on, man," I say, struggling to get any slack in the leather. I try to lift Ryan with one hand and undo the knot with the other. Tears build up in my eyes, blurring my vision, making it harder and harder to see what I'm doing. I claw at the gaps in the leather, my nails bending and chipping in the process.

Finally, I'm able to dig my fingers into the knot and jerk it loose, the makeshift noose coming undone. The belt buckle clanks to the floor, and Ryan's torso and head slump forward. The deadweight catches me off guard, pulling me to the ground with him. I roll him flat onto his back and remove the belt from his neck. The skin underneath is black and blue with splotches of red from burst blood vessels. There's a small line of blood on his neck from where the leather cut into his flesh. I search for a pulse but there's nothing. I check his nose, holding my hand less than an inch from his nostrils, hoping I'll feel hot air, but I don't.

"You're not going out like this, Ryan," I say, tipping his head back and lifting his chin to open up his airway. I place my hands against the lower half of his sternum, one on top of the other, and press down hard, beginning chest compressions at 110 BPM. In the distance, I can hear boots on the ground, or at least I hope that's what I'm hearing.

"Come on, man!" I say, bearing down harder and faster. Something inside of his chest cracks, but I keep going because I know broken ribs happen often during CPR. It's as though God calls back to his original deal with Adam, removing a rib to create life again. I pause only to give Ryan air, then start compressions again.

"Oh fuck!" a voice says in a panic. I briefly look up to find Officer Clark standing in the doorway. All the blood has drained from his face, and he looks like a deer in headlights.

"You said you checked on him!" I shout, saliva spraying the room in a wide mist.

"I did. He was asleep."

"Who the hell let him keep his belt!?"

Clark stammers. "I . . . I don't know."

Two paramedics push past the officer and drop to their knees beside me. They start hurling questions. *How long has he been out? How long have I been doing compressions? Was he breathing when I found him?* I answer them the best I can, but I don't know if my responses are correct. I can't even hear the words leave my mouth. One paramedic straps an oxygen mask over Ryan's mouth and nose while the other handles compressions. Sinking into a seated position, I scooch away until my back hits the bars of the cell.

My gaze goes to Officer Clark, standing near the security door. He's trying to make himself look as small as possible. Sweat pools at the edge of his receding hairline, and his eyes dart in all directions. He makes the mistake of briefly locking eyes with me.

I lift my hand, pointing a finger at him. "You better hope he lives."

12

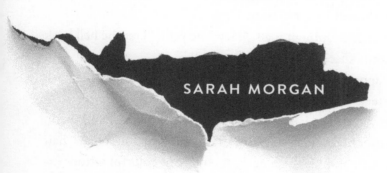

SARAH MORGAN

I'm greeted with an unpleasant but expected sight when I pull my Range Rover into the Morgan Foundation office parking lot. A half dozen reporters are leaning up against their respective news vans. Cameramen stand at the ready, waiting for me, eager to get the first sound bite. They're probably the same ones who were lingering at the end of my driveway this morning when I left to run some errands and drop Summer off at school. I'm sure as soon as I was out of sight, they packed up their stuff and raced to beat me here.

I park in my designated spot, which is thankfully numbered rather than marked with my name. It gives me a moment to gather myself before anyone notices my arrival. I considered staying home for the day, but the foundation needs me, and I have work to do. Stealing a glimpse of myself in the rearview mirror, I check my makeup and find in my reflection the woman I need to be today. *There she is.* She looks almost the same, but there's more depth behind those green eyes. I reapply my lipstick and smile back at her.

As soon as my stilettos hit the pavement, I hear it.

"There she is!" followed by hurried footsteps as reporters race, trying to get to me first.

I close my car door behind me, toss my bag over my shoulder, and start walking.

"Ms. Morgan."

"Sarah!"

They swarm, yelling over one another, making it impossible to hear any of their questions—not like I'd answer them anyway. Cameras click and flash, and microphones are thrust into my face. One of them bops me in the mouth, and I swat it away.

A deep voice cuts through it all. "Hey!" he yells. "Get the hell back and give her some space."

Alejandro appears from within the crowd, pushing through the flock of pesky reporters. When he reaches me, he turns and stretches his arms out at his sides, creating a barricade of sorts between myself and them. My eyes skim over his back, taking him all in—his broad shoulders, hair cut short and neat, and his thick neck. A collage of colorful tattoos extends the length of it, continuing beneath his fitted, long-sleeve Henley. Alejandro flicks his hands at the reporters, demanding they move back. He has the physique and stature of a bodyguard paired with the hardened look of a criminal, so they do as he says.

The media falls silent as they take their new places, a safe distance from me. Satisfied, Alejandro looks over his shoulder and bobs his head. I press my lips firmly together and return the gesture, signaling to him that I'm good. He then steps to my side, giving me full view of the crowd.

One reporter finally speaks up, saying, "Ms. Morgan, will you be making a statement?"

I steal a deep breath and nod, knowing I have to say something but unsure as to what that something should be. I know what they want to hear. I can see it on their faces. I should be outraged, crushed, devastated. Given the news of Sheriff Stevens's connection to the Kelly Summers case—which was only news to them, not me—I should want to scorch the earth beneath me. That's the sensationalism they crave, so that's what I'll give them. I clear my throat before I begin and summon a sadness from somewhere deep inside. Emotion sells, and what they're looking to sell is outrage.

"Good morning. My name is Sarah Morgan, and twelve years ago, I defended my husband Adam in a court of law after charges were brought against him for the murder of Kelly Summers and her unborn child. As his wife, I knew he was innocent. I knew he was incapable of murder, but I was unable to convince a jury of that fact, and now I know why. One of the great unknowns in the Summers case was the identity of the third set of DNA found inside the victim. The Prince William County Sheriff's Office assured me they had done their absolute best to uncover the truth." I dramatically scan the crowd, watching them hang on my every word. "That was a bald-faced lie because they were playing by their own rules. My husband did not receive a fair trial, which was his right under the Constitution of the United States, one I swore to uphold, and one former sheriff Stevens swore to uphold too. Only one of us kept that oath." I pause for a moment because it's a nice sound bite, and I hope the media will run with it.

"I started the Morgan Foundation because I believe in justice, but I also believe in reform and second chances. To learn that my Adam never got a chance to begin with is beyond devastating." I stare into the lens of the camera belonging to the biggest news station. "And what I can't stop thinking about, what kept me up all last night, and maybe what will forever keep me awake . . . is what Adam's fate might have been if the truth had been allowed to present itself in that courtroom all those years ago." I conjure thoughts that I know will bring me to tears—my beautiful daughter lying in a casket, me standing over her, looking at a life cut short. Losing her is the only thing I'm afraid of. My eyes instantly well up.

"Sorry," I say, pretending my emotions are raw and out of my control. I clear my throat and continue. "My husband was taken from me at the hands of the commonwealth of Virginia, in the name of justice. But you tell me—how is it justice when the evidence that could have set Adam free was buried? How is it justice when the person overseeing the investigation was engaged in an illicit affair with the victim? That's not justice at all; that is corruption; *that* . . . is *murder*." I add some fire to the word *murder* as I make eye contact with each reporter, ensuring they not only hear my words but feel them too. I want them to remember this moment, and I want them to carry it with them when they go off and do their reporting.

"If our legal system isn't able to provide justice . . . then I will. Thank you, and I won't be taking any questions at this time."

There's a moment of stunned silence when I finish my statement, and Alejandro immediately escorts me through the crowd, toward the office building. The haze that has overtaken them wears off after only a few seconds, and they start to swarm again, trailing behind us, questions erupting in a fury. The media can never help themselves. They always want more. Give them an inch, and they'll take your whole life. I keep walking with the intention of not saying another word. But one question stops me dead in my tracks, and a reporter following closely behind collides with me due to my sudden halt.

"Get back!" Alejandro yells, creating more distance between us and them. He leans into me and whispers, "Are you all right?"

I lock eyes with him and nod before slowly turning to face the ambush of reporters one last time.

"Can you repeat that?" I say to the woman who asked the question.

All eyes fall on her, and she clears her throat. "What's your reaction to the statement Eleanor Rumple gave to the media this morning? Adam's mother . . . your mother-in-law or former . . ."

I hold my hand up to cut her off. "I know who Eleanor is, but unfortunately, I haven't had a chance to listen to her statement, so I can't comment on it."

"Eleanor stated that she plans to file a lawsuit against the Prince William County Sheriff's Office for concealing exculpatory evidence, and if successful, she'll follow that up with a wrongful death suit. Do you support her?" The reporter extends the mic in my direction.

I consider my answer, but I can't bring myself to say I support Eleanor.

Instead, I land on, "I support justice."

"How do you feel about the fact that she's also accused you of mishandling Adam's case?" the same reporter quickly adds.

How am I even supposed to answer that stupid question? *I feel great. I love that my crypt keeper of a mother-in-law is continuing to screw with me after all these years.*

I should refuse to comment any further, but I know that old, vile woman is watching, grinning ear to ear, and if I can wipe away the smug smile that's surely plastered across her face, I will.

"I'll be honest, it saddens me that Eleanor would even think that, let alone say it out loud, but I do have to give her grace. She lost her husband before she lost her only son, so she's been alone for a long time. Eleanor has spent many of her golden years grieving, and given her age, she may not have many more left, but I *do* empathize with her."

I bite my tongue to stop myself from chuckling because I know the mention of her age will piss her off more than anything. "I'd also like to note that Eleanor's memory of her son's trial is not the best, and with the recent discovery of new DNA evidence, I can understand how confusing that must be for an elderly woman." I'm sure she's blowing a gasket now. Maybe I'll get lucky, and her heart will give out, and she'll just drop dead. Then again, Eleanor never had a heart to begin with.

"Despite what my mother-in-law has falsely claimed regarding my legal work, I'd like to make it clear that I did everything in my power to defend my husband Adam. However, when pertinent evidence was intentionally withheld from the case, that power was taken from me, and now that the truth has finally been revealed, I *will* be taking it back. Thank you."

I turn to leave, and Alejandro walks in step with me while the media, once again, follows closely behind, yelling over one another. But this time, I won't answer any more of their questions. I've given them enough to run with.

We reach the office building, and Alejandro holds open the lobby door so I can pass through first. He jerks it closed behind him, leaving reporters shouting on the other side. I walk farther into the empty lobby, my heels clicking along the tile floor. Roger, the building's security guard, isn't at the front desk, and I assume he's out on a cigarette break since he takes at least a dozen of those a shift.

Alejandro strolls toward me, a look of concern plastered across his face.

"What are you doing here?" I ask before he can say anything.

"I was driving by when I saw all the news vans and curiosity got the best of me, so I decided to stop and check out what was going on. Then I saw you and figured you could use some help dealing with them." He shoves his hands in the front pockets of his jeans.

"Well, thanks. I appreciate what you did out there." I tightly smile.

"Of course." He shrugs. "It's the least I could do, especially considering you're giving me something no one else has."

"And what's that?"

"A second chance."

His eyes lock with mine, and it's like we're studying each other, deciding on boundaries, whether to keep them where they are or maybe push them a little. The reporters are still standing outside, yelling muffled questions.

"It's the least anyone can do," I say.

He smiles, and then his face turns serious. "Ya know, I don't know everything that's going on . . . I picked up the gist of it from those banshee reporters." Alejandro motions to the door. "But I'm here if you wanna talk."

"Thanks, but I'm fine," I say because this isn't something I want to talk about with him or anyone, for that matter. This all should have stayed in the past where it belongs.

"How's the apartment?" I ask only to change the subject before he pries any further.

"It's great. I wasn't expecting it to be so nice."

"It's meant to reflect what you're capable of achieving. Sometimes we have to see ourselves as the person we want to be before we can become that person."

"That's a good sentiment," Alejandro says. "The clothes fit nicely too." He gestures to his outfit.

My eyes skim from the white tennis shoes to the blue jeans to the waffle-knit, long-sleeve top that fits like a second skin.

"They do."

He rocks back on his heels and cracks a small smile. "Well, I should leave you to it. I don't wanna take up any more of your time, and I've got some more job applications to fill out anyway." He folds his lips in.

"How's that going?"

"Really well . . . that is, until they find out I have a felony conviction." He shrugs. "I've actually been looking for a while, but I'm hoping with the help of your foundation's career resources, I won't be looking for much longer."

"I hope so too. Removing the barrier to employment for people with felon status is a major focus for the foundation." I stare into his eyes, mulling over an idea that'd be mutually beneficial for the two of us. "You know, I might have something for you. If you're interested. It's temporary, but it'd give you something to do and some extra cash."

"I am," he says without hesitation. "I'd take anything at this point."

"Anything?" I arch a brow.

"Anything legal, I mean."

I notice a shade of crimson settles onto his cheeks as I fish a pad of paper and a pen from my purse and scribble down an address.

The sound of heels rapidly crossing the lobby floor catches my attention, and I glance over my shoulder to find Anne racing toward me. I tear the paper from the pad and fold it up before slipping the pen and notebook back in my bag.

"Sarah! Oh, thank God, there you are!" Anne exclaims, slowing her pace now that she's located me. "I'm so sorry. One of the associates just noticed all the news vans parked out front. I swear they weren't here when we arrived. Did they swarm you? Are you okay?"

"I'm fine, and yeah, they did. But luckily, Alejandro happened to be in the area, and he got me out of there."

Anne looks up at him, grinning as she extends her hand. "That is lucky. It's nice to see you again."

"Likewise," he says, shaking her hand.

"What the hell is going on out there?" Roger yells as he shuffles into the lobby. He's an older man with a bad back and a nicotine problem. Despite that, he's tough as nails.

"It's the media, Roger," Anne says.

"You mean, fake news?" He chuckles to himself. The stench of cigarette smoke reaches us before he does. "What do they want?"

"Doesn't matter what they want, because they always want more," I say.

"Ain't that the truth." He makes a *humph* sound. "Buncha bloodsuckers."

"Can you make sure they stay out of the building?" Anne tightens her eyes.

"That won't be a problem at all." He grins and pats the revolver clipped to his hip.

I press my lips firmly together. "Roger, you can't shoot them."

An amused look settles on his face as his other hand goes to his Taser. "Who said anything about shooting?"

Anne scolds Roger while I extend the folded paper to Alejandro. "Saturday morning at seven," I say loud enough for only him to hear.

He takes it from me and bobs his head as he pockets the slip. From a professional standpoint, I shouldn't be offering him this, but I feel like I owe him. Plus, there's something intriguing about him, and I want to find out what that is.

I turn my attention to our security guard. "Roger, would you mind escorting Alejandro through the back entrance?"

"Sure thing, boss. I could go for another cigarette anyway." He looks to Alejandro, beckoning him with his hand. "Let's go, Muscles."

Alejandro mouths *thank you* to me and then waves before he and Roger exit to the back, disappearing around the corner. My gaze veers to the lobby door, where reporters are still loitering, peering through the window to try to get a better look inside. I'm going to be under a microscope until this whole thing gets settled, and it's the last thing I need. All eyes on me, the devastated widow. It's not what I want right now, but I can play that part and I can play it well. Because I've done it before. It's like I'm an actress reprising a role that fans just couldn't get enough of.

Anne rests a hand on my shoulder, startling me, and I turn my head to meet her gaze. "I saw the news segment. I can't believe it. Does this mean Adam was innocent?" she says softly, furrowing her brow.

"He always was to me."

"I know, but legally, I mean . . . What's going to happen now?"

I blow out hot air before I speak. "I'm not sure. There's no road map for these sorts of things, but I presume the sheriff's office will be forced to reopen the Kelly Summers investigation, due to the blatant corruption involved with their initial one."

Anne tucks her chin in like she's thinking about the question she wants to ask next. "Do you think Sheriff Stevens killed Kelly?"

"I don't know."

She squeezes my shoulder and then drops her arm back to her side. "You already have so much going on with the divorce, and now . . . I can't even imagine. The timing is just insane."

Anne's right about that. With the impending divorce . . . things could get messy, twisted even. The truth and Summer are the only things tying Bob and me to one another—but it feels more like a bow that could easily be unraveled rather than some intricate fisherman's knot. If I had known this was going to come out, I would have waited until it blew over before I started the separation process. But it's too late now. I can't unring that bell. Plus, I really don't want to. I acknowledge Anne's sentiment with a nod.

"Shall we?" I say, motioning to the elevator that will take us to the Morgan Foundation offices. Anne gives me a tight smile, and we start toward it.

The word *timing* swirls around my brain as we wait for the elevator. The doors open, and Anne and I step inside, pressing the button for the third floor. The *timing* is a little too perfect. Last night after the news hit, Bob begged me to stay with him, to be a unified front, so we could get through this together. But now I can't help but think: Did he have something to do with leaking it to the media? Like me, he has friends in all places, both high and low. Would he be that stupid or desperate? Would he think it would stop me from leaving him? No, I'm being paranoid. I shake the thought away.

"If the sheriff's office reopens the investigation, what does that mean for the courts?" Anne asks. The doors close and the elevator starts to ascend.

"Nothing yet, but if they're going to move on this, we should try to get ahead of it."

"And how do we do that?"

I take a deep breath. I know the right answer, the one that will look best in the public's eye. But it could make me vulnerable, and that's the last thing I want to be. Doing nothing, though, might cast suspicion on me. The elevator doors open, and Anne steps out first. I stay put, mulling it over. I know what I have to do even though I don't want to.

"We need to file a motion with the court to reopen Adam's case," I say.

Anne turns back, a determined look on her face.

"I want you to get a couple of associates on it right away. Plus, get in contact with our friends in DC. See what strings we can pull or favors we can cash in to get this moving through the court system ASAP."

"I'm on it," she says. The doors start to close, and she thrusts her hand out to stop them.

My phone rings, and I quickly retrieve it from my purse, seeing the word *Unknown* splayed across the screen.

"You coming?" Anne asks.

"No," I say. "I've got some things I need to take care of, and I should answer this."

"Okay. I'll be in touch with any updates. Let me know if you need anything. But don't worry. You've got the whole Morgan Foundation team behind you, Sarah."

"Thanks, Anne." I softly smile. "I don't know what I'd do without you."

She withdraws her hand, allowing the doors to close.

I press *1R* on the elevator, so I can go out the back to avoid the reporters. My phone continues to ring, and I hit *Accept* before bringing it to my ear. "Sarah Morgan speaking."

"Sarah, this is Sheriff Hudson."

I'm not surprised to hear his voice. I figured he'd be in touch sooner rather than later. The fact that it's a call and not a visit tells me how ashamed and embarrassed he must feel. He's got to backpedal and plead for forgiveness, or at least some understanding, during this trying time at the department.

"I assume you're calling about the Kelly Summers case."

"No," he says. "That is now an open investigation, so I can't share any details on that matter."

It appears someone in that department finally knows how open investigations work. I liked it better when Stevens was the sheriff. He did nothing by the book, sharing details of the case with me and allowing me to walk through crime scenes—although that was all just to cover his own ass. I won't be getting that type of insider information this time around, but I don't think I'll need it.

"Then, what's this about, Sheriff?"

"I was calling to inform you that your client Ryan Stevens attempted suicide a little over an hour ago. He's currently in critical condition at UVA."

The elevator doors open, and I exit into a dimly lit back vestibule.

"I'm sorry to hear that, Sheriff. Stevens is no longer my client, though, but I do appreciate the call," I say, hanging up the phone.

13

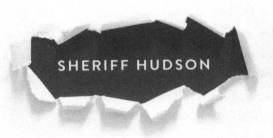

SHERIFF HUDSON

"The press is ready for you," Marcy says, poking her head in my office just as I set my phone down.

I acknowledge her with an "Okay."

Sarah's reaction to Ryan's suicide attempt doesn't surprise me in the slightest. I figured she'd drop him as a client, given the media leak. She might have even been happy to hear the news. I tightly close my eyes, unable to get the image of Stevens out of my head. His frozen eyes. The belt taut around his neck. His skin a mix of burst blood vessels and bruised discoloration. I inhale deeply, trying to expel it, but it's still there—right in front of my eyes, whether they're closed or not, only for me to see. The doctors think Ryan will pull through. They said I got to him just in time. A minute later and he would have been dead. When he does wake up, I'm sure he's gonna be just as pissed at me for saving his life as I am at him for ruining mine.

I look at the piece of paper on my desk, my statement to the media. I didn't write out a full one, just about a dozen words, reminders of what to say and what not to say. I don't want it to come off as too rehearsed. I figure the public and the media will think our office knew about the corruption for a long time if I do. But the shit storm Ryan's caused has barely begun. It's gonna hang over my head, raining down accusations, lawsuits, terminations, budget cuts, firings, smear stories in the press—like tennis ball–sized hail trying to crush everyone and everything in this building. That's my forecast for now and for years to come. But I'm a better sheriff than Ryan ever was, so I'll get us through this no matter what it takes. With the statement in hand, I stand from my desk and make my way to the front of the station.

Marcy is waiting for me in the lobby with a tight-lipped smile, like she's saying, *Sorry you have to go through this.*

Me too, Marcy, I think. I hold my head high and pin back my shoulders, exiting the sheriff's office. Reporters and cameramen are lined up at the bottom of the concrete steps. A half dozen deputies are positioned off to the sides of the podium, where I'll be delivering my statement. Beyond the media, there are barricades in place with more officers standing guard in case the public gets out of hand. About forty or so people have gathered, many holding signs. I scan the crowd, quickly reading each sign, trying to garner their overall sentiment.

Adam's innocent!!

ACAB

Send Stevens to the electric chair!

Kill all cops!

Recall Sheriff Hudson!

I take the steps slow, and before I can even reach the podium, reporters are already shouting questions and the crowd is frenzied, shouting and chanting. Their mouths are moving, but I can't make out their words. I'm sure whatever they're saying is just as vile as the signs they're holding. A couple of my deputies look to me, displaying their solidarity with me and this office. The sun shines bright on us today, even though it shouldn't. I briefly glance at the sky, reminding myself that this is all so small in the grand scheme of things, and then I return my attention to the crowd. My mind is racing a hundred miles an hour down a busy highway, and I can feel my heart beating in every part of my body. I've gotta slow my thoughts down, so I steal a firm, deep breath and focus on myself in this moment. Three things I see: Gretchen Waters from Channel 5 News standing poised a couple feet in front of her colleagues. It's hard to pick out two more things when there's so much chaos in front of me. A small dog cradled in the arms of an older woman. A man wearing a baseball cap, pulled down to shield his eyes. A thick blond beard covers what I can see of his face. He looks like he's trying to blend in, but he stands out, thanks to his posture, which makes him appear like he's ex-military or former law enforcement. He's dressed in plain clothes, and he's taller than nearly everyone around him. I know this man, but I can't place him, at least not right now.

"Sheriff," Lieutenant Nagel whispers from my side, pulling me from my frantic thoughts.

I take another deep breath and acknowledge him with a nod before looking out at the crowd.

"Good morning, I'm Sheriff Hudson of Prince William County," I start. People shush one another and a silence falls over them. "I'd like to start off with some news regarding former sheriff Ryan Stevens . . ." When I finish telling them what has occurred, several people in the crowd yell out inflammatory comments. They're beyond cruel, and each one feels like a punch in the gut.

Good.

Let's finish the job.

Stevens sucks at everything, even suicide.

He deserves to die.

They don't see Ryan as a human being. They see him as a uniform, just like the rest of us that have sworn to protect and serve. But unlike Ryan, I've kept my oath. I swallow hard and continue with the statement, moving on to what they're all really here for. They want to know what we're doing to right this ship.

"As many of you are aware, new information regarding the Kelly Summers homicide investigation has come to light as a result of Ryan Stevens's recent arrest." The crowd begins to quiet again.

"I want to assure each and every one of you that no one is above the law, including the former sheriff. That is why he was promptly arrested for the DUI crash that took the life of forty-four-year-old Jackie Clarke. My department followed protocol by entering Ryan Stevens's DNA into CODIS to see if there was a connection between him and a hit-and-run accident that occurred last summer, resulting in the death of Tim Redding. No link was found, but I speak on behalf of the entire Prince William County Sheriff's Office when I say that we were just as shocked and devastated as all of you were to learn there was a connection between Ryan Stevens and the Kelly Summers case. I know how upset this community is. Believe me, I share your sentiment." My mouth forms a hard line, and I pause to scan the assembled crowd.

"As sheriff, I swore to protect and serve this community and that is exactly what I will continue to do, as I have done since I took office a mere five months ago. This new information undeniably calls into question the validity and handling of the Summers homicide investigation. Like all of you, I want justice, and I want to be one hundred percent certain the person responsible for this murder pays for their crime . . . no matter who it is. As of this morning, I have ordered the investigation into Kelly Summers's murder to be reopened." Whispered conversations ensue after this announcement.

"It is now an open and active investigation, so I will not be taking any questions. Thank you." I fold the piece of paper that I never even looked at once and slip it into my pocket.

The media erupts with questions, reporters screaming simultaneously. The crowd is in an uproar too, but their sentiment is now split. Some are cheering. Others are still spewing hateful remarks. At least I got a handful of them on our side. This is already going to be a tricky investigation given how long ago the murder took place, so having the public's support is vital. I turn from the spectacle before me and begin to climb the steps to the sheriff's office, taking each one nice and slow so I don't appear like I'm running away from this.

At the top of the steps, Marcy holds the door open. "Great job, Sheriff."

"Thanks," I say, entering the lobby. "I'll be in my office if you need me."

She delivers a small smile as I part ways with her. Rounding the corner, I run smack-dab into my second-in-command here and first-in-command at home, Chief Deputy Pam Olson. She's petite but tough as hell, which is why she's not sent reeling backward when we collide. The pad of paper and folders she was carrying fall to the floor, and I quickly bend down to pick them up for her.

"Sorry, Marcus," she says. "I mean, Sheriff Hudson."

She calls me Marcus outside of work and Sheriff or just Hudson here, but sometimes she mixes them up, which I find endearing. We've been dating for over two years, long before I made sheriff. Even though I'm in charge now, I don't play favorites—as much as I would like to with Pam because I wouldn't be where I am without her.

I stand and hand the folders back to Olson. "What's the rush?"

"I came to find you," she says, restacking them.

"Is there another closed investigation coming back to bite me in the ass?" I say it teasingly, but I'm serious.

"Negative, but I just met with a woman named Deena Walsh. She came in to file a missing person's report on her roommate, Stacy Howard. She hasn't been seen or heard from in nearly three days."

"Okay, so put out an APB on Ms. Howard and assign a deputy to it," I say, starting to walk away because I'm not sure why she's bringing this to my attention, considering the shit show we're dealing with.

"Hudson," she says firmly. "You're gonna want to hear this."

I sigh and turn to face her, noticing the seriousness in her eyes. "This better be good, Olson."

"Deena said she received a text from Stacy on Monday night around five p.m., saying she wouldn't be home when Deena got off work, which would have been just after ten p.m., because she was planning to meet up with a guy she'd been seeing."

"Okay, and . . . ?"

"The guy Stacy said she was going to meet is Bob Miller."

14

BOB MILLER

Sitting in an interrogation room in the Prince William County Sheriff's Office is something I expected, due to the reopening of the Kelly Summers investigation—but not this soon. I assume they're dotting their i's and crossing their t's. I just didn't think I'd be the first i they dotted. There've been a couple updates since the last time I was in this room. The lights are a little brighter. The chairs are new, a bit more uncomfortable. Maybe that was the intention behind replacing them.

I received a call a couple hours ago from a Chief Deputy Olson, asking if I would come in for questioning. I said yes because saying no would make it appear as though I'm hiding something. I'd never advise my clients to accept—but I'm a lawyer, and I know what I'm doing. Hudson has a lot to prove to this community, at least that's what I gathered from his statement to the media, and I'm sure they want to wrap up this reinvestigation swiftly so they can put it behind them once and for all. We're on the same page there, and I'll do what I can to help me—not them.

The door swings open, and Sheriff Hudson and a female deputy walk in. She's much smaller than him. Her hair is pulled back in a low bun, and her mouth forms a hard line like she's got something to prove. They must have some sort of good cop–bad cop routine going on.

"Thanks for coming in to speak with us, Mr. Miller," Hudson says, slapping a folder down on the table. "This is my colleague Chief Deputy Olson." He gestures to the woman wearing the scowl. That's the one who called me.

"It's no problem at all, Sheriff Hudson, and it's nice to meet you, Chief Deputy Olson." I nod at both of them as they take their seats across from me.

When neither Hudson nor Olson speaks, I add, "And I assume this is about the Kelly Summers case."

The two of them exchange a look, narrowing their eyes slightly before returning their attention to me. I can tell by their expressions that I've already made more than one mistake. I shouldn't be here . . . because I know now this isn't about Kelly Summers.

"No." Sheriff Hudson furrows his brow. "Why would we call you in for that?"

Shit.

My shirt collar suddenly feels too tight around my neck. A bead of sweat trickles down my back, and I tense, trying to keep from squirming at the sensation. My heart rate hastens. I can feel it in my wrist, beating against this cold metal table. I need to pivot, and I need to do it fast. Readying myself to go into full lawyer mode, I clear my throat and my mind.

"I caught your statement on the news earlier, Sheriff Hudson," I calmly say. "With the investigation reopened, I assumed I would be reinterviewed, since I had known the victim. I will note, my alibi was verified, and I *was* cleared of any involvement in her murder, but I understand you need to get your ducks in a row, as they say, so that's why I figured I was called in."

"Nope." Hudson slightly shakes his head. "Don't need anything there, but good to know for the future in case we *do* have some questions." He flips open the folder, removing the photo on top and sliding it across the table. "Do you recognize this woman?"

The photograph is of an attractive woman in her midtwenties with long red hair, high cheekbones, and plump lips. She looks familiar, very familiar. But I can't place her. My brain is finding her in figments and waves, a blur in the background of memories but nothing solid. And nothing solid means . . .

"Not that I can recall," I say, pushing the photo toward them.

"You can't recall?" Chief Deputy Olson asks.

"No, I can't."

She raises a brow at my answer like she's judging me for it. "From what we've heard," Olson says, "you two are friends. One might even say closer than friends. Why don't you take another look?" She slides the photograph back to me.

I squint, my eyes darting back and forth between the two of them. Then, I drop my gaze, reexamining it, taking in every detail. A smattering of freckles sprinkled across the bridge of her nose. Her skin bronzed from what I assume is a spray tan. A silver necklace with a letter *S* pendant that rests against the center of her chest, just below her collarbone. I've seen it before. A memory stored somewhere deep inside my brain resurfaces. It's that necklace . . . the cold pendant brushing against my cheek. Her long, soft hair cascading all around my face as she rode me fast and hard. I quickly blink it away.

Shit. Another mistake. This is the woman I slept with, and I've just told them I don't recognize her. How do I backtrack? Explain that I was blackout drunk when she and I were . . . together and that I don't remember her. *Wait.* Why are they asking me about her? I try to keep my composure, maintain a neutral expression. But every muscle in my face is twitching. I wonder if they notice it. My eyes swing between them. The female deputy wears a look of disgust like she's staring at a pile of rotting garbage rather than the prestigious lawyer I am. Something happened to the woman in the photo, and it's clear they think I had something to do with it.

"So, are you sticking with you don't recognize this woman?" Hudson lifts his chin. "Or do you have something to tell us?"

It might be time to lawyer up. Even lawyers need lawyers. But

I have to know what exactly they're accusing me of or what they think I'm involved in.

"I recognize her necklace," I finally land on. It's the truth. It's what jogged my memory, and I'm not technically backtracking or changing my story with that answer.

"From where?" Olson asks.

I swallow hard as the memory of that night resurfaces. Her hot, sweaty skin pressed against mine. Her moans and cries as I thrust up into her. The silver pendant swinging above my head, lightly tapping my face. My tongue touching the cold metal as it slipped into my mouth when I was close to coming. I can practically taste its metallic tang right now. I have to disclose the one-night stand I had with this woman because they're going to find out one way or another. From the sounds of it, they already know and they're just waiting to see if I'll tell them the truth.

"I had a one-night stand with this woman a few weeks back. Other than that, I don't know her. It only happened once, and I was drunk. I barely remember it, and I don't remember her. But . . . I do remember that necklace." My voice is emotionless as though I'm stating a series of facts. I keep direct eye contact with Hudson to convey I'm telling the truth. He's the one in charge, so he's the one I need to get through to. The other one already despises me anyway.

Olson leans forward in her chair. "Her name is Stacy Howard," she says with a hard tone.

I briefly look at her and then to Hudson. There's no point in responding. It doesn't matter what her name is. The only thing that matters to me is why I'm here, sitting in this interrogation room.

"When was the last time you had contact with her?" Hudson asks.

"Three weeks ago."

He cocks his head. "You sure about that?"

"Positive."

"Interesting," Olson says. "Because we've heard otherwise." She pulls a piece of paper from the folder and places it in front of me. It's a screenshot of a text conversation.

STACY HOWARD

Hey, D! Going to meet up with that guy I told you about, so I won't be here when you get home from work. Could be a late night or an early morning 😉

DEENA WALSH

The lawyer?

STACY HOWARD

That's the one . . . for now 😉

DEENA WALSH

Remind me of his name, just in case he's a psychopath 😂

STACY HOWARD

Bob Miller

DEENA WALSH

Bob? What is he sixty?

STACY HOWARD

No, midforties tops

"This is a text conversation between Stacy and her roommate, Deena, from Monday night." Olson taps her finger on one of the messages. "Do you recognize that name, Bob?"

The name she's pointing to is my own.

"That's bullshit," I scoff, pushing the paper back toward the deputy. "I haven't had any communication with this Stacy woman in weeks."

"Not according to these texts."

"What's this all about?" I ask, growing beyond frustrated.

Hudson leans forward in his chair. "Stacy's roommate, Deena, filed a missing person's report. No one's seen or heard from Stacy in three days. So, can you tell us your whereabouts on Monday night?" He cocks his head.

Fuck! I exhale through my nose and think back a few days. My hand tingles, and I glance down at the bandage wrapped around it. I'm surprised they haven't asked about the injury. Why the hell would this chick tell her roommate we were meeting up? That's not true. I don't even know her.

"I picked up my daughter from her friend's house after work."

"What time was that?" he interjects.

"Around seven."

He nods.

"I had dinner with her and my wife at our home on Lake Manassas."

"Time?" Hudson interjects again.

"Like seven thirty. Then, I drove back to DC, and I went to bed."

"Why'd you drive to DC? Why not stay at your house with your wife and child?" Olson squints, clearly judging me.

"I have a place in the city, since I work there. Makes the commute easier when I have early meetings or I'm due in court," I explain.

"Can anyone verify that you drove back to DC?"

"Yeah, my wife and my daughter."

"I mean after you left. Can anyone other than yourself verify that you drove to your house in DC and stayed there all night?" she clarifies.

I press my lips firmly together and shake my head. "No, I was alone."

"Speaking of your wife, does Sarah know about your affair?" Hudson asks.

I slide my tongue over the front of my teeth and then bite it to keep myself from laughing like a crazy person. *Sarah. That evil, conniving, vengeful . . .* This has her written all over it. My eyes flick to Hudson and then Olson and back again. How can they not see it? Her first husband, Adam, had an affair and his mistress was found murdered in cold blood. My one-night stand (because I wouldn't constitute her as a mistress) is now missing. She's screwing with me, has to be.

"Not that it's any of your business, but yes, Sarah is aware of the mistake I made." I tilt my head, hoping they'll see the writing on the wall.

"Sarah must be pretty pissed," Hudson says.

There we go. I think he's getting it. He's putting the pieces of this fucked-up puzzle together and realizing there's no such thing as coincidences when it comes to Sarah.

"She filed for divorce."

"Good for her," Olson says with a slight smirk.

I need to put an end to this. They're connecting dots that shouldn't be connected. I've given them enough of my time, probably too much of it, because if Sarah *is* behind this, then I may not have much of it left. She might just be trying to scare me so I'll stop fighting the divorce, or she might have a much more sinister plan in place. I never know with her.

"Am I free to leave?" I ask.

Hudson leans back in his chair. "Yeah, you're free to go."

I stand, immediately heading for the door. It feels like I've got a clock hanging over my head, except it's not keeping time, it's counting down.

"Hey, Bob," Hudson calls out just as my hand grips the handle.

I pause, glancing back at him.

"Don't leave town."

I give the sheriff an amused look and shake my head. "You must know you have no legal authority to enforce that."

He smirks. "I'm well aware. But I also know that *you know* exactly what that means."

Blood starts to pool in my face, so I leave before my temper gets the best of me.

And yeah, I know what that fucking means. It means I'm their number one suspect.

15

SARAH MORGAN

My daughter, dressed in a black one-piece swimsuit, climbs onto the starting block and gazes up at the bleachers. When she spots me seated at the very top, she beams. I smile back and clap my hands. She's the only thing in the world that matters to me. Summer readjusts her goggles and focuses on the pool, readying herself. The other parents are seated down in front, mingling. Sometimes I join them, but most times I sit alone.

A whistle blows, and the kids dive into the water, with Summer taking the lead. She's the best on the team, and I couldn't be prouder of her. I'm not proud because she's the best. I'd feel the same way if she were the weakest swimmer. I'm proud because she puts her all into it. She works hard. She practices. She doesn't give up. Effort is what I admire because you don't get results without it.

Shoes clomp heavily against the bleachers, shaking them. It seems intentional, like someone wants me to be aware of their presence. I look to my left and find Bob stomping toward me with tapered eyes and lips pursed so tightly they could burst. I'm not in the mood to deal with him right now, so I shake my head and return my attention to Summer.

Bob takes a seat right beside me because he doesn't understand boundaries.

"Where the fuck is she?" he seethes.

"Jesus, Bob." I give him an incredulous look and scoot a few inches away. "Summer's in lane four."

"You know that's not who I'm referring to," he says, clenching his jaw. "I'm talking about Stacy Howard."

"Who?"

"The woman I slept with." His words come out in a strained whisper like they're coated in shame and guilt.

"I didn't realize it was my job to keep tabs on your mistress."

"She's not my mistress." Bob grits his teeth so hard I can almost hear it.

"My mistake . . . your whore." I roll my eyes and return them to my daughter, watching her flip around at one end of the pool and use her feet to push herself off the wall. She glides through the water with grace and speed.

He lets out an exasperated sigh. "Stacy, the woman I was with . . . she's missing."

"That's unfortunate. Were you looking to hook up again?"

"No!" he practically yells.

His outburst catches the attention of a parent seated down in front. She turns and looks up at us. Bob and I acknowledge her with waves. She smiles casually and faces forward again.

"I got called into the Prince William County Sheriff's Office today, and they questioned me about her disappearance," Bob says in a strained voice.

He wants me to react, to be concerned, to be in his corner, but I'm not going to do any of that—because I don't care what trouble he's in.

"And what does that have to do with me?" I ask.

"It has everything to do with you, Sarah. You and I both know that, so tell me what you did with her."

When I don't answer, he grabs my arm and squeezes it. "Where is she?"

"Let go of me," I say, trying to pull free from his grip. He refuses to let go, so I thrust my elbow back. Connecting with his jaw, it makes a cracking sound. Bob grimaces and releases my arm.

"Don't you ever touch me again," I warn, readjusting myself and scanning the bleachers below us to make sure no one saw.

He rubs a hand against his jaw to expel the pain. "You're not fooling me. I know exactly who you are, Sarah, and I'm well aware of what you're capable of."

"No, you aren't, Bob. If you were . . . I think you'd be a little nicer to me."

He huffs and shakes his head. "So, what's your plan then? Are you going to frame me for her disappearance? Is she already dead, and I've got a murder charge waiting in the wings? Or are you just screwing with me until I go through with the divorce? Which is it, Sarah?"

"It's none of those. Now, before you continue throwing accusations my way, ask yourself, what do you know about this girl?" I squint, staring at him. "Do you know anything at all?"

He's quiet for a moment, contemplating, eyes flitting. It's obvious he doesn't know a damn thing about this woman.

"Is she a prostitute?"

He answers right away, telling me no.

"What about a drug addict? Criminal? Wild party girl? Is she seeing anyone else?"

Bob doesn't say a word. He just sits there with a blank expression on his face.

"Exactly. You have no idea who you slept with. You don't know what she may or may not have been wrapped up in. And how long has she been missing?"

He looks down at his lap and then back at me. "About three days."

"That's not long at all. She could be out on a bender. She could have left town. And from what your coworker told me, she's young too, and young people do dumb things."

"Stacy told her roommate that she was meeting up with me the night she went missing," Bob says with a small sigh.

"I didn't realize you two were still seeing each other."

"We're not. I haven't had any contact with her in weeks, so I don't know why she would tell her roommate that."

"Maybe you pissed her off. And now, she's the one messing with you. Women don't like to be fucked and forgotten, Bob. Or did you not know that?"

He buries his head into his hands, letting out an even deeper sigh. I return my attention to the pool just in time to see Summer finish first. I'm immediately on my feet, cheering for her. In my peripheral view, I notice Bob hasn't even looked up, doesn't realize the race is over and his daughter came in first. Summer rips off her goggles, grins ear to ear, and waves at me excitedly, her head floating just above the water.

"Smile at your daughter, Bob," I say, never taking my eyes off her.

He slowly lifts his head and stands, waving his arm dolefully at Summer, his lip quivering from the strain of his artificial smile.

16

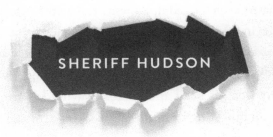

SHERIFF HUDSON

Pam and I are seated across from one another in a booth at a small bar, mostly frequented by cops—which is good, because we need distance from the public while we work to undo the mess Ryan's gotten us in. The place is dimly lit and quieter than usual. Aside from the two of us, a couple of older guys on the force are bellied up to the bar, arguing over the evaluations of some company showcased on an episode of *Shark Tank*. They don't care what this town thinks of them because they'll be able to take off those uniforms soon enough, collect their pensions, and live the peaceful lives they've worked the last forty-odd years for.

Pam pulls her chin in and clasps her hands around the beer bottle set on the table in front of her. "So, how are you feeling . . . about Ryan?"

She and I haven't really talked about it yet because each time she's asked, I've changed the subject. The image of Stevens slumped forward with a belt cinched around his neck flashes before my eyes again. I've seen far worse, but I'm usually primed for it. When I'm called to a crime scene, I've already gotten a heads-up on what's happened and what I'll be encountering, so I can somewhat prepare myself. But with Stevens,

I had no idea what I was walking into. The moments that shock you are the ones that live with you forever.

"Marcus?" Pam snaps her fingers a few inches from my face.

I blink several times, and she comes into focus again. She always brings me back.

"I'm just glad he's going to be okay," I say, staring into my glass at the brown liquid.

"That doesn't answer my question."

I lift my head and give her the faintest smile, knowing she's not gonna let me talk my way out of talking this time. Before Pam came into my life, I bottled up everything, pushed it all down, so it would fester and build. I thought it was a good way to cope with the trauma that comes with the job, but it took its toll on me. I've been on the force for thirteen years now, witnessing the worst of the worst. I've seen all forms of evil, gruesome crime scenes, bodies in every stage of decay. You carry all of that with you even if you don't want to. The best way to deal with it is to talk about it—or at least that's what Pam says.

I look to her. "I don't know exactly what I'm feeling, but when I do, I'll let you know."

She holds my gaze for a moment and then nods, accepting my answer because it's the honest one, and she knows it. Pam takes a swig of her beer and sets it back on the table.

"Okay, how are you feeling about our interview with Bob Miller?"

"I think he's hiding something and not just about Stacy Howard's disappearance." I sip whiskey from a highball glass.

I've never been a beer guy. I like the hard stuff because it burns when it goes down. Some things in life are meant to be enjoyed and some aren't. I always thought alcohol fell into the latter category. Like the truth, just give it to me straight, no matter how much it hurts.

"I got the same feeling," Pam says. "Like why would he assume we brought him in to talk about the Summers case?"

I rotate the glass, busying my hands. "I have to admit, he did have a good explanation for that since he was a suspect at one point, but he really downplayed why he was ever a suspect to begin with."

"What do you mean?" She squints.

Pam started working at the station five years ago, so she doesn't have firsthand knowledge of the Summers case. Prior to that, she lived in Florida, but it does feel like she's always been here. Maybe that's just because she fit in so well, right from the start. I haven't had a chance to catch Pam up on the Summers investigation, and I know she hasn't had a chance to go through that behemoth of a case file.

"Kelly was married to Bob's brother, Greg. She went by Jenna back then. The two of them lived in Wisconsin. Greg was murdered, and she was charged with it, but the case against her fell apart when key evidence went missing during the trial. After that, Jenna changed her name to Kelly and relocated down here to Virginia to start a new life."

Pam's mouth slightly parts. "That's quite a motive."

"It is, and we—well, Stevens—explored it back then, but as Bob mentioned, he had a solid alibi. He was out of state at the time of Kelly's murder."

"Unless he hired someone to do it," she says, lifting her drink and taking a quick swig. "Did the department ever look into his finances?"

I tuck my chin in and shake my head. "No, Stevens had tunnel vision on Adam. Everyone else that could have been a suspect was cleared almost immediately, when really, they shouldn't have been. Back then, I tried to do some digging on my own, but it was Ryan's investigation, so I was just met with lots and lots of red tape."

"Did you think Bob did it?"

"I don't know, maybe." I lean forward in my seat. "For the longest time, I actually thought it was Sarah."

Pam gives me an amused look, waving a hand at me. "Why? Because it's always the wife?"

"No," I say with a small but serious grin. "She had motive. The victim was sleeping with her husband after all. But Ryan ruled out opportunity."

"How?"

"Sarah was out for drinks in DC at the time of the murder with her assistant, Anne."

"And that was corroborated with a bar receipt, security or traffic cam, or other witnesses like a bartender or a server?"

"No," I say, staring into my glass. I'm embarrassed at how sloppy our police work was. Everyone thinks because we have protocol, that means we always follow it. Yes, we take an oath, and we wear a uniform—but underneath that uniform, we're human just like everyone else. We're flawed. We make mistakes, sometimes accidentally, sometimes intentionally. It's clear what Ryan did was deliberate. He saw Adam as a slam dunk, and he needed that investigation closed as fast as possible so no one would ever find out about his affair with Kelly. I even question how Adam was able to escape from jail following his arrest. It never made any sense to me, but maybe Ryan set him up, gave him the opportunity to run. It would make Adam look even more guilty, and it did—because innocent people don't run.

"What about fingerprints on the murder weapon?" she asks.

"It was never found."

"That's convenient," Pam says, tilting her head. "Do you really think Sarah could have set Adam up for the murder of his mistress?"

"She represented him in court. It'd be quite the play. But Kelly was stabbed thirty-seven times, so I find it hard to believe that a woman could do that to another woman."

"I've learned that anyone is capable of anything if they think they're doing it for the right reasons. Look at Ryan. He withheld and tampered with evidence, failed to recuse himself from the investigation, and didn't disclose his relationship with the victim. He must have thought he was doing it for the right reasons." Pam swigs the rest of her beer and sets the empty bottle on the table.

"Like covering for himself?"

"Those would be the right reasons for him."

"I could kill Ryan right now."

She reaches her hand across the table and rests it on my balled-up fist, her touch instantly relaxing it. "No, you couldn't, Marcus. Your reasons are right because they're moral, not because they're what's best for you."

"I hope that's true," I sigh.

"I know it is."

I bring Pam's hand to my lips and kiss the top of it. She has more faith in me than I've ever had in myself, and I don't know where she found it.

"The only thing I know," I say with a determined look on my face, "is that you and I are going to figure this out, and we're gonna do it right this time."

17

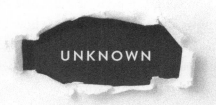

UNKNOWN

Something slaps against the concrete floor, jolting me awake. An even louder item thuds near me, bouncing several times, before it hits the wall, rolls, and settles into place. A door slams. It sounds like it's about ten feet above me and a little off in the distance, like a basement door at the top of a set of stairs.

"Hello?" I say cautiously to the dark room. "Is someone there?"

Loud, heavy footsteps stomp across the ceiling. They sound like work boots, the kind a man would wear at a construction site.

I search for the objects that were tossed down to me, hoping it's food and water again. I've received them twice before. One I found shortly after I first woke up here. The other was tossed down a while later. I think I'm provided them each day, but I'm not sure on the timing because there's no light. I find the object that bounced into the wall. It's a plastic bottle. Unscrewing the cap, I smell it first, just to be sure. It smells like nothing, so I know it's water. My throat is parched, and I chug the entire thing in seconds. Immediately, I regret drinking all of it because I'm still thirsty, and I'm not sure when I'll get more.

Rummaging around, I find the other object. It's about eight inches long, soft and squishy with a layer of plastic wrap on the outside. It's a sandwich, but what kind? I peel away the plastic, and the scent of it takes over, painting a picture for me. Bread, mustard, onions, tomato, lettuce, and I think ham. The last one was roast beef, which I'm not a fan of, but I ate it anyway. Kidnappees can't be choosers. I take a bite, confirming the meat is ham. I nearly choke from eating so fast and have to remind myself to slow down. I chew until each bite becomes a paste, and then I swallow. I really wish I hadn't drunk all the water.

I don't know how long I've been here because I mostly sleep, and when I'm not sleeping, all I can think about is how I wish I was asleep. I gave up screaming for help because no one's come, except for whoever tosses the food and water. But they're clearly not helping me. They're keeping me alive, and I don't know what for.

I searched around for a while, trying to find something that could help get me out of here. All I have to show for that is a sliver lodged in the palm of my hand. It throbs, and I've tried to push it and bite it out, but I can't see it—so I guess it's a part of me for the foreseeable future, just like the thick metal chain cuffed around my ankle.

I'm not sure who's doing this, but I can think of at least five people who have good reason to want to hurt me.

18

BOB MILLER

I check my phone again to see if Brad's texted me back: still nothing. I told him last night he needed to find everything he could on Stacy Howard. He said he'd have something to me this morning—but it's almost noon now and it's been nothing but radio silence.

After sleeping on it, I realized Sarah was right. She might be trying to lead me in another direction, throw me off her scent, but she did have a point. I don't know anything about Stacy Howard—not a single detail. Well, actually, I know two things.

One, she's a thief. The morning after she and I had sex, I woke up to find she was already gone—along with my Rolex and all the cash in my wallet.

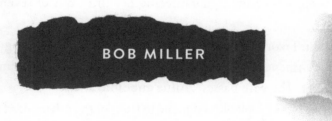

And two, she's an extortionist. Less than a week after Stacy and I hooked up, I received a text from her demanding that I pay her or else she'd tell my wife about us. She got my number from the business card she took from my wallet. I was going to pay her at first, just to keep her quiet, but by the next day, Sarah already knew, thanks to some jackoff at my firm. So, I just ignored Stacy's text as well as her follow-up attempts to extort money from me. Her telling her roommate we were seeing each other is a total lie. I never saw her again after that night, and that's why I need to find out who she is.

"Bob," Anne snaps. "How do you vote?"

I look to Sarah, seated at the opposite head of the conference table for this quarter's Morgan Foundation board meeting. Her thumb is up, so I put mine down. I don't even know what I just voted on. Anne is on her left with her thumb also pointed up. She's the facilitator, so she also gets a vote, which basically means Sarah gets two votes. I used to go along with Sarah, guaranteeing her three out of seven, but not anymore.

"Six in favor and one opposed in the vote for donating premium feminine hygiene supplies to women's prisons across the commonwealth of Virginia. The vote passes," Anne announces.

Great. Now I look like a douche in front of the other board members, who are all highly valued members of surrounding communities—the warden of a prison, the CEO of an accounting firm, the owner of a PR agency, and another man that owns a lobbying firm based in DC. The warden gives me a peculiar look. He's older with a hardened face and a booming voice, no matter at what volume he speaks. I lower my head and rub my brow, so he'll think I'm ill rather than inattentive and unfocused.

"You all right, Bob?" the warden asks.

"Yeah," I say. "Just have a migraine." I pour myself a glass of water from the pitcher set in front of me and chug it while peering over the rim at Sarah, who sits prim and proper, like everything is just peachy fucking keen. With our marriage falling apart and the reopening of the Kelly Summers case, I don't know how she can appear so calm and demure. I set the glass down and refill it once more.

Sarah pays me no mind, not even glancing in my direction. I wish I knew what she was thinking, what thoughts were coursing through that brilliant, diabolical mind of hers. I'd love to rip open her skull and poke and prod at her brain, see what makes it tick, see where she hides her darkest thoughts and deepest secrets. Even if I could hear her thoughts, I don't think I'd be able to hear all of them. Sarah can cube parts of who she really is, as well as the horrible things she's done, like sides of a die. Only one side can be face up, and that's just the one she wants to show you. Right now, she's a respected business owner, a board member, a strong pillar of the community, an activist, a loving mother, a caring friend, and a wonderful leader. Or at least that's what these other five bozos think because that's what she wants them to think. Most psychopaths can compartmentalize, and that's exactly what Sarah is. It's why she was able to stab Kelly thirty-seven times and then show up for work the next day like nothing out of the ordinary had happened. She and I are alike in that sense.

Anne clicks around on her laptop and says, "That brings us to an update on Case Fifty, Alejandro Perez. First, congratulations to Bob for a successful nomination."

There's a quiet round of applause. Even Sarah claps, and this time she makes eye contact with me, delivering a pleased smile. It's all for show, I'm sure. I pull my lips in and nod.

"Alejandro has settled into his apartment," Anne reads out loud from her computer screen. "He's passed his first drug test, and he also saved Sarah here from getting ambushed by reporters yesterday."

Sarah's smile tightens. The board members clap again, offering sympathetic looks.

"What about work?" the warden asks. "Any luck on finding a job?" He leans back in his chair and crosses his arms over his barrel-sized chest.

"He's secured a temp job," Sarah says. "But when it finishes, he'll continue with his job hunt. Alejandro did express he was already having a difficult time finding permanent work prior to being accepted to the Morgan Foundation program, due to his felon status."

"I'd like to address that," Kendall says, lifting her hand. She's an elegant, wispy woman, always dressed to the nines, and she owns a renowned public relations firm. It's all about image for her, but she's great at what she does—which is just spinning bullshit and presenting it as gold.

Sarah nods, giving her the go-ahead to continue.

"We have several upcoming national media pieces that will push to reclassify the term *felon* as a derogatory label and educate the public that people who were previously incarcerated are actually members of an underrepresented community. This narrative should invigorate the younger generation to rally around this group, like they've done for so many others. And we think the added pressure put on businesses and corporations should generate a positive impact on employment outcomes for this community," Kendall explains.

The warden cocks his head. "What are you gonna call them then?"

"My team is brainstorming a list of new labels that we feel are positive and more politically correct, and I should have it ready to present at the next board meeting."

"If we throw an *-ist* or a *-phobe* behind anyone that doesn't accept or use the new label, we could have ourselves a movement," Corey says, raising his perfectly plucked brows. He's a DC lobbyist, sporting overstyled hair that looks like it belongs on a Ken doll. If you want something done in DC, you go to Corey. I swear he's got dirt on everyone in that city.

"That's exactly our plan." Kendall grins.

"Good, I look forward to seeing what your team comes up with." Sarah nods. She looks to Corey. "Any updates on your end?"

"Yes, I'm close to pushing through a bill on the Senate floor that will offer additional incentives to employers that hire felo . . . I mean, people with a felon status," he says.

Sarah steeples her fingers in front of her face. "Is that on top of the Work Opportunity Tax Credit that's already in place?"

"That's right." He nods. "If this goes through, it will double the WOTC and give employers access to even lower healthcare premiums for all employees."

"How confident are you that it'll pass?" Sarah asks.

Corey delivers a devilish smile. "Very."

"That's what I like to hear," she says with a pleased look.

Nods and smiles all around as Anne takes notes and moves on to the next item on the agenda. My phone vibrates against the table, causing a small disturbance. Sarah's eyes tighten, but she doesn't say anything. I silence it, but not before I glance at the text Brad sent. I almost let out a sigh of relief.

> Background check on Stacy Howard came back. She was charged with extortion for blackmailing a sitting congressman a few years ago but got a slap on the wrist for it.

I text back.

> Did she have an affair with the congressman and threaten to tell his wife?

He replies right away.

> Umm. Not sure. It's a sealed record, but I'll see if I can find a way around it.

It looks like I wasn't Stacy's first rodeo. Before I can reply, Brad texts again.

> There was something else that might be a red flag.

> What!?!?!

I chew on my lower lip, waiting for him to message me back. Finally, it lands on my screen, and I can feel my face flush. The thick vein in my forehead starts to throb as I read it.

Stacy's name came up on the Morgan Foundation's external payroll list. Still trying to figure out what exactly she was paid for as it's listed as "contractor." More to come.

My hands ball into tight fists, and I slowly lift my head, scowling at my wife seated at the other end of the table. *I knew it.* She's plotting against me. Probably has been since the moment she found out I had an affair.

Before I can think it through, I grab the ballpoint pen lying beside my phone and launch myself at her. No one has time to react, and in an instant, I'm on top of Sarah, sending her reeling backward in her chair. We crash to the floor, her little blond head cracking against it, instantly putting her in a daze. Gasps and screams fill the room. With the pen clenched in my hand, I raise it above my head and thrust it into her eye socket. Blood spurts out of the wound, spraying red onto my white button-up. I plunge the ballpoint into her face over and over again until she's completely unrecognizable, just a mangled mess of skin, blood, cartilage, and exposed bone. I can't help but laugh manically. *Ding dong, the bitch is dead.*

"Bob," Sarah says with an ounce of concern in her voice. I shake away the fantasy, finding myself still seated in the conference room right across from her. Her head is slanted to the side, and her brows are pulled together. The ballpoint pen was clenched so tightly in my hand, it snapped in half, causing red ink to spill out from my closed fist and drip onto the conference table. The other board members are looking at me the same way she is.

"How do you vote?" she asks, relaxing her face to a neutral position. Her hand is raised out in front of her with a thumb up.

I release the pen from my grasp and hold out my red-stained fist, rotating it slowly into a thumbs-down. Sarah doesn't know it yet, but she's met her match.

19

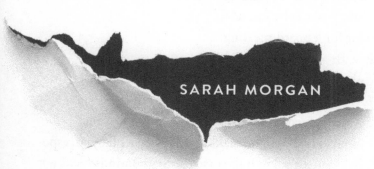

SARAH MORGAN

Anne places two mugs of coffee on the purple table and takes a seat across from me. We're at a quaint coffee shop just a few blocks from the office. The café has an eclectic style, featuring a hodgepodge of mismatched chairs and tables, but it somehow works. It reminds me of Bob and me until he showed his true colors and made me realize he couldn't be trusted. But I don't think I ever really trusted him . . . at least deep down.

"What was up with Bob at the board meeting? Was he intentionally voting the opposite of you on every issue?" Anne takes a cautious sip of hot coffee. The steam is still wafting from it, but she's never been a patient person. Only with me, she is. When the liquid touches her lips, she winces and sets the mug back on the table.

"You noticed that too?" I say, raising a brow.

"It was impossible not to."

"He's acting out because of the divorce. Must be in the anger phase of his separation grief, which was a quick progression from groveling and denial." I bring the mug of coffee to my lips, sipping slowly. It burns, but I have a high pain tolerance, so I don't mind it.

Anne furrows her brow. "And was his hand bleeding at one point too?"

"Pretty sure that was red ink from the pen he snapped in half," I say, rolling my eyes.

Bob has always refused to use blue or black ink on anything, even signing his name or adding a tip to a receipt. It has to be red. It's a stupid little power move that I've always thought made him look like a jackass, rather than an alpha male as he intended.

"Odd behavior for a board meeting."

"Very," I say with a nod.

"What's the plan after the divorce? Is he going to stay on the board?"

"My hope is that he'll agree to step down as part of the divorce settlement, but he hasn't agreed to anything, not even the divorce."

"That's ridiculous. He should be making things easier on you, especially after what he's done, and with the case . . . that reminds me. I got a call from Sheriff Hudson today asking if I would come in for questioning in regard to the Summers case. Is that normal?" Anne raises an eyebrow over her mug as she drinks.

"Yes, it is. With the investigation reopened, they have to reinterview everyone connected to the initial one."

"But it was over a decade ago. How do they expect me to remember anything?"

"They don't, really. It's just protocol," I say.

She bobs her head. "Are you at all worried about the Summers case?"

My eyes tighten, but I relax them before she notices. "What do you mean?"

"Like if they discover Adam wasn't the one that killed Kelly Summers?" She pauses and peers down at her mug of coffee before meeting my gaze. "I don't know how you would be able to live with that, especially since it's too late to make things right now. I would be so angry and devastated. I don't know what I would do."

I let out a small sigh. "I'm just trying not to think about it."

She reaches her hand across the table and rests it on mine, gently squeezing. "I'm always here for you. No matter what, Sarah."

"I know, Anne."

My phone vibrates in my pocket, and I pull my hand away to retrieve it. A text from Bob lights up the screen.

> I know exactly what you're up to, Sarah, and you're not going to get away with it. Stop all of this now or I will stop it . . . permanently.

"What is it?" Anne asks, noticing my eyes are glued to the phone.

I lift my head and quickly repocket my cell.

"Nothing. Just one of those spam texts," I lie.

As much as I'd like to think Bob's threats are empty, I know they're not.

20

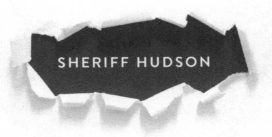

SHERIFF HUDSON

"We appreciate you coming in today, Anne," I say as Chief Deputy Olson and I escort her out of the interrogation room, where we just spent the last thirty minutes going over her whereabouts the night Kelly Summers was murdered.

"Of course." Anne smiles tightly. "I wish I could be of more help, but it was so long ago."

"We understand," I say. "And if we have any more questions, we'll be in touch."

"Of course." She nods. "Enjoy the rest of your day," Anne says, backing up a couple steps before turning on her heel and heading down the hall toward the front entrance.

When she's out of earshot, Olson bumps her shoulder into mine. "What do you think?"

I look to her and shrug. "There's not much to think. She didn't have anything new to add, and she could barely remember her original testimony."

"Almost like it wasn't her testimony." Olson raises a brow. "It's too bad we can't verify her story with something concrete like a receipt from that bar she and Sarah were at or traffic cams or cell tower pings."

"Well, I could have back then, if Stevens hadn't—"

Olson cuts me off. "There's nothing we can do about that now, so let's just focus on what we can control."

The corner of my lip lifts as I gaze into her big brown eyes, appreciating how she always keeps me grounded, anchored in the present, not regretful of the past or anxious about the future. Before Pam, I'd either react with anger or completely shut down. She helped me find the balance between the two, but unfortunately, with everything going on, I've been finding it more and more difficult to keep that balance, even with her help.

"Where are we at on the Howard disappearance?" Olson asks, pulling me from my thoughts.

"Hospitals and jails in the surrounding areas came up empty. I've got Lieutenant Nagel and a couple deputies interviewing friends, family, coworkers, neighbors, anyone that may know of her whereabouts."

"Hopefully, we get a lead there or she just turns up. And who all do we have left to reinterview for the Summers case?" she asks.

I slide a small notebook from the front pocket of my shirt and flip it open. "There's Bob, but I want to save him for last, given the Howard investigation."

"Best not to rattle him about this now." She nods in agreement.

"Scott Summers, Kelly's husband, but we haven't been able to locate him, and I'm not sure we ever will, unless, of course, he wants us to find him."

"What do you mean?"

"Scott skipped town after the trial. No one's seen or heard from him since."

"That's rather suspicious, right?" Olson tilts her head. "Guilty people run."

"Yeah, they do. I always thought he was guilty of something, but I don't think it had to do with Kelly's murder."

She raises a brow, but before she can ask another question, I steer the conversation forward. "There's also Jesse Hook, the guy who was stalking Kelly, but he died of a drug overdose three years ago."

"Stalking?"

"The defense described Jesse as a stalker. The prosecution said he was just a guy who was a little too infatuated with Kelly. Stevens cleared him, but we know now that doesn't mean he was actually cleared."

Olson shakes her head in dismay.

"And then there's Sarah," I add. "But I wanna be careful with her."

"Why's that?"

"She filed an appeal with the court to reopen Adam Morgan's case, and I got a tip from someone over at Judge Carmack's chambers that they're going to grant her request. It'll leave the department extremely vulnerable to legal action, so I'd rather not tick her off until I absolutely have to."

"It's being granted that fast?" Olson's tone is skeptical.

"Sarah's got friends in all places. If she wants something done, it'll get done, and it'll get done quickly."

"The fact that Sarah filed an appeal to reopen the case kind of makes me think she didn't have anything to do with Kelly's murder, because why file then?"

"It'd look suspicious if she didn't file, given the new information."

"True." Olson nods. "She could just be playing the game. What about Stevens? Did we hear back on how his surgery went?"

I look down at my wrist, checking the time. "No, not yet. But he should be out soon. Regardless, the surgeon informed me that following his operation, he wouldn't be able to speak for a few days, and that's if everything went well."

"Damn," she says.

"Damn is right, and the public wants definitive proof as to who killed Kelly. Unless we get some lucky break, I don't think we'll be able to give that to them." I deeply exhale through my nose.

"If we push hard enough, maybe the truth will come out."

"Maybe. But I only see that happening if there were two people involved in Kelly's murder, and one of them turns on the other. Whoever did this has kept this secret for twelve years now, and as they say, two can keep a secret if one of them is dead."

"Let's hope there's two of them, and that they're both still alive then." Olson wistfully smiles.

We're cut off by the sound of my phone ringing. I unclip it from my belt and bring it to my ear. "Sheriff Hudson."

"Sheriff, it's Lieutenant Nagel. We found Stacy Howard's vehicle."

"Where?"

"Over on Lawson Road."

"I'm on my way," I say, ending the call.

Chief Deputy Olson and I walk toward the scene that's unfolding on a dead-end street in a subdivision. There are plots of land for sale with several houses in different stages of construction, but none of them are complete. Deputies are spread out, surveying the area. The forensics crew is already hard at work examining Stacy's vehicle, a black Hyundai Santa Fe, and Nagel stands near the abandoned SUV with his back to us.

"Lieutenant Nagel," I call out as we approach.

He turns to face us and nods. "Sheriff Hudson. Chief Deputy Olson."

"Fill us in," I say.

"A patrol car spotted the SUV and called it in. I've got deputies searching for clues, and field techs are processing the vehicle for forensic evidence."

I look to the forensics team and then back at Nagel. "They find anything yet?"

"Yeah, what appears to be dried blood on the steering wheel, so I think we're looking at a possible abduction, sir."

"Can we verify that it belongs to Stacy?" Olson chimes in.

"Not without a DNA sample. She's an only child. Her mother passed when she was twenty, and her dad ran out on her when she was a kid, according to her roommate. However, I have Sergeant Lantz en route to Stacy's apartment to collect a hairbrush and toothbrush; hopefully the lab can use one of those items for DNA comparisons."

"Good," I say. "And yes, I agree this is a possible abduction, which upgrades Stacy's status from a missing person to a critically missing person. Has she been entered into the National Crime Information Center and the Virginia Criminal Information Network?"

"I'll get Deputy Lane on it back at the station."

"Once that's entered"—I look to Olson—"I want you to consult with the Bureau of Criminal Investigation."

"You got it," she says.

"What about putting out a critically missing adult alert or a media release?" Nagel asks.

"We have to consult with BCI first, and they'll take it from there, coordinating with state police to activate an alert and with the Public Affairs Office to put out media releases and social media posts," I say, scanning the area. "I'm guessing there's no traffic cams out here."

"That's unfortunately correct, Sheriff," Nagel says.

I blow out a breath and shake my head. "Whoever dumped it here either got lucky or they knew it was a surveillance blind spot. Find anything else in her vehicle?"

"A cell phone was found on the floor of the passenger's side. It's dead though, as we expected, since its last known location, according to Stacy's cell provider, was in the vicinity of her apartment."

"Make sure that goes straight to the lab, so they can start working to unlock it."

"It's already en route," Nagel says.

"Good. Hopefully, they'll get it open so we can actually see her text messages, since her cell phone carrier doesn't store them."

"What about Stacy's roommate?" Olson asks. "We should get ahold of Lantz, since he's already headed to Deena's apartment for the DNA collection. Maybe she knows Stacy's password."

"Good thinking," I say. "Reach out to Sergeant Lantz so he can ask about that while he's there."

Nagel nods again. "There's also this, Sheriff." He holds up an evidence bag containing a white business card with red typography.

"Bob Miller," I read the card aloud.

"Should we bring him in for questioning again?" Olson raises a brow.

I shake my head. "No, not yet. We just interviewed him, and he already admitted to meeting her, so that's circumstantial at this point. And I don't have enough to hold him anyway, but have it sent to the lab."

"Yes, sir. Anything else?" Nagel asks.

My gaze veers to the vehicle, where the forensics team is dusting for prints and collecting every shred of evidence. Stacy's been missing for four days now. We missed the first forty-eight hours, which are the most crucial. With her cell phone left behind, her vehicle abandoned, and the dried blood on the steering wheel, this is clearly an abduction—or possibly worse. My gut tells me Bob had something to do with this, but I can't allow my vision to be tunneled. That's why we're in the middle of a shit storm with the Summers case. Maybe there's another angle here I'm missing.

"Sheriff," Nagel says, pulling me from my thoughts.

I look to him and then Olson. "Has anyone pulled a background check on Stacy Howard?"

They both shake their heads.

"I want that too."

"I'm on it," Nagel says, turning on his heel. He gets on his radio, alerting Sergeant Lantz and Deputy Lane to his new requests, and then he calls his team over to dispense instructions on next steps.

"Background check?" Olson squints.

"Just a gut feeling," I say.

"And you're sure we shouldn't bring Bob in for questioning again?"

I scan the scene before me, taking it all in.

"No, I'm not sure," I say. "But we interviewed him yesterday, and until forensics comes back on this scene, we've got no direct evidence tying him to Stacy's disappearance. So, we have nothing new to question him about . . . at least not yet."

21

SARAH MORGAN

I clamp the metal tongs down on the sizzling bacon and pull each one from the hot pan, transferring them to a shallow bowl lined with paper towels. Two pieces of bread suddenly pop from the toaster, startling me. I'm worried about Summer, what this will do to her, what effect it will have on her. All I want to do is keep her safe.

Summer's feet slap against the hardwood floor as she barrels down the hallway, racing to the kitchen. It's my favorite sound in the world, and I cherish it more than anything because I know it's temporary. One day, her steps will be sluggish, the excitement to see me having completely worn off. And then there will come a time when I won't hear them at all. Dressed in a nightgown, Summer's blond hair goes in all directions. She sleepily rubs at her eye with the back of her hand.

"Good morning, sweetie," I say with a smile as I serve her up a plate of bacon, toast, and a slice of spinach-and-gouda quiche.

"Hi, Mom," she croaks.

"Did you have a good night's sleep?"

"I think so." The chair skids across the floor as Summer settles at the table.

"Well, I hope so." I carry a glass of orange juice and her plate of food to the table, setting them in front of her. "Are you hungry?"

"Starved. I haven't eaten since yesterday."

"No, you haven't." I laugh. "Let me get you some silverware." I cross the kitchen to fetch her a fork.

"Mom!" Summer screams.

My head whips around, and I see her arm extended, pointing at the glass sliding door.

"What? What is it?" I ask, racing to her side.

"There's a man outside."

I sigh with relief, following her gaze to Alejandro, dressed in jeans, work boots, and a tight white tee. He's kneeling on the deck with his hands on a drill and the sun beating down on him. The power tool buzzes as he presses down, forcing a screw into a fresh wooden board.

"That's Alejandro, honey. I hired him to fix the deck."

She drops her arm and furrows her brow, watching him. "Why does he have so many tattoos, Mom?"

"Because he wanted them, and that's his choice," I say, handing her silverware.

Summer's eyes light up as she takes the fork from me. "I want tattoos."

"Maybe when you're older." I smile and leave her side, crossing the kitchen to plate my food.

"Like thirteen?"

"Not even close."

"What about getting my ears pierced? Can I get that when I'm thirteen?"

"Maybe," I say, returning to the table and taking a seat.

"But my friend Courtney got hers pierced when she was a baby. She doesn't even remember it." Summer pouts.

"I said maybe, sweetie. That's not a no, so let's not push it right now."

She sighs and chews on a piece of bacon.

"Are you excited to spend the day with your dad in DC?" I ask, changing the subject.

"Kinda."

"Why kind of?"

Summer tucks her chin in. "Because I wish you were coming too."

I run a hand over her head, smoothing out her soft blond locks. As much as I've tried to keep her in the dark regarding Bob's and my separation, on some level she already knows. Children are perceptive because they're still developing and still trying to make sense of this world that can be so cruel and so beautiful at the same time.

"I know, sweetie. I wish I was too," I lie. "But I have work to do." Another lie. "Plus, it'll be nice for you and your father to spend some time together, just the two of you." That one's the truth.

She stabs her fork into the quiche and takes too large of a bite. I encourage her to take a drink so she doesn't choke. She's nine years old, but it's just a force of habit from her toddler years and a defect as a mother to always worry. My gaze falls on Alejandro again. He carries a board over his shoulder and sets it down, lining it up tightly against the one he just secured to the deck. He must feel me watching because he lifts his head and looks in my direction. I avert my eyes, refocusing my attention on Summer, who is shoving another massive bite of quiche into her mouth.

"Take a drink and take smaller bites next time," I remind her.

She brings the glass of OJ to her mouth and chugs half of it, leaving behind a mustache of orange juice clinging to her top lip. I pick at my food, my eyes flicking back and forth between my daughter and the stranger outside. I'm not sure if it's a good idea to have him around as I don't know what he's capable of. I know what his file says, what he's done, or at least what he was held legally responsible for. But that doesn't mean it entails every horrible act he's ever committed. After all, *my* record is clean as a whistle.

"All done," Summer declares. Only the crusts from her quiche and toast are left on the plate.

"Why don't you go shower and pack?" I say, glancing down at my watch. "Your dad should be here soon."

She jumps from her chair and takes off down the hall. The bathroom door closes, and a moment later, I hear the shower turn on. I should have canceled this sleepover after Bob threatened me, but it wouldn't be fair to punish our daughter for her father's erratic behavior. I just hope he can pull it together and, at the very least, provide Summer with an enjoyable and memorable night in the city.

My eyes are on Alejandro again. He tugs his shirt up to wipe his face, revealing wet, chiseled abs. I pull myself away, collecting the dishes and bringing them to the sink. But I can still see him through the window above it, screwing a wooden board onto the deck, his forearms bulging, his skin perspiring. I've never really watched anyone work with their hands. Adam never did any manual labor, and Bob wouldn't even know what a screwdriver is. Alejandro pauses to take a drink of water, finishing off the bottle. He's been out there for a couple hours now, and I'm sure he must be hungry. I prepare him a plate, pour him a glass of OJ, and walk to the sliding door, pushing it open. Alejandro lifts his head and smiles as soon as he hears me.

"I figured you might be hungry," I say, extending the food and orange juice to him.

"You figured right." He crosses over the hole in the deck where the boards have been removed, awaiting replacements, and takes the plate and glass, thanking me.

I pull the sliding door closed and carefully cross over the area with the missing deck boards. "It's looking good," I say.

"Thanks. I should be finished in a few days." Alejandro pops a piece of bacon in his mouth and chews.

"There's no rush."

He nods and continues eating, clearing his plate in less than a minute. "You must have been starving," I say, collecting it from him.

Alejandro licks his upper lip. "Sorry, force of habit. If you didn't eat fast, you didn't eat." He polishes his OJ off in one big gulp.

"What was it like on the inside?"

His eyes lock with mine, and he's quiet for a moment as though he's trying to decide how to answer my question. "Let's just say I never wanna go back."

I've noticed Alejandro's not much of a talker, or at least not with me. But he does like to ask questions. I extend my hand, taking the glass from him.

"Well, that choice is yours."

As soon as the words leave my mouth, I think of Adam. He didn't have a choice because I made it for him. Sometimes we suffer the consequences of our own actions, and sometimes we suffer the consequences of others'. Then again, in a way, Adam sealed his own fate.

"Ya know"—Alejandro crosses his arms over his chest—"I don't think I had a choice the first time around."

I tilt my head, intrigued by his answer. "And why's that?"

"I was young. My father had run out on us, and my mother wasn't capable of being a mother. She chose her own vices over her children, and it left me looking for a place to fit in, to be accepted, to feel like a part of something. People looking for belonging find it fast and easy within a gang," he says, barely able to meet my gaze.

His answer reminds me of my own upbringing. My father passing. My mother spiraling, using drugs to cope. Losing everything. Being forced to live in motels. Her bringing strange men back to our room, ones that would give her a fix in return for the only thing she had left to offer them . . . herself. And sometimes, even that wasn't enough. They would look to me after she'd passed out, like I was some sort of a bonus. I always fought them off . . . one way or another. You do what you have to do to survive. Most of us have never had to make a choice between life and death. But I can tell you, once you do, once you're forced to make that choice, it changes you forever.

"It's a shame that's what I fell into," he adds, his gaze meeting mine.

"Yeah," I say. "You and I aren't so different after all. We just fell into different things."

Alejandro offers a tight smile. "And what did you fall into, Sarah?"

"Survival."

I don't have to elaborate because I can see it in his eyes. He knows exactly what I mean.

22

BOB MILLER

I slam the car door behind me and look up at my house surrounded by woods. Seeing the large wraparound porch and big bay windows used to bring me joy. Now, it's just a reminder of what I've lost, or rather, what Sarah's taken from me. I know she's behind everything. She has to be. It can't be a coincidence that Stacy worked for the Morgan Foundation. My guess is Sarah hired her to seduce me. But what I can't understand is why she would do that.

Brad did a little more digging and discovered that Stacy had been hired as an event staffing model for a fundraising gala put on by the Morgan Foundation six months ago. Meaning, she was a hot waitress, eye candy to get the male donors to open their pocketbooks. I wonder if that was when Sarah got the idea in her head. Maybe she caught me looking at her and decided to test me, see if I'd stay faithful. Or maybe there was something more she wanted?

Sarah was the one who suggested using that same catering and event staffing company for the celebration my firm threw to honor my being named partner. On the night of my party, Sarah said she couldn't go because Summer was sick, and she didn't feel comfortable leaving her with a sitter. I was so disappointed. No, I was pissed. At the time, I thought she didn't want to see me in her old position, perhaps due to jealousy. But now I know why Sarah couldn't be there. Because if she had been, how could Stacy test me?

A shooting pain in my jaw drives the thoughts away, and I realize it's from clenching too tightly—so I relax, hold my head high, and stride toward the house. At the door, I don't knock because it's my home too.

"Summer," I call as I stroll in.

There's a glow under the bathroom door in the hallway, and I can hear the hum of the fan and the sound of running water. Just as I step foot in the kitchen, the glass sliding door opens, and Sarah enters, carrying an empty plate in one hand and a cup in the other.

"Morning, Bob," she says, closing it behind her and walking to the sink. She's trying to be nonchalant, pretend like nothing is wrong and that I'm the only one acting out. She did the same thing to Adam, made him crazy, while she slowly destroyed him in the background. The only difference is that I'm onto her.

A blur of movement on the back deck catches my eye, and I immediately recognize him. Case Fifty, Alejandro Perez. He carries a board over his shoulder and pauses when he catches me looking at him. Alejandro meets my gaze and nods.

I shake my head and turn my attention to Sarah. "I see you hired a criminal."

"He's reformed, Bob." She rinses a plate and sets it in the drying rack. "And he was your nomination. Do you not feel confident in your selection?" Sarah glances over her shoulder at me, raising a brow.

"That's not what I said." I take a step farther into the kitchen, lowering my voice. "But I'm not comfortable having him around Summer."

"I'd never let anything happen to her." She pauses her dishwashing and shoots me a look. "And besides, the foundation has a hundred percent success rate of non-recidivism."

"It only takes one to drop that percentage." I press my lips firmly together.

"Everyone deserves a second chance."

"Oh yeah. What about you and me? Where's my second chance, Sarah?"

"You'll have your second chance with your next wife, Bob." She doesn't look at me when she says it; instead she pulls the plug from the drain and dries her hands with a towel.

I let out a single sarcastic *ha* and take another step toward her. "When did you know?"

"When did I know what?" She squints.

"When did you know you were going to divorce me?"

"The second I found out you fucked another woman."

"You knew before that," I challenge, lifting my chin.

Sarah simply scoffs and goes back to tidying. She's treating me like this kitchen, like I'm just another mess she has to clean up.

"I know you hired her," I say.

"Hired who?"

"Stacy."

"I don't know what you're talking about." She wipes down the countertop, busying herself to make it clear this conversation isn't worth her full attention.

"Why the fuck is Stacy on your company's payroll?"

Sarah tilts her head in confusion but doesn't say a word.

"Yeah, that's right. I took your advice, and I looked into her. Stacy was hired as an event model or cocktail waitress or whatever it was for a gala your foundation put on six months ago." I cross my arms over my chest, thinking, *Checkmate, bitch. I'm onto you.*

Maybe I should have held my cards close, but I have other cards that are snug up against me. I need Sarah to know that I'm fully aware of what she's doing, so maybe she'll realize none of it's going to work, and she'll stop.

"Are you telling me how you meet other women, Bob?"

Always with the clever remarks.

"No!" I say, clenching my jaw. "I'm telling you that you and Stacy are connected. I'd call it a coincidence, but it's never a coincidence with you."

She pauses her cleaning to meet my gaze, staring intently at me. "Do you really think I hire the fucking cocktail waitresses? I'm the founder and CEO of the company. Anne and her assistant take care of things like that."

"Like Anne makes any decisions without your blessing . . ."

"Yes, she does. That's why companies have employees."

"You're not fooling anyone, Sarah," I say, shaking my head. "I know you hired Stacy to sleep with me."

She tosses the dishrag into the sink. "My God. You have lost your mind."

"No, you're the one who's lost their fucking mind. Why'd you do it? Why'd you set me up? Did I piss you off? Did you decide you don't need me anymore? Did you stop loving me?" My voice gets louder with each question, and I can feel a vein start to throb in my neck as the anger inside of me flourishes. "Is there someone else? Or maybe it's because you couldn't stand me taking your partner position? Is that it? Did I make you feel *small*?"

Sarah doesn't respond. She just stands there, calm as can be, with a look of pity on her face. That's the last thing I need from her.

"Which is it?" I shout. "Why'd you decide to destroy our family?"

My heart is beating so hard and fast, it feels like it could shoot right out of my chest. Sweat gathers at my hairline, and my fingers ache from how tightly my hands are clenched. I'd love to wrap them around her pretty little neck and squeeze until her head pops off. My breaths turn shallow and quick like a bull's snorts before it charges a matador. I slam my fist against the granite countertop in an attempt to release all the fury I've been holding in since she served me with those stupid divorce papers. Something in my hand cracks. But I can't feel it. Because all I feel is rage.

"Tell me why you did it!" I yell.

"I can't," she says.

"Why?"

"Because I didn't do anything. Your actions have consequences, Bob, and I'm sorry you're incapable of accepting that."

"Dad," Summer calls out. I turn to find her standing in the archway of the hall. A backpack is slung over her shoulder, and she's looking at me like she's scared of me. "Why are you yelling at Mom?" Her voice trembles.

I let out a heavy sigh, allowing the tension in my body to melt away. My shoulders drop and my chest deflates. "We just had a little argument, honey. Sometimes grown-ups do that. But everything's okay now, so there's nothing to worry about." I seal my words with a smile. "How about you run outside, and I'll meet you in a minute."

"Okay," she replies apprehensively, like she's studying me. She's clever just like her mother. Too clever sometimes. Summer rushes past me to Sarah, giving her a hug. "Bye, Mom. I love you."

Sarah hugs back and kisses her on the forehead. She almost looks like a real human in this embrace.

"Love you too, sweetie. Be good for your dad." Her tone is cheerful as she sends her off.

"I will," Summer says, and she heads for the front door. I wait for her to leave the house before I continue because I don't need to make myself look like the bad guy any more than I'm sure Sarah already has.

"This isn't over." I grit my teeth.

Sarah stares at me for a moment, studying me, trying to gauge how serious I am and how much of a fight I'll put up.

"It is, Bob," she says, but I notice there's very little conviction in her voice—because deep down, she knows we're just getting started.

23

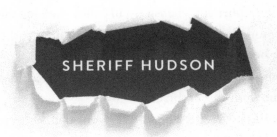

SHERIFF HUDSON

The sound of a ringing phone stirs me awake, but maybe I was already awake to begin with. Stress and anxiety will do that to you. They'll make you feel like you haven't slept a wink, no matter how long you've been lying in bed with your eyes closed. I splat my hand against the nightstand, my fingers tapping around in search of my cell. Finally, they touch the cold metal, and I hit *Accept* before pressing the phone against my ear.

"Sheriff Hudson," I whisper, my voice croaking. I glance over at Pam. She's sound asleep beside me, her long hair spread across the pillow.

"Sorry to wake you, sir. It's Deputy Morrow. But . . . umm . . . I figured you would want to hear this right away . . ."

"Spit it out, Morrow."

"Stevens is dead, sir."

My eyes widen in disbelief, and I swing my legs out of bed, planting my bare feet on the floor. I rub the side of my temple, wondering if this is a dream.

"What the hell do you mean he's dead? His doctor told me yesterday that surgery went well, and he'd make a full recovery."

"This isn't from natural causes, sir." Morrow goes quiet on the other end, save for his labored breaths. "Stevens was murdered," he finally adds.

Less than twenty minutes later, Olson and I arrive at the hospital. As soon as she heard me getting out of bed, she was up and ready to go before I was, insisting she come with. I didn't argue because I know once she's made up her mind, there's no changing it. We make our way to Ryan Stevens's room—or is it his former room now? Does it stop being his room if his body still occupies it, even with no life inside? Deputy Morrow is standing watch. Not sure why he wasn't doing that before Stevens was murdered. There's police tape stretched across the doorframe behind him, so it seems he's done one thing right, but that doesn't make the wrong he did any better.

"Sheriff Hudson, I don't—" he says with a look of fear.

I put my hand up, stopping him. "Save it. I'll deal with you later." He steps aside, and I lift the police tape for Pam to duck under first.

A doctor seated in a chair in the far corner of the room is on his feet as soon as Pam and I enter.

"Hello, Officers," he says, walking toward us with a clipboard clutched in his hand. "I would say good evening but . . ." He trails off, looking to the lump lying under the blood-soaked sheet in the hospital bed.

"Yeah, helluva way to spend a Saturday night, Doc," I say, shaking my head. "I'm Sheriff Hudson, and this is Chief Deputy Olson."

"I'm Dr. Boyd. It's nice to meet you both, although I wish it was under different circumstances." He pulls his lips in.

I nod and cross the room, pausing at the side of the bed. The sheet is soaked red just under Ryan's head, so I already have a good idea as to what I'll find underneath. There's no Schrödinger limbo here. I know he's dead, and that's not going to change by waiting. I slowly pull the sheet down, revealing the face of a man I've known for many years, but I've never seen him like this. His eyelids have disappeared up into his forehead. He must have opened them in shock, his last agonizing seconds spent staring up at the person who had just taken his life. Farther down is the wound that ended everything for him—a long, deep gash beneath his chin, spanning from ear to ear. Blood trickles down his neck. The white sheet has absorbed a great deal of it, allowing the stain to grow and spread even farther.

A thought creeps into my mind. The deputy said it was homicide, but I can't be sure that's true, at least not yet. I retrieve a pair of latex gloves from my utility belt and stretch them over my large hands. Given why Ryan was in the hospital in the first place, he might not have even been murdered. Honestly, as horrible as it is to think, suicide would be the better cause of death here. Otherwise, we've got a killer on the run. I glance over at Deputy Morrow for a moment, squinting at him in displeasure. His face is as white as the sheet used to be.

"Who found him?" I ask.

Morrow clears his throat. "I did, sir."

"Did anyone move anything?" My eyes swing between Morrow and Dr. Boyd.

"I checked for a pulse and then pulled the sheet over his head to cover him," the doctor says.

I bend down and look under the bed to see if any objects were dropped, say a scalpel. But there's nothing. I then lift the pillow and Ryan's head, sliding my hand beneath the tops of his shoulders, finding nothing.

"Olson, can you help me lift him?"

"Sure." She puts on her own gloves and helps me with Ryan, tipping him to the right and then to his left.

"It's very unlikely he would be able to do that on his own," Dr. Boyd says.

I open Ryan's hands, examining them for any marks or objects. Nothing there either.

"Why's that?" I ask.

"A person could only make a quick slash across their neck in a straight line before the body would go into shock and seize up but . . ."

The doctor walks to Ryan's body and indicates the starting point of the cut under the ear. "This cut pattern, going from under the ear, curving along the throat and back up to the other ear, would require a steady hand throughout. Plus, I mean I'm not an expert on postmortem wounds, but this cut is very deep and consistently so. The odds that he would be able to maintain that amount of force in that curve the entire time are extremely unlikely."

I look down at the wound, inspecting it even closer this time. It's nearly an inch deep throughout the entire incision. Never getting any shallower, even at the ends.

"Thanks, Doc," I say, pulling off the latex gloves and tossing them into a nearby waste bin.

"Of course, Sheriff."

I turn my attention to my deputy. "So, tell me what happened."

"I don't know. I was . . ."

"That part I already know. I already know that you don't know what happened. I know that you don't know who did this. I know you weren't here and weren't doing your goddamn job. All of that I already know. So how about you save me the time and skip to the part where you explain why the hell you weren't standing guard at that door!" I seethe, gesturing to the entrance of the room.

Deputy Morrow's mouth opens, but nothing comes out.

"I don't have time for you to clam up. We have a killer on the loose, and I need to know everything. So, where were you?"

"I was in the bathroom, sir." Deputy Morrow is unable to look me in the eyes, choosing to stare at the floor instead.

"The bathroom? What were you doing in the bathroom that gave someone enough time to notice you were gone, sneak in, unplug a heart monitor, slit Stevens's throat from ear to ear, and then leave, all with you seeing nothing? Were you installing a fucking toilet?"

"It's the vending machine food and coffee here, sir. It runs right through me. I was in the bathroom pissing out my—"

"Enough! I don't need the details of you shitting your brains out, Deputy. Now, what time did you leave your post?"

"Uhhh, I think around one fifteen a.m."

"And when did you return?"

He looks down at the floor and mutters, "One forty-ish."

"Jesus," I groan, pushing out a heavy sigh as I take a step toward him. "You know what you're gonna do now? You're gonna walk up and down every hallway on this floor, and you are going to ask every single person who isn't confined to a bed if they might have seen something while you were on your porcelain throne. And then you're going to do the same with everyone working at the front desk and anyone who has come in or out of this building in the past three hours."

"Sir, that's gonna take . . ."

"All night, I'm aware. So, you'd better get started." I stare at Deputy Morrow, the fire in my eyes burning right through him until he leaves the room.

I turn back to face the doctor. "What kind of surveillance do you have in the building?"

He stammers but regains his composure almost instantly. Like me, he's in a line of work where one mistake can be the difference between life and death.

"We have cameras in every hallway, elevator, at every floor station and every exit, and there are several positioned at the front desk and in the waiting area. We also have surveillance covering the parking lots," Dr. Boyd says.

"Perfect. Could you please have your security or IT person, whoever oversees the cameras, come meet us? I'll need all footage pulled from this evening."

"Of course. I'll go call him now." He leaves the room with much more urgency than my deputy.

"Who could have done this?" Olson asks, glancing at the blood-stained sheet covering Ryan's body.

"Anyone," I say, shaking my head. "I know you weren't at the press conference, but people were furious. You should have seen them. It may as well have been a mob with pitchforks and torches. They wanted blood." I point to the bed. "They wanted *his* blood."

She furrows her brow. "I don't think it's that simple, Marcus. Sure, they're angry, but this is beyond that." Olson gestures to the former sheriff. "Whoever did this is someone who was willing to risk it all. They knew Stevens was guarded, but they came in here anyway, and they slit his throat without any hesitation. This isn't some nameless member of the public who was so enraged they decided to take justice into their own hands. This was personal."

I know she's most likely right, even though I don't want her to be. Her theory is much more dangerous than mine. If this person targeted Ryan because of something he did in the past, then anyone involved in that case or incident could also be in danger.

"If your theory's correct, who would be pushed far enough to do this?" I ask.

"What about the family of Jackie Clarke, the woman Stevens hit and killed? Do we know anything about them? Any ex-cons or former military? Because whoever did this was very skilled."

Again, that's a good theory. If someone had killed a family member of mine, I would certainly want them dead. But what Olson doesn't know is all the other filth and dirt from Ryan's past. I don't even know it myself. If the average person sat down and tried to put together a list of people who would be willing to slit their throat, 99 percent of them would just have a blank sheet of paper. But I'm sure Ryan would have had no problem compiling an extensive list. The question is, whose name would be at the top?

24

SARAH MORGAN

News vans line both sides of the road, and as soon as they see my vehicle, reporters and cameramen scatter, ready to get their shot, hoping I'll stop to answer questions. I lock eyes with a few of them as I turn slowly into the long driveway that curves and cuts through the woods, giving them no view of my house. Even on a Sunday morning, they're out here trying to get whatever scraps they can for their story. They weren't here when I left an hour or so ago, and aside from the run-in at the office, I've been able to avoid them for the most part. The media are like freshly hatched lake flies, an overwhelming nuisance that swarms all at once, but they only live a week or two, just like a news story. I can't wait for this all to be over with, for them to move on to the next salacious news piece, one that doesn't involve me.

I kill the engine and exit the vehicle, grabbing two bags of groceries from the back seat. I had a few errands to run in town and figured I should take care of that before Summer got home. Rays of sunshine splice through the branches that create a sort of canopy over the house. I can hear the small waves from the lake lapping against the shore. A loon wails a haunting and beautiful call from somewhere in the distance, its sound carrying effortlessly across the water.

Inside, I unpack the groceries and steal a glimpse out the kitchen window to check on Alejandro. He swipes a brush along the fresh deck boards, coating them in a stain the shade of cedar. I left the sliding door unlocked while I was gone, in case he needed to use the restroom, but I'm not sure if he even came inside or not. I survey the living room and kitchen, checking to see if anything is out of place, moved even a centimeter. My eyes go to the rug lying in front of the door that leads to the deck. The corner of it is kicked up. He was inside.

I make my way to the bathroom and flick on the light. My fingers graze the basin of the sink, testing for dampness. It's bone dry. The toilet seat is down. The hand towel hung on the matte black ring is still perfectly in place. I catch my green eyes in the mirror and stare back at them, finding her in the reflection. Letting out a heavy sigh, I leave her be and return to the kitchen.

With the toe of my shoe, I flip the corner of the rug flat and observe Alejandro through the glass door. He's kneeling, one hand on the deck to hold himself upright. His back is toward me, so he doesn't notice my presence. Through his white T-shirt, I can see the muscles in his back tense up, and then he pulls his hand from the deck, quickly bringing it to his line of sight. Alejandro drops the stain brush and sits up on his knees, craning his neck forward as though he's inspecting something.

I slide open the door and pop my head out. "Are you okay?"

"Yeah, just got a splinter," he says, holding up his hand.

"Come inside then. I'll help you get it out."

"It's fine. I'll take care of it later."

"It could get infected or wedged into your skin even farther," I argue.

He sighs and cocks his head. "All right." Alejandro gets to his feet and follows me inside.

He sits at the table while I retrieve a small sewing kit from the hall closet. When I reenter the kitchen, I notice he's scanning his surroundings, taking it all in.

"Got it," I say. His gaze snaps back to me, and he tightly smiles.

I pull out a chair in front of him and sit. Our knees bump into one another but neither of us acknowledges it. With a needle pinched between my fingers, I hold out my other hand, and he places his in mine, palm up.

His skin is warm and soft with colorful tattoos covering the entirety of his forearm. Up close, I can see what some of them are now. A cross wrapped in barbwire. A rising sun. The face of a woman surrounded by flowers and flames. A skull. And the words *Fear nothing, for fear is nothing but a defect.* I wonder if he actually believes that. To have no fear is ignorant. It's what keeps us on our toes, ensures we're one step ahead. Knowing his background, it's clear he's fallen steps behind more than once in his life, which is why he's here—sitting across from me in my kitchen. I know what he is, but he has no idea what I am.

I lift his hand, bringing it closer to my line of sight. The skin surrounding the sliver is bloated and red. I press the needle into it, scraping and digging.

"Does that hurt?" I ask, pausing to look up at him. I've never seen him this close-up before, and I pick out small details I hadn't noticed. A small inch-long scar protruding from the arch of his right brow. His facial hair is dense but trimmed close to the skin. There's a black spot on his iris, like a beauty mark of sorts.

"No," he says.

I return my attention to his hand and lean forward, dropping my head and flicking my hair over my shoulder. Piercing his skin with the needle point, I push and prod in an attempt to wiggle the small foreign object free. His hot breath sweeps across the tip of my ear and the side of my neck, sending a shiver down my spine.

"You're tense," he notes.

"Well, I'm trying not to hurt you."

"I don't think that's even possible."

I can't tell if he intends his words to be playful or challenging, so I meet his gaze again, trying to get a read on him. I lock onto the tiny dark spot surrounded by the sage green of his iris. It has the magnetism of a black hole, and I wonder how many people it's pulled in.

"It is," I say matter-of-factly, lowering my head again.

This time, I press the needle a little harder into his skin, piercing a new hole for the sliver to exit. You can't always leave the same way you enter. That's true for both splinters and people. His forearm tightens and several veins swell up, creating long, purple ridges from his wrist to his elbow. He sucks in air through his teeth, the tiniest wince of pain.

"Did that hurt?" I smirk.

"Not at all," he lies.

There's a moment of silence before Alejandro speaks again. "You know, yesterday, I overheard that argument you and your husband were having. The way he spoke to you." He shakes his head, letting out a puff of hot air. "It took everything in me not to intervene. I wanted to knock him out."

"It's good you didn't."

"No man should speak to a woman like that, especially a husband."

"I know . . . that's why I'm divorcing him."

"Really?"

I look up at him, but his gaze is a little lower than mine, staring right at my lips.

"Really," I say, returning my focus to his hand.

He clears his throat. "If you don't mind me asking, how long have you two been together?"

"I mind."

"Sorry," he says.

"I mean . . . because it doesn't matter how long we've been together. Time isn't an anchor. It's not something to hold you in place just because of how long you've been in that place. Like, for instance, how long were you in prison?"

He stammers for a moment. "Ten years."

"If you'd only been in one year, would you still want to do another nine?"

"Well, no." Alejandro shakes his head. "But that's different."

"It's really not. We're all confined in one way or another. Some of us just can't see the cages we're locked in."

The tip of the needle finally forces the splinter out of the fresh hole I pierced into his skin.

"There you are. Good as new," I say, looking up at Alejandro.

His expression is serious, his eyes flicking all around my face. And then he leans in, brushing his lips against mine. They're warm and soft, and he presses into me a little harder. I'd say this was unexpected, but I could tell from the first moment we met, he wanted to do this.

The front door opens, and we break apart.

"Mom!" Summer yells. Her shoes thud against the wall one at a time as she kicks them off.

She stops in her tracks when she spots Alejandro seated at the table, rubbing the palm of his hand.

"Oh, hi," Summer says with wide eyes.

Alejandro nods and says, "Hey there."

"Alejandro, this is my daughter, Summer. Summer, Alejandro."

"It's nice to meet you," he greets.

"Nice to meet you too. I like your tattoos."

He cracks a grin, briefly examining his colorful arms. "Thanks."

I hear another set of shoes clomp into the house. Bob rounds the corner, walking down the hallway without even a glance in our direction. His footsteps are heavy, and a moment later, the bathroom door shuts with a thud.

Summer runs to me and wraps her arms around my waist. I kiss her head and return the hug.

Alejandro gets to his feet and flicks his head at me, signaling he's going back to work. I nod, all business. His gaze is intense, and he doesn't take his eyes off me until he's out on the deck, pulling the sliding door closed behind him.

"Did you have a fun time?" I ask, lifting my daughter's chin with my hand and inspecting her pale face.

"Yeah," Summer says, looking up at me. An inch or so below her bottom lip, right on her chin, I notice a bruise, shaded with hues of blue and purple. It's small, only the size of a nickel—but it's there and it wasn't there yesterday.

"What happened here?" I graze a finger over it.

"I slipped when I climbed up on the counter to reach the peanut butter, and my chin smacked the countertop."

"You know you shouldn't be climbing on counters."

"I couldn't reach the peanut butter, Mom. I'm too short," she says, slightly nudging away.

"Your father could have gotten it for you."

"He wasn't home," she moans.

I tilt my head, squinting at her. "What do you mean he wasn't home?"

"Dad said he had to go do something." She crosses her arms over her chest. "But that means I don't need Anne or Natalie to watch me anymore, right? I was fine all by myself."

"How long was your father gone for?"

"I don't know." Summer shrugs. "I watched a few episodes of *Stranger Things*, so like three hours."

I press my lips firmly together. I'm livid with Bob. He asked to have Summer stay overnight with him in DC and then he leaves her home alone—to do what?!

"I was fine, Mom," she huffs, picking up on my displeasure.

I relax my face because she's not the one I'm mad at, and I don't want her to ever be afraid to tell me things, even things that will royally piss me off.

"Why don't you go unpack and get your homework done?" I say in a calm, happy voice.

Summer groans, and before she can protest, I tell her, "Now." Her shoulders slump, and her head lolls forward, but she does what I say, picking her backpack off the floor on the way to her room.

"Bob," I say as soon as he appears from the hall. My voice is full of anger, but he doesn't seem to pick up on it.

"Ready to talk?" he asks, strolling toward me.

"Why did you leave Summer home alone?"

He squints like he doesn't know what I'm talking about but then raises his chin in defiance. "That's none of your business."

"Bullshit. She's my daughter."

"She's my daughter too!"

"Really? Because what kind of father leaves their child home alone for hours, especially one that rarely sees her anyway?"

"It wasn't hours, and she was fine," he says nonchalantly.

"I don't care if it was for twenty minutes. She's got a bruise on her chin, Bob, so she wasn't fine, and she could have gotten seriously hurt," I spit.

"Yeah, but she didn't. You really need to stop coddling her."

"Coddling her? You mean being a parent, keeping an eye on her, making sure she's safe. She's nine years old for fuck's sake." I raise my chin to match his. "Now, what could you have possibly needed to do that required you leaving her home alone?"

"We aren't together anymore, Sarah, so I don't have to answer to you."

"Yeah, that's because you can't be trusted as a husband or a father," I say, shaking my head. "When I'm done with you, Bob, you'll be lucky if you even get visitation rights."

"I doubt that. You have no idea who you're messing with." He narrows his eyes. "And I'll be petitioning the court for full custody, so I can ensure Summer doesn't end up like you."

I take a step toward him, staring into his dark eyes. "The only way that will happen is if I'm dead."

He whispers his response, but it doesn't register right away. My brows shove together. "What was that?"

The smallest smile settles on his face. "Nothing, Sarah. Nothing at all."

Finally, his words register. *Or in prison* . . . and for some reason those three words send me into a rage. Maybe it's fear that does it. Fear of what would happen to Summer if I wasn't around. Fear that he'll take her away from me.

"Get the hell out of my house, Bob!"

"It's our house," he says with an air of cockiness.

"Get out!"

We stand mere inches away from one another. He's got half a foot on me, but right now, he seems so small. Maybe I've always seen him that way, and that was my mistake.

The deck door slides open just as I tell him to get out again. This time my voice is calmer and more controlled. I've regained my composure, reminding myself that when you lose your temper, you lose.

"She asked you to leave," Alejandro says firmly.

Bob's eyes bounce between me and somewhere behind me, just off to my left, where I'm sure Alejandro is standing. I don't have to turn around to know what he looks like right now. I can imagine it's the same as when he protected me from that horde of reporters the other day. Chest puffed out. Shoulders pinned back. Chin raised. And a stare so intense, it comes off more as a threat than a look of scrutiny. Bob's eyes practically disappear behind his lids as he tightens them, deciding whether he should challenge Alejandro or back down.

"I've got someplace to be anyways." He looks at me and smirks. "Some loose ends to tie up."

I know it's a threat, but I don't know what exactly he's threatening or what it is he has up his sleeve. The words *or in prison* swirl around my brain. I always knew he couldn't be trusted, but this confirms it. Bob leaves without another word, just a lingering stare for as long as he can hold it. The front door slams closed behind him. I let out a deep breath and turn to Alejandro, who appears exactly how I pictured him. With Bob gone, his chest deflates, and his shoulders and chin return to a neutral position.

"Thanks," I say.

"No problem, and I didn't mean to intrude. I was just coming in to use the restroom."

I motion toward the hallway. "Second door on the right."

He nods and makes his way around the kitchen table and down the hall. I exhale deeper this time, trying to release all the pent-up frustration inside me. But it's still there.

There's a knock at the front door, three knocks to be exact. The thorn has returned to my side. I stomp toward it, ready to rip Bob's head off.

Hurling the door open, I say, "I told you to . . ."

But I stop midsentence because it's not Bob standing on my porch. It's someone far worse, someone who's been a thorn in my side far longer than my husband has.

"Hello, Sarah," she says, delivering her classic smug grin.

"Eleanor."

25

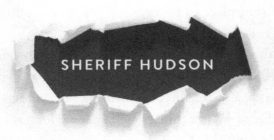

SHERIFF HUDSON

“Morning,” I say, entering the chatty briefing room, which resembles any high school classroom. There are rows of tables with deputies seated at them, all facing forward. They fall silent and sit up straight as I walk to the front. Olson and Nagel stand off to the side, their hands clasped together in front of them.

I take a seat, fire up the computer, and select the document detailing updates on our open investigations. The computer screen projects three bullet points onto the whiteboard behind me.

- Ryan Stevens MURDER
- Kelly Summers REINVESTIGATION
- Stacy Howard DISAPPEARANCE

Lifting my head, I look out at my team. “Obviously, you all heard the news that Ryan Stevens is dead. He was murdered while asleep in his hospital bed at around one thirty this morning.”

I tap the mouse, and a blurry image of a man standing in the hospital hallway projects onto the whiteboard. He’s dressed in scrubs, a doctor's coat, and a surgeon's cap and mask. "The victim's throat was slashed ear to ear by this man." I point to the image rendered from a security camera.

It feels weird to refer to Ryan as a victim. He was the sheriff for a long time, then he was a drunk, and then he was a pain in my ass. But he's never been a victim.

"Did we locate the murder weapon?" a deputy sitting in the front row asks.

I shake my head. "No, but the medical examiner believes the weapon was a scalpel."

I look to Pam. "Olson, do you want to update us on what you and your team have so far, regarding security footage and witness statements?"

She nods and steps forward, addressing the room. "We're still in the process of reviewing all the footage, but we know he entered the hospital through an employee entrance shortly before one a.m. and exited the same way at one forty. He kept a low profile and waited for Deputy Morrow to leave his post. He kept a close eye on Morrow while moving in and out of other nearby rooms as though doing hospital rounds. He never removed his mask or surgeon's cap, so identifying him will be difficult, but we would guess he's a white male, anywhere from six foot to six four, average build, age somewhere between midthirties to midfifties. It's hard to tell though, given how much of his face was covered."

"How did he get through an employee entrance? Don't those require a code or a fob or a badge?" a deputy seated in the back questions.

"He used an employee badge belonging to a nurse on staff. She said it went missing sometime between her previous shift on Thursday and her shift last night, but she hadn't reported it to the IT department yet," Olson says.

Sergeant Lantz clears his throat. "Do we believe her?" He's been on the force longer than I have, but he's got an attitude problem, which is why he hasn't moved up in rank—and why he probably never will. I can tell by the sad yet angry look on his face he's not taking the news of Stevens's murder well.

"Her story was corroborated by another nurse who swiped her in when they started their shift yesterday afternoon. I'll note she was very upset when we questioned her," Olson says.

"Why didn't she report her missing badge to IT at the beginning of her shift? Stevens is dead because of her," Sergeant Lantz seethes, his face turning red.

"She's well aware, Sergeant." Olson purses her lips. "But Stevens is dead not because some nurse misplaced her badge or had it stolen from her. Stevens is dead because someone murdered him." She turns her attention back to the room. "Whoever this man is, he knew what he was doing. He acted calmly, never changing his pace, even after he killed Stevens. We interviewed several witnesses that encountered the suspect, mostly just passing him in a hallway, and not one person could tell us a single detail about him. He blended in seamlessly, bringing no attention to himself, so identifying him is going to be extremely difficult, if not impossible."

A hand goes up in the back. "Do we think this is related to the Clarke woman Stevens killed?"

Olson looks to me for the answer.

"We're not ruling anything out," I say.

She nods in agreement. "My team will start putting together a list of possible suspects that fit the physical description as well as had motive and opportunity. Stevens received a number of death threats, mostly online, so we'll be following up on each of those as well."

"A statement will be released to the press, so expect additional media coverage and, potentially, some civil unrest," I add.

"Why would the public be upset? Didn't they want Stevens dead?" one of my more senior deputies scoffs. He's leaned against the back wall with his arms crossed over his chest.

"Some did, but others might think this was a cover-up to make the Summers investigation go away," I explain.

His brows shove together. "*Pfft.* That's ridiculous."

"It is," I say with a nod.

Right now, this is a nothing burger of an investigation and everyone knows that. It's just one of those cases that will require a lucky break to crack it. Actually, that's nearly the majority of murder investigations these days. In the eighties, the murder clearance rate was around 71 percent. But now, it's only half. Our technology and forensics are more advanced than they were forty years ago, yet 50 percent of homicides go unsolved. It doesn't make any sense.

"Any other questions or comments on the Stevens case before I move on?" I scan the room. No one says a word, and several shake their heads.

"Moving on to the Kelly Summers case." I click the mouse, projecting a new slide onto the whiteboard.

- Ryan Stevens—DECEASED
- Jesse Hook—DECEASED
- Scott Summers—WHEREABOUTS UNKNOWN
- Anne Davis—REINTERVIEWED, NO NEW INFO
- Bob Miller—PENDING
- Sarah Morgan—PENDING
- Adam Morgan—DECEASED

"These are the suspects and/or witnesses from the initial investigation. As you can see, several of them are deceased, which makes reexamining the case all the more difficult. We also didn't get a chance to speak to Stevens regarding his concealment of DNA evidence and his involvement with the victim before his untimely passing. Olson and I reinterviewed Anne Davis, but she provided no new info, and due to how long ago this all happened, we are unable to verify her story."

"Jesus, what a crapshoot," an officer comments.

"The JonBenét case would be an easier one to solve than this," Sergeant Lantz adds. The mention of the infamous unsolved Ramsey case gets everyone going, and they start throwing out theories.

"Everyone knows her mother did it," says one deputy.

"No, it was the brother. The parents just helped cover it up," says another.

"All right, settle down." I stretch my arms out and wave my hands to quiet the room. "Let's focus on our own unsolved cases."

"What if we already got the right guy? What if Adam Morgan did kill Kelly?" Deputy Lane ponders.

"We may have, but regardless, we still have to reexamine the case, especially since the reason it's going through the appeals process is due to the shoddy investigation that was conducted by our office. I know most of you weren't here or involved with that case, but it's our responsibility to make sure it's done by the book this time," I say firmly as I make eye contact with my most vocal officers. They nod and their mouths form hard lines, confirming that even though they're frustrated, they accept it.

I point to three of my patrol deputies seated at a table together. "I want you three to pull all the physical evidence related to the Summers case from homicide row."

Since homicide has no statute of limitations, we have to keep that evidence forever, so it's all tucked away in the last aisle of our storage facility. The Summers case evidence hasn't seen the light of day in over twelve years, but maybe a reevaluation of it will help shed some new light on the investigation.

The three deputies nod.

"That's all on the Summers case for now," I say, knowing there really isn't anything new on the matter. Another case with not much to go on. I tap the mouse with my pointer finger and look to Nagel.

"Lieutenant, fill us in on the Stacy Howard disappearance." I glance at the photo projected on the whiteboard behind me. It's a picture of Stacy in a tight black dress that stops a few inches above her knees. A glass of white wine is clutched in her hand. Her long red hair hangs freely in loose curls, and her mouth is partially open as though the picture was taken midlaugh.

Nagel nods and takes a step forward. "Just as a recap, Stacy Howard was reported missing by her roommate, Deena. Cell phone data tracked her last location near her apartment before her phone either died or was shut off. She hasn't been seen or heard from in six days now. Her last point of contact was a text to Deena around five p.m. on Monday night, saying she was planning to meet up with a man she was seeing by the name of Bob Miller. Sheriff Hudson and Chief Deputy Olson interviewed Mr. Miller. He denied meeting her on the night she went missing and said he had only met her once, nearly four weeks ago, when the two engaged in a one-night stand. With the recent discovery of Stacy's abandoned vehicle, Bureau of Criminal Investigation was consulted. A critically missing adult alert went out this morning as well as social media posts and a media release."

"Did we get anything back from the lab yet?" I interject.

"Yes, BCI expedited the DNA tests. The dried blood found on the steering wheel was compared to a strand of Stacy's hair collected from a hairbrush her roommate turned over. It was a match."

"What about the background check I asked for?" I meet Nagel's eyes.

"We just got that back. Stacy was previously convicted of blackmail and extortion of a federal employee."

Olson and I look to one another, each raising a brow.

"Say more."

"According to the court documents, Ms. Howard had an affair with a sitting congressman, and she threatened to go public with it unless he supported her financially. The congressman did comply with her demands for a while but eventually went to the feds. She served two years of probation, paid a hefty fine and restitution."

"Is that Bob guy, the one Stacy told her roommate she was going to meet up with, married?" Deputy Lane asks.

"He is," I say.

"Well, do we know if Stacy was blackmailing or extorting him?" Lane asks.

"It's a possibility, but we haven't confirmed that," I answer.

"That would definitely be a motive," another deputy comments. "And what about Bob's wife? What do we know about her?"

"A lot actually. Bob Miller is married to Sarah Morgan, who you all know was the wife of Adam Morgan, so there's some overlap between the Howard disappearance and the Summers case," I explain.

"Sounds like the wife did it," Sergeant Lantz calls out.

"We're looking into all possibilities, but we don't want to jump to any conclusions given the sensitive nature regarding reopening the

Summers case." I look to Nagel. "Please continue with the debrief on the Howard disappearance, Lieutenant."

"We were able to unlock the cell phone found in Stacy's abandoned vehicle, and we're still going through all of it," Nagel continues. "But there was a text to a phone number saved under the contact labeled 'Bob Miller' on the night Stacy disappeared, confirming they were meeting up. However, that phone number is unregistered."

"So, a burner phone?" one of my greener deputies asks.

There are nods all around.

Deputy Lane raises his hand. "Did that unregistered number text Stacy back?"

Nagel shakes his head.

"What about fingerprints or DNA? Did forensics find anything on the vehicle, Lieutenant?" Olson looks to him.

He continues shaking his head. "Unfortunately, it was wiped clean, save for that bit of Stacy's blood on the steering wheel."

"Has Miller been reinterviewed?" Sergeant Lantz calls out.

"Not yet," I say.

Lantz squints. "Shouldn't we bring him in again?"

I take a moment to think it over. We don't have his prints or DNA on or in the vehicle. The number attached to his saved contact in Stacy's phone isn't registered to anyone, so we can't confirm it even belongs to Bob. I know we don't have enough for a search warrant, and Bob's a seasoned lawyer, so we won't be able to rattle the truth out of him like we could with any other Joe Schmo.

"No," I finally land on. "But, Lieutenant Nagel, I want you to put a surveillance team on Bob Miller. You and three deputies. Teams of two on rotating twelve-hour shifts, starting as soon as you can pull your team together. Be discreet. Bob already knows he's on our radar, but I don't want him tipped off that he has a tail."

"What about bugging his phone or obtaining a search warrant?" Lantz asks.

"I don't have enough evidence to get a judge to sign off on any of that, Sergeant." I pull my lips in. "Let's just hope Bob leads us to Stacy."

The room nods in agreement.

"Dismissed," I say.

Chatter ensues, and my team filters out of the room. I shut the computer down and get to my feet as Olson approaches, holding her head high.

"We need to bring Sarah in for questioning," I say.

She furrows her brow. "I thought you said you wanted to wait, given the appeal."

"I did, but with Stevens dead, I'm running out of people to question. Plus, I need to find out what she knows about her husband's relationship with Stacy and then decide if she's a suspect."

26

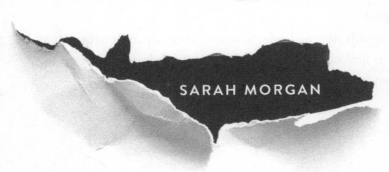

SARAH MORGAN

I hold the front door open, allowing Eleanor to enter my home. If she weren't so elderly and feeble, I would have turned her away, but I know that would reflect poorly on me, given the circumstances. She's traded in her Manolo Blahnik heels for sensible flats, and I'm sure she hates them, especially now that I have several inches on her. Her classic scent of Chanel No. 5 permeates my nose, but she wears too much of it now—most likely trying to overcompensate for her old-lady smell. It's nauseating, to say the least. It's been a little over a year since I last saw Eleanor, and she's aged so much since then. I'm not surprised though. It must be difficult to live with the fact that she watched her only son die right in front of her eyes, and she couldn't do a damn thing about it. The skin on her face is pulled so taut, it looks as though it could snap at any moment, like a rubber band stretched beyond its limits. It's clear she's done everything she can to slow the aging process, but her efforts have only left her botched.

Eleanor doesn't ask whether she should remove her shoes and instead floats into my home like she owns the place. In the kitchen, she pauses to survey it, her hands gripping the back of a chair to keep her body upright.

"It's quite small in here," she notes.

I ignore her gibe and offer her something to drink.

"Coffee," Eleanor says, jutting her chin.

I retrieve a mug from a cupboard, filling it from the pot I made this morning. I remember she takes it black just like her cold dead heart.

She stands near the kitchen table waiting for her beverage. I hand her the mug of coffee and pull out a chair for her. "Would you like to sit?"

Eleanor doesn't answer but takes a seat anyway. Her hands tremble as she grips the cup and brings it to her lips. The last thing I want to do is have a conversation with her, but I know she won't leave until she says whatever she came here to say, so I pull out a chair and sit too.

Shakily, she sets the mug down, making a sour face to show her displeasure for the beverage. "Are you having money problems, Sarah? This coffee tastes poor."

"I'm doing just fine, Eleanor. Now, what brought you here today?"

"Well," she says, narrowing her eyes, "I caught your little stint on the news."

I figured that was the reason for her unforeseen visit. She needs to have the last word, the last dig. I knew she was watching and that she'd be furious. But I didn't expect her to show up at my doorstep. I assumed she was too old to make the trip. Then again, she's always been driven by spite.

"I heard the statement you put out as well."

"Sarah, it's no secret how I feel about the legal representation you provided for my son. I made that clear twelve years ago, and those feelings have not changed. But obviously, your feelings for me have."

I lean back in my chair, furrowing my brow. "I'm not sure what you mean, Eleanor."

"I know we've had our differences, but you were my daughter-in-law, and I always treated you as such." She lifts her chin a little higher.

I keep my composure, forcing my eyes to stay put and not roll around in their sockets from her complete and utter delusion. Either she's suffering memory loss or she's messing with me, trying to act like she's always been the bigger person. My gaze goes to her wrinkly hand adorned with gaudy rings and long scarlet nails. I remember that same hand slapping me across the face so hard that blood was drawn. The words she uttered before the strike echo in my head: *You wouldn't know a mother's love, you little bitch.* I guess that's what she considers appropriate treatment for a daughter-in-law.

Boots clomp down the hallway, and Alejandro emerges into the kitchen, pausing when he spots us. He eyes me and then my former mother-in-law, or at least her side profile. Eleanor stiffly swivels in her seat to get a better look. Her head bobs as she surveys him before returning to her original position.

"I see your taste in men has deteriorated, Sarah," she says, attempting to raise a critical brow. They're permanently lifted though, stuck in a position of constant surprise.

Alejandro squints, but I faintly shake my head, signaling that I don't condone her rudeness and that it's not worth an acknowledgment. He picks up on my nonverbal cue and relaxes his face. Folding his lips, he returns the nod and heads for the door.

"Why are you here, Eleanor?" I ask curtly, my patience wearing thin. I think it was thinning as soon as I laid eyes on her.

The glass door slides open, sucking all the air out of the room. Alejandro steps onto the deck and closes it behind him.

She waits to speak until he's left the room. "A couple of reasons."

"Let's hear them," I say.

"The recent news regarding the former sheriff having been intimate with Kelly Summers was extremely disappointing, to say the least, and it was something *you* as Adam's lawyer should have uncovered."

"It was hidden from the prosecution and the—"

She lifts her frail hand. "I don't want to hear excuses, Sarah. It's far too late for that."

If Eleanor knew the truth—that I had uncovered the affair between Stevens and Summers in the midst of the trial and chose to keep it hidden—I'm sure she'd drop dead from pure shock and utter rage. But I can't count on that. Like I said, she's driven by spite and her resentment of me.

"Okay," I say. "Why else are you here?"

"I want to know what you're doing for my son's case."

I don't owe her an explanation, but I'll give her one if it'll help shorten this visit. "I've already filed an appeal with the courts because of the Prince William County Sheriff's Office's concealment of exculpatory evidence. The process was expedited due to internal corruption and mishandling of the investigation as well as some connections I have, so we should hear back soon. With the media attention, I assume it'll be in our favor," I say matter-of-factly. "And if it has to go back to trial, the Morgan Foundation will be handling the case."

"So, the world will finally know my Adam was innocent?" Her eyes develop a sheen to them.

"An appeal alone doesn't prove his innocence. It's just a small step in the legal process, which can take years. But we're lucky they're even reviewing it this quickly."

"Lucky?" she scoffs. "My son is dead, or have you forgotten?"

"No, Eleanor, I haven't forgotten."

"Mom," Summer calls from the other end of the house. Her feet slap against the hardwood floor, growing louder. She calls for me again as she rounds the corner dressed in a pair of leggings and a plain long-sleeve top, and stops just a foot or so in front of me.

Eleanor squints her wrinkly lids, eyeing her suspiciously. There's not a shred of kindness on her face, and I know exactly what she's thinking.

"I finished my homework just in time," Summer says.

"Just in time for what?"

My gaze keeps bouncing between my sweet daughter and the wicked old woman shooting daggers at her, merely because of her existence. Summer's a reminder of what I never gave Eleanor, and something she will never ever have. A grandchild.

"I told you last week that Courtney's mom was going to take us to the movies today for her birthday." Her voice is high-pitched, showcasing her frustration.

I furrow my brow. "I don't remember you telling me that."

"I did!" she groans.

"Is Courtney's mother going to watch the movie with you two?"

"Yes, Mom." She rolls her eyes.

"What did I tell you about rolling your eyes, Summer?" I softly scold.

"Sorry," she says, looking down at her feet.

A car horn honks twice in quick succession.

"She's here." Summer lifts her head and smiles. "Can I go?"

I move my mouth side to side, mulling it over. Did she really tell me? Maybe she did. I've had so much on my mind lately, I can barely keep it all straight. I can't tell her no if I already told her yes, and she needs as normal of a life as I can possibly give her. Plus, the last thing I need right now is to have a spat with my daughter in front of Eleanor. She already has enough to say as it is, and I don't need her judging me as a mother.

"Yeah, you can go."

"Thank you, thank you, thank you," Summer squeals as she wraps her arms around my neck and gives me a big hug. Pulling away, she races toward the front door to put on her shoes.

"Take forty dollars out of my purse for your ticket and concessions for you and Courtney," I call out.

I hear my purse unzip and rezip. "Bye, Mom. Love you," she says before she leaves the house.

I return my attention to Eleanor. Her wilted lips are firmly pressed together, and I can hear her teeth—actually dentures—grinding as she clenches her jaw, moving it back and forth.

"Who's the father?" she asks.

"My husband."

Eleanor scowls. "Did you *ever* even love my son?"

"Of course, I did," I say. "But he's been gone a long time."

"No, he hasn't. It's only been a little over a year." She narrows her eyes and shakes her head in disgust.

"You know what I mean, Eleanor."

"No, I don't know what you mean, Sarah. Adam wanted nothing more than to be a father, and you withheld that from him. Besides, what kind of name is Summer anyway? It's not even a name. It's a season."

I don't answer her because she wouldn't understand, and I wouldn't explain it to her either. Giving my daughter the name Summer was my gift to Kelly Summers, a way to honor her and her unborn child. After all, she was just a casualty in my war against Adam, and it was Kelly who freed me from him. I'm forever indebted to her for her sacrifice, although she didn't have a choice in it. Wrong place, wrong time, as they say. And that wrong place was my husband's dick, and that wrong time was the duration of our marriage. Bob never put two and two together, never even questioned it. I told him summer was my favorite season, and that was the reason for the name.

"Was that everything you came here for, Eleanor?"

"No," she says, lifting her chin. Her bony hand disappears into her oversized designer bag and reemerges with a manila envelope clutched in it. "I thought I'd do you the courtesy before it was official."

I squint as she extends it to me. "What's this?"

She smirks. "Open it."

I don't want to give her the satisfaction, but I bend the clasp, lift the flap, and pull out a small stack of papers, quickly scanning them. "You're suing me for defamation?" I say, meeting her gleeful gaze.

She nods. "That's right. You made false statements about my mental state, which is detrimental to the civil lawsuit I'm bringing against the Prince William County Sheriff's Office. I would have sued you for legal malpractice in Adam's case, but lucky for you, the statute of limitations lapsed."

"You know you can't legally serve me. You're a party in the lawsuit," I say, cocking my head.

"I know." Eleanor rises from her seat and picks up her purse, gripping the handles. "You'll be properly served soon enough. I just wanted to give you the courtesy of knowing what's to come." She turns on her heel and starts toward the front door, signaling that her work here is done.

"I think you just wanted to revel in it," I say.

Eleanor pauses, briefly glancing over her shoulder. "That too." She smirks again.

I don't say anything back, because I know if I do, she'll just keep talking. The front door slams, punctuating her exit, and I sigh out of annoyance, flinging the papers onto the kitchen table. I'll let her have the last word because it's all she has left in this world.

27

BOB MILLER

Walking through downtown Manassas at night reminds me just how little the town has to offer, especially compared to DC. But what DC has in nightlife, restaurants, entertainment, and everything else you would expect from the seventh-largest metro area in the country, Manassas makes up for in other areas. It's quiet, peaceful, safe (for some), and one can easily find solitude. The sound of my own footsteps echoes off the brick façades, and I can even hear the buzz of the few streetlamps illuminating the closed shops. The ring of my phone startles me. I fumble with my pocket to finally retrieve it. *Brad Watson* is splayed across the screen.

"Hey, Brad," I answer as I dip into a nearby alley and lean against the side of a building.

"How ya hangin' in there, Bob?"

"How do you think I'm doing? My wife is divorcing me and trying to take my daughter, and the woman I had an affair with has vanished into thin air." I flail my free hand, even though he can't see it.

"Look, I know this isn't easy but you just gotta stay cool. Losing your shit isn't going to help you get custody of Summer. I need your mind sharp, okay?"

"That's easy for you to say."

"True, but you also know I'm right."

"Fine. I need answers though, so I need to find Stacy."

"What do you mean? Even if she randomly reappears, you don't want to be seen anywhere near her until your divorce is finalized."

"I get that would be messy, especially if I'm seen with her . . ."

"Messy? Bob, it would be a disaster. You're trying to claim that this was a onetime screwup and that, at your core, you are still the loving husband and father you've always been. How is that going to play out if you're seen getting cozy with the woman who's the other half of this sordid affair? I can tell you how it'll play out: Sarah will eat you alive, and we might as well just throw in the towel on all your demands." Brad's voice is steadily climbing to a near yell.

"But Stacy's the only one who can tell me the truth about what Sarah did."

"What Sarah did? What are you talking about?" His anger has changed to confusion.

"Sarah hired Stacy."

"Yeah, we already know that, or at least someone on her staff hired her to work a gala. That's old news."

"No, not the gala. Sarah hired this woman to sleep with me."

"Whoa, whoa, whoa. You think your wife hired a prostitute to sleep with you?" Brad begins to laugh, his guffaws cracking through the speaker. "Come on, man!"

"I'm serious! I think she hired Stacy to seduce me. She set the whole thing up just to take me down. Probably gave her money to disappear too."

"Why would Sarah do any of that?"

"To get full custody of Summer, obviously."

"No, I mean, why do any of this at all? What's the catalyst for her setting you up to cheat?"

I sigh heavily. "I'm not sure. I'm still trying to figure that out."

"I'm sorry, Bob, but what you're saying doesn't make any sense. The whole reason Sarah filed for divorce is because you had an affair. If you didn't cheat, no divorce. So, why would she set up a scenario to have you cheat? Do you see how clunky that all sounds?"

"You don't get it. Sarah is always scheming. She's two steps ahead in every situation." I nearly spit because I'm so angry.

"No, I do get it. You're making your wife sound like some evil mastermind out to get you, and you don't even have an explanation as to why. I love you, man, and it pains me to say this, but it sounds like you just don't want to take responsibility for your own fuckup. That's all it was though, a screwup. And so what? You cheated. You aren't the first guy to do it, and you certainly won't be the last."

"Brad, listen to me. You have no idea what Sarah's capable of."

"Right now, I think she's capable of getting full custody of Summer and more than half of all your shit if you don't get your head screwed on straight."

I pound my fist against the brick wall and grimace.

Brad just doesn't get it. He doesn't understand the full scope of what's really going on. He doesn't know what Sarah's done or what she's willing to do to protect herself. I check my watch and realize I'm late for my hair appointment.

"I've gotta let you go," I say.

"Fine, but where are you at with compiling all your . . . ?" Brad starts to ask, but I pull the phone from my ear, his voice faintly coming through the speaker as I end the call.

I arrive at the salon six minutes late, which isn't like me. I'm always punctual, and I pride myself on that. It's a small building with a glass façade. White calligraphy sprawling across the window reads, *Cuts by Carissa*, accompanied with a graphic of a large pair of scissors that looks like it's about to cut the words in half. I pull on the door handle only to find it's locked.

The lights are on inside though. I peer through the glass, looking for signs of movement, but there aren't any. I wonder if she closed already. It is after hours. Slipping my phone from my pocket, I'm about to call her when movement in my peripheral view catches my eye. Carissa emerges from the back room, moving at a half jog with an apologetic expression on her face. She looks more like the lead singer of a punk rock band than a hairstylist, sporting a half dozen piercings in each ear and long bright-pink hair. She clicks the dead bolt out of its slot and pushes the door open.

"Sorry! I forgot I locked it up after my last client. Please, come in." Carissa motions with her hand.

"Don't apologize. You're the one who's keeping the salon open past hours for me." I remove my suit jacket, hang it on the coatrack, and undo the top button of my Oxford shirt.

"You're my most regular client. It's the least I can do." Carissa smiles and closes the door, relocking it.

I have a seat, and she takes her position behind the chair, peering at me through the large mirror hung on the wall.

Carissa tosses a cape over me and secures the Velcro around my neck. "So, what'll it be today? Liberty spikes? Mohawk? Maybe add some funky colors?" She smiles as she runs her fingers through my hair, checking its length.

"Dealer's choice." I smile back.

"Green liberty spikes it is then." She grabs a clipper with no blade guard and starts cleaning up my hairline. "So, how are Sarah and Summer doing?"

I debate as to how to respond to that question but decide to stick with the cookie-cutter answer. The expected answer. I can't and won't dump all the shit that's going on in my life on her. Plus, this is a place for me to relax and escape for an hour, not wallow about my divorce.

"They're good," I say. "Sarah's busy with the foundation, as usual, and Summer's doing well in school and focusing on swimming right now. She actually just won her last swim meet."

"Good for her," Carissa says without pausing her work.

"She definitely doesn't get it from me." I force a laugh. "How about yourself?" I ask to get the spotlight off me. "What's new?"

"Same old, same old. Just here, working. When I'm not cutting hair, I'm cleaning or ordering inventory or balancing the books, paying bills, running payroll." She turns the clippers off and quickly glances at the locked door to her right. "I could really use a vacation one of these days."

"Yeah, I hear you. Ever since I made named partner at my firm, it's just work, work, work."

"Mmhmm," Carissa replies, slightly nodding her head. "Let's get you over to the washing station, and I'll give that big brain of yours a nice scalp massage."

I chuckle as I get to my feet and follow her. "I know I've already kept you late, so you can skip the hair wash if you'd like, even though the scalp massage sounds great right about now."

"Nonsense." She flicks a hand. "I've got nowhere important to be anyway."

It's nice talking to a woman who isn't jumping down my throat every chance she gets. Sarah could really learn a thing or two from Carissa. As we walk through the salon, I notice she scans the back door, past the restroom and her office. She checks her watch and does a once-over on the front entrance again.

"Are you sure you've got nowhere to be? I don't want to hold you up."

Her mouth opens but it takes a moment for words to come out. "Yeah, I'm sure. Go ahead and take a seat."

She seems nervous or maybe anxious, but I decide not to press any further.

"Let me know if this is too hot," Carissa says, turning on the sink.

Warm water gushes over my hair, completely saturating it.

"It's perfect," I say, letting my eyes close and my mind go blank.

I must have dozed off because all of a sudden, there's a tap on my shoulder, and Carissa leans down, whispering, "All done. I'll meet you back at the chair."

I blink several times and slowly rise, watching her as she walks to her station. She's still double-checking the office, the back door, the entrance. I follow and take a seat in the chair.

She strokes the hair on my neck with her thumb. "Would you like a shave with the straight razor tonight?"

"Sure, why not."

Carissa pulls out a razor and looks over the blade, feeling the edge of it. She places a hot, moist towel over my throat and says, “Just lean back and relax,” before beginning the process, applying preshave oil and taking slow passes up my neck. I can hear the scrape of the blade as the hairs give way, leaving nothing but smooth skin behind. If this goes on long enough, I could fall asleep again. The smell of the shaving oil mixed with the soothing— Then a sharp pain bites at my throat just under my chin.

“Shit!” Carissa blurts out before covering her mouth. “Oh God. I’m so sorry.”

I reach my hand up to the spot where the pain is, touching it before bringing it to my line of sight to find blood clinging to my fingers. More of it trickles down my neck, underneath the cape, no doubt staining my shirt. Some blood dribbles over the cape and drips to the ground. I don’t think she nicked me that bad, but when the skin is warmed, it softens, and the neck already has a ton of blood flowing through it.

“Get me a towel and something cold!” I yell in a panic. “Now!”

“I’m sorry!” She races into her office, appearing no more than a moment later with a large dry towel and a can of sparkling water. “Here,” Carissa says, pressing the towel against my neck and extending the can to me.

“What’s this for?”

“It’s the only cold thing I have.”

I alternate between applying the towel and the cold can against my skin while Carissa stands over me, watching and anxiously biting her nails.

She closes her eyes for a second, taking several deep breaths, in through the nose and then out through the mouth. “I’m really, really sorry, Bob.”

“It’s fine,” I huff. “Accidents happen, but do you have a first aid kit?”

Carissa gives me an odd look before nodding and scurrying off.

I hear a ruckus, things being dropped and moved around, and then she returns with a small kit. It takes two Band-Aids to fully cover the wound.

“If you wanna skip the haircut, I understand,” Carissa says, tears welling up in her eyes.

"I'm already here, so there's no point in not getting my hair cut. Just keep the scissors away from my neck," I joke, attempting to put her at ease.

She laughs nervously. "Are you sure?"

"Yes."

"Okay, but it's on the house."

I can't accept that because I know she only makes enough to stay afloat. Plus, she's had her fair share of problems and unfair circumstances. "How about this?" I look at her in the mirror. "I'll pay for the haircut, and you'll pay for my dry cleaning."

Her eyes dance around my reflection until she finally says, "Deal."

I stare back at Carissa, wondering why she hesitated or even had to consider my generous offer to begin with.

28

SARAH MORGAN

"Are you sure you want to do this?" Jess asks, taking the envelope from my hand. She's seated across from me, dressed in a muted pantsuit. "If we go this route, there's no going back."

"I'm sure." I lean back in my chair, looking out the large windows that line the sidewall of my office. The morning sky is a sea of gray overstuffed clouds, ready to burst at any moment. Even they can only take so much before they fall apart.

"I just want to be certain," Jess says. "I know initially your main goal was to keep your separation private and quiet, and I can't guarantee that anymore with this route. If anything, I can guarantee the opposite. It will be messy."

I swivel my head from the window. "It already is."

"Okay, I'll get it filed right away and will request an emergency hearing to expedite the process." She slips the envelope into her briefcase and gets to her feet. "I'll be in touch," Jess adds as she heads for the door.

Before leaving my office, she pauses and delivers a sympathetic look. "Take care of yourself, Sarah."

"I always do."

Jess tightly smiles and exits my office, leaving me alone again. I didn't want to have to go this route, but Bob has left me with no other choice. I know he's got something up his sleeve, some plan he's working on. The warning he whispered under his breath—*or in prison*—changed everything. Plus, I can't trust him to take care of Summer. The one night he had her, she got hurt because of his negligence, and I can't take that risk again—not with my daughter. I wanted this separation to be quick and quiet. But no, he had to make things difficult.

That reminds me. I pick my phone up from my desk and type out a text.

> Hey, Alejandro. It's Sarah. I just remembered that I forgot to pay you for your work.

Three dots appear on the screen seconds later, bouncing up and down.

> Did u forget on purpose just so u can see me again?

> Did you purposefully forget to ask for payment, so you could see me again?

His message hits my screen before I can even set my phone down.

> . . . Maybe ;)

I move my mouth side to side, deciding what to say.

> I can swing by today and drop it off.

> If it's no trouble. Otherwise, I can come by your place.

It's fine. I'll come to you.

Do you need my address?

Already got it.

Stalking me??? ;)

I literally gave you the keys to your apartment . . .

There are two soft knocks on my office door before it clicks open and Natalie, the foundation's receptionist, pokes her head in. "Sarah, sorry to bother you, but there are two police officers asking to speak with you."

I keep my composure while trying to think of all the reasons they'd be here. I know Bob's been up to something, but would he involve the police any more than they already are? He wouldn't be that stupid, would he? There's also the reopening of the Kelly Summers investigation. I know they have to reinterview everyone, but I figured that would be much more formal, like setting up a time for me to come down to the station. Regardless of why they're here, I can't turn them away.

"Go ahead and send them in, Natalie."

She nods and disappears from the doorway. Letting out a heavy sigh, I sit up straight in my chair and stretch my neck from side to side, cracking it in the process. *Let's get this over with.*

29

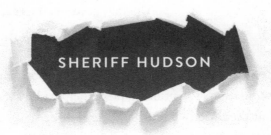

SHERIFF HUDSON

The Morgan Foundation receptionist scurried off a couple minutes ago to see if Sarah was available to speak with us. I told her we're willing to wait, no matter how long it takes. I need answers, and I can't afford to come back another time to get them. Olson and I decided to show up at her office rather than bring her in for questioning because we figured she might be a little more forthcoming if the visit was less formal and on her own turf. The elevator dings, and the doors open behind us. I turn to find a man dressed in khakis and a button-down. His eyes widen when he looks up from his phone, noticing our presence. He forces a tight smile and a quick nod before speed-walking past us. This isn't an uncommon reaction when we show up somewhere unannounced, which is exactly why I wanted to arrive unannounced. Sarah always has all the right answers, and the last thing I want to do is give her time to prepare even more perfect ones.

"Think she's going to make us wait?" Olson asks.

"No, they never do."

In my experience, people want us gone as quickly as possible. Two fully kitted-up cops standing in the middle of an office for a long time only makes things more uncomfortable for everyone. It just fuels gossip and theories as to why we're here.

The receptionist returns and waves for us to follow her. "Sarah can see you now," she says. "Would either of you care for a beverage?"

"No," I say.

"I'm good," Olson adds.

"Are you sure? We have coffee, bottled water, tea, and kombucha. We also have beer, wine, and prosecco on tap."

Olson and I shake our heads but exchange an envious look. We don't have that type of beverage selection down at the station. It's Folgers or water from the drinking fountain. Guess we're on the wrong side of the justice business.

We weave our way through the large open-concept office, around desks, tables, and even sitting areas with ridiculous ball-shaped chairs. The layout and décor are more fitting to a tech company than a non-profit. Heads pop up from laptop screens as employees do a double take upon seeing two uniformed officers waltz through their workspace.

The receptionist knocks lightly on Sarah's office door and then outstretches an arm, directing us inside. Sarah doesn't acknowledge us when we enter and instead keeps her eyes on her computer screen, typing away. Unlike the rest of her employees, she's unfazed by our appearance here—or at least she's pretending to be.

She beckons us farther into her office with a wave of her hand, eyes still on her monitor. "Please sit down," Sarah says, pointing to the two chairs positioned in front of her desk.

The receptionist closes the door behind her.

"Sarah, this is Chief Deputy Olson," I say as we take our seats.

She finally pulls her eyes from her screen and looks to Olson and then at me. "Nice to meet you, Chief Deputy Olson, and nice to see you again, Sheriff Hudson."

We nod and return the greeting.

"To what do I owe the pleasure of two such esteemed officers of the law making an in-person visit to my office?"

Olson has had little to no interaction with Sarah, and I can see by the look on Pam's face that she's thrown off by the mixture of supreme confidence laced with sarcasm and wit coming from the woman in front of us. But I know Sarah very well, and if I want to get anything of value out of her on the Stacy Howard disappearance and the Kelly Summers case, I'll have to play her games—otherwise, she'll shut us out cold. She may already have. As a lawyer, she knows knowledge is power, which is why she holds it tight.

"I'm sure you're aware at this point that we've reopened the Kelly Summers investigation," I say, figuring I should start with the likely reason she assumes we're here.

"You mean the murder your department helped wrongfully convict my husband of? The same one in which one of your colleagues concealed exculpatory evidence as well as his sexual involvement with the victim. That investigation?" She cocks her head to the side, studying our faces.

"Just because a piece of evidence was . . ." I put my hand up to stop Olson.

"No, Sheriff Hudson, please let her continue." Sarah gestures with her hand.

Olson looks to me for guidance on how to proceed. I shake my head softly, signaling for her to drop it. If Sarah wants to play it like this, then we need to dial her back.

"Obviously, in light of everything that's happened since the withheld evidence was made public—"

"Yes, the suicide attempt plus the manslaughter charges certainly don't help the county's image at all," Sarah interrupts. "How's the former sheriff doing by the way? I hope he's recovering quickly because I have a lot of questions for him."

"Actually, that's one of the things we wanted to talk to you about, in addition to the Kelly Summers investigation."

"I already answered every single question your sheriff's department could throw at me a dozen years ago. If you want to know more about the Kelly Summers case, I suggest you go ask the guy who withheld evidence from it."

"We can't," I say.

"And why's that?"

"Because he's dead," Olson answers before me.

Sarah's mouth parts but then snaps closed. Her eyes swing between us, slightly squinting. "So, you're telling me that the man who led Kelly Summers's investigation and the only person that could answer for key evidence having been withheld is dead? Right before the county will most likely be hit with a mountain of lawsuits due to his shoddy police work? If you ask me, that sounds rather convenient for the Prince William County Sheriff's Office," she says, leaning back in her chair.

"It's actually not at all convenient for us," I respond, narrowing my eyes to match her demeanor.

Sarah turns her head toward me slowly. "Oh yeah, and why's that, Sheriff?"

"Because Stevens was murdered. Someone slit his throat while he was asleep." I'm only telling her this because I need Sarah to grasp the severity of the situation. Public information be damned.

"Okay, so what's this have to do with the Summers case?" she asks, indifferent to the gruesome details I just revealed. Then again, she's a lawyer; she's heard about many murders in gory detail over the years, including one in her own home.

"We're not sure it has anything to do with it, but with the investigation reopened and Stevens dead, we're running out of people to question, so I'd appreciate your cooperation." I press my lips together and hold her gaze.

Sarah nods and flicks a hand. "Please proceed then."

I slip a pen and a pad of paper from my front pocket. "The night Kelly Summers was murdered, you previously stated that you were out at a bar in DC, having drinks with your then assistant, Anne Davis. Is that correct?"

"Yes, that's correct, and Anne has corroborated that as well. In fact, she works here with me and can verify it again if you like." She begins to rise from her chair.

"No, no. That won't be necessary." Olson gestures for her to sit back down.

It's clear Sarah is still toying with us. She's pissed, and she wants us to know it—so she'll continue to jam it down our throats every chance she gets.

"What time did you go home?" I ask.

"I don't remember, whatever I said twelve years ago."

I glance at the pad of paper. "A little after midnight," I say.

"Sounds about right."

"And where did you and Ms. Davis have drinks?"

She shrugs. "I don't remember, whatever I said twelve years ago."

I pull my lips in. This line of questioning is a dead end. If I'm being honest, this whole investigation is. It's been too long, and the work that was done is a mess and mostly incomplete, thanks to Stevens. He didn't even ask Sarah or Anne *where* they were having drinks for Christ's sake.

"Did you ever provide proof of your whereabouts or were they ever verified?" Olson asks.

"Besides a direct statement and an eyewitness account from an upstanding citizen with no criminal record?"

"Yes, do you have a receipt from any of the bars you were at that night?"

"Do I have a receipt from a bar that I was at twelve years ago?" Sarah rolls her eyes and begins to shake her head. "Unfortunately, I only save my receipts for eleven years."

Olson presses on. "Were you aware that Adam was having an affair prior to the murder of Kelly Summers?"

"Do you think I would still have been married to him if I knew?"

"We understand that you have filed for divorce from your current husband, Bob Miller," I say, changing the subject to what we're really here for. "Is that correct?"

Sarah's eyes flick to me, slightly tightening. "Yes, that's correct."

"Care to share the reason for your separation?" I ask.

"I'd prefer not to, but if you must know, Bob had an affair," she says, lifting her chin and resituating herself in her seat.

"Do you know a woman named Stacy Howard?"

"Not personally, no, but I'm aware that's the name of the woman my husband had an affair with," Sarah says, holding my gaze.

"Can you tell us where you were last Monday night between the hours of five and ten?" I ask.

She's quiet for a moment, thinking over her answer. "I was here at work until closer to six, then I went home and had dinner with Bob and my daughter. Afterward, I cleaned up, played with my daughter, read a little, and I was in bed by ten."

"What time did Bob arrive?"

"Around seven thirty."

"With your daughter?" Olson confirms.

"Yes. He picked her up from a friend's house and drove her home," she says.

"And what time did Bob leave?"

"Shortly after nine. Is there something I should know, Sheriff?" Sarah tilts her head.

"Stacy Howard was reported missing, and from our understanding, Bob may have been the last person to see her. Do you know if the two of them were still seeing each other?"

"I don't know. You'd have to ask him," she says.

"Bob stated he hadn't seen Stacy in weeks, do you believe that?" Olson chimes in.

"I don't believe anything my husband says."

My radio crackles to life. *Chhhhkkk. "Lieutenant Nagel for Sheriff Hudson, over."*

"Go for Sheriff Hudson."

"Sir, we need you down at the salon on Center Street."

"Why? What's up?"

"That B&E is looking more like a possible 187."

Shit. Just when things didn't seem like they could get any worse. "Sorry, but we're gonna have to cut this short," I say, already standing from my seat. "I appreciate your cooperation today, Sarah, and we'll be in touch if we have any additional questions."

"I'm a very busy woman, Sheriff, so I would appreciate a heads-up the next time you decide to drop in," she says, already averting her attention back to her computer.

"I'll keep that in mind." I nod and turn to leave with Olson in step right behind me.

In the elevator, I press the button labeled *Lobby*. When the doors close, I ask, "What do ya think?"

"Sarah's a real treat." Olson smirks.

"I warned you about her. She's tough."

"Yeah, something like that."

"Ya know, the timing of Sarah's story does align with Bob's, but it still leaves his whereabouts before seven thirty p.m. and after nine unverified, so he has opportunity there."

"But we don't know the exact time Stacy went missing either. We could assume it was shortly after five, while she was in the vicinity of her home, which was her last known location based on cell records, or perhaps it was later in the night and her phone died or was shut off," Olson says.

"True. Well, we've got eyes on Bob as of this morning, so hopefully we get a lead there."

"I did find one thing strange about Sarah's interview."

I tilt my head. "And what's that?"

"She didn't ask how Stevens died." Olson raises a brow.

"Huh?"

"You told her Stevens was dead, and Sarah's first response was to insinuate that his death was convenient for our office. She wasn't shocked in the slightest."

"So, you think Sarah already knew Ryan had been murdered," I say.

"It sure seemed that way, and the only way Sarah would know is—"

"If she was tipped off," I interject.

"Or she was a part of it," Olson offers.

30

BOB MILLER

My knee bounces twice for every second that passes. I'm seated in a small reception area outside my boss Kent's office, waiting for him to summon me. He called last night, requesting that I speak with him first thing in the morning. He said he wanted to discuss something, and it needed to be done in person. I'm not sure what it could be about. I'll admit, I've been a bit MIA recently—but my junior team's been on top of everything. Nothing has slipped through the cracks. I've made sure of that.

Kent's admin, Candace, eyes me with disdain from her desk. She wears a sour look like she's been sucking on a lemon, but that's just her face and attitude. I wouldn't be surprised if she came out of the womb frowning, disappointed that the room wasn't the right temperature or that the doctor didn't have designer skincare products on the hands he was pulling her out with. Her last name is Williamson, as in Williamson, Miller & Associates—but it's her uncle's name on the building, not hers. My name's up there too, but it comes after Williamson and, apparently, after nepotism as well.

I push up my sleeve, checking the time on my Rolex. I've been sitting here for fifteen minutes already, so I know this isn't going to be a good chat. Kent likes to make people wait when he's pissed at them. It's one of his power plays. Sweat it out and marinate in all of the possibilities that could be coming, make you think about every bad thing you've ever done and how Kent could have found out about it. But I truly don't know what I'm supposed to be thinking about.

"Do you know how much longer he'll be?" I ask.

Candace looks to me, squinting. "I don't," she says, dropping her chin to refocus on her work.

"Could you check?"

She sighs, lifting her head back up as if it's the greatest physical feat a human has ever accomplished. "He'll see you when he's ready to see you." She seals her comment with a smirk.

Candace turns her attention to her cell phone, angling her body away from me. I whisper *bitch* under my breath.

It's another ten minutes before Kent's admin/niece gives me the go-ahead that he's ready to see me. I deeply exhale as I rise from my chair.

"Good luck," Candace says, putting an extra high-pitched emphasis on the word *luck* as I walk past her into Kent's office.

I ignore her sarcastic well-wishes and close the door behind me. Kent is seated in an oversized swivel desk chair, the best money can buy. His office is tidy, not a single item out of place, and his eyes are fixed on his laptop.

"Morning, Kent," I say, pulling my lips in and clasping my hands together in front of my waist.

He lifts his head. "Bob, just the man I wanted to see," Kent says nonchalantly, closing his laptop and motioning to one of the two chairs positioned in front of his desk. "Have a seat."

I nod and do what he says. When I'm settled, Kent props his elbows on the desk and leans forward, interlocking his fingers. He sports a full head of silver hair, a hardened face, and a watchful eye. He's near retirement age but he'll never retire. This firm is his life, his legacy. Removing that from him would be the same as pulling the plug on someone's life support. He'll probably die right here in this very office. It's essentially a coffin waiting for a body.

"So, how've you been, Bob?" he asks in a jovial tone—well, jovial for him.

I know what Kent's doing. He's trying to act as though everything is fine and dandy, get me to lower my defenses, so I can be on my heels the second the conversation turns south. But everything is not fine, and I've witnessed this tactic far too many times before. I'm just waiting for the hammer to drop.

"Fine, and how about yourself?"

Kent leans back in his chair, swiveling back and forth. "Well, I was fine until I received some unfortunate calls last night from two of our biggest clients. Do you have any idea what they'd be calling me about, Bob?"

I swallow hard. "No."

"I figured that much." He cocks his head. "They informed me that they are not too happy with the lack of attention they've been receiving from the senior team. Apparently, they've only had direct contact with our junior members for the past month or so."

"Yes, that is true," I say, quickly pivoting. "I thought it'd be a good idea to elevate my team and give them more responsibility. More direct client interaction with tasks typically reserved for senior leadership would make them grow all the faster. Being thrown into the fire, so to speak."

"Putting in face time with our biggest clients is not a responsibility you just hand off to the junior team."

Kent sees right through my bullshit. Honestly, I knew I'd been slipping at work because I've been so focused on the divorce, and now the stuff going on with that missing woman. But I didn't think I'd slipped enough for anyone to notice. "You're right, Kent. I apologize."

He lets out a deep sigh, exhaling through his nose, signaling that he's just getting started. I already know an apology isn't going to cut it with him. He wants me to beg for forgiveness. Grovel at his feet.

"You know, Bob, it took me a long time to find someone that I felt was worthy enough to become named partner at my firm. I mean, Sarah Morgan's stilettos were incredibly large shoes to fill." He lets out a small laugh.

I bite my tongue to stop from interrupting. With Kent, you have to let him finish because he's going to get out every word he intended to say regardless. The only difference my interruption would make is to the delivery of his remarks, and I prefer condescending over angry.

"But I chose you, despite your prickly personality. Because when push comes to shove, you've always shoved back harder." He firmly nods. "However, over these past few weeks . . . I've been questioning if I made the right decision."

"You did make the right decision, Kent. I'm your hardest worker. I've proven that to you, and I'll do it again. I apologize for having fallen short recently. I really do. It was not my intention." I pause, rubbing my temple. "I've just been dealing with some personal stuff but—"

"I know all about your personal life, Bob." He raises a brow and then continues with his prepared speech. "But that doesn't excuse you not showing up at the office or having junior staff run meetings with my firm's top clients. You've been a ghost around here. The echo of your cheap loafers and the lingering scent of what you call a cologne are the only things that let me know you were once a valuable asset." Kent's anger is starting to rise, and his voice is following suit. Now would not be the time to argue with him that my Ferragamo loafers are anything but cheap and that Creed Aventus is most certainly a cologne. "The only time I hear your name in a sentence around this office now is when your colleagues are asking, 'Where's Bob?' or 'Has anyone seen Bob?' I put your name on the goddamn building!" Kent pounds his fist onto the desk, shaking the contents like an earthquake. "That means you should practically be living in it, especially for how much I pay you!"

I hold direct eye contact with him to show him that I'm listening, but I'm not—because I'm still stuck on one sentence he said. It's echoing in my head. *I know all about your personal life, Bob.*

"What do you mean you know all about my personal life?" I ask, tightening my eyes.

Kent sits there silently staring back at me. Letting the seconds pile up until they nearly become minutes. Why isn't he answering? He's never at a loss for words because he enjoys hearing himself speak so much. Unless . . .

"You," I say, pointing a finger at him. He doesn't react. He remains calm, holding steady eye contact. "*You* told Sarah. How the hell could you do that to me?"

"Now, now. Settle down." His tone is just as condescending as his remarks. His hands flap in a downward motion as if he expects my nerves to follow suit.

"I can't believe you." I shake my head. "I'm your partner. We're . . . bros. We're supposed to have each other's backs."

"I'm a sixty-five-year-old multimillionaire. I own a prestigious law firm. I'm both a Princeton and Yale grad. I'm a member of the American Bar Association, and I sit on numerous boards around the DC area. I'm a father and a grandfather and a loving husband. Do you notice what isn't on that list? A bro. I'm not your fucking bro, Bob!"

"There was no goddamn reason for you to tell her. It was a onetime thing, a huge mistake, and now you and your big mouth have blown up my family. Why the fuck would you do that?" I yell.

Kent looks out his floor-to-ceiling windows for a moment before meeting my gaze. "Because Sarah is like a daughter to me."

"Bullshit. When she worked here, you two were at each other's throats. She thought you were an arrogant asshole who acted like you were better than her."

"I *am* an arrogant asshole, and I *was* better than her. Just barely as a lawyer but certainly as a businessman. I was hard on Sarah for a reason. I molded her into the lawyer I knew she was capable of becoming. How do you think she made named partner so young? Do you think that happens by me taking it easy on someone, never pushing them to reach their full potential? It was tough love because that's how I love. I care for Sarah deeply, and I wasn't going to stand by and allow *you* to make her look like a fool."

"You have no idea what you've done," I say, clenching my fists, which are resting in my lap. It's taking everything in me not to fly across this desk.

"You did this. Not me. You're the one that couldn't keep your dick out of a hot waitress. I was merely the messenger." Kent lifts his chin.

"Oh, fuck off. Like you haven't dicked down most of your secretaries. We've all heard the rumors."

"Careful, Bob," he warns.

"Is that why your bitch of a niece is your admin now? Did your wife finally put her foot down and force you to hire someone you legally couldn't fuck?"

"That's it," he says, slamming his fist against his desk. "You're on suspension. Three weeks without pay. Go sort your shit out and come back with a severely improved attitude."

"I'm a named partner. You can't suspend me."

"Oh yes, I can, or did you forget that my name is on the fucking building."

"So is mine," I say, gritting my teeth.

"Keep this up and it won't be."

I grind my teeth side to side. Heat radiates off every inch of me while beads of sweat trickle down my back. I force myself to swallow all the words I want to scream at him because I don't want to lose this job. Kent stares back at me with narrowed eyes and a raised chin. He never argues in court anymore, so I know this is a thrill for him, a throwback to his glory days. Fire burns behind his fleshy lids and it for sure won't be extinguished anytime soon. I stand from my chair too quickly, making it topple over and thud against the floor, but I don't bother picking it up.

I throw open his office door, letting the handle slam into the wall.

"That's six weeks now!" Kent yells.

Candace doesn't look up from her cell phone. "Enjoy your time off, Bob," she says in a cheery voice.

I flip my middle finger up over my shoulder as I storm out of the office.

31

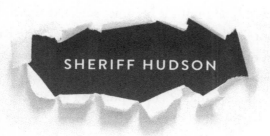

SHERIFF HUDSON

"What do we have here?" I take a wide step over the broken glass; it's strewn all about the floor, nearly impossible to avoid. My boots crunch over the shards as I walk farther into the Cuts by Carissa hair salon.

The scene in front of me is more than just a smashed window as initially reported. The place has been ransacked—chairs knocked over, salon supplies scattered across the floor, broken mirrors. I bend down, eyeing several crimson stains near one of the stylists' stations, as well as scattered dark-brown, almost-black hair clippings. There's blood, a lot of it, which is why I'm here. The forensics team is already on scene, collecting evidence and photographing every square inch of this place.

"I'm not sure, Sheriff," Nagel says. "Deputy Lane arrived on scene for a reported B&E, but when he realized it was possibly more than that, he requested a supervisor. Once we got inside and saw all the blood, well, I called you." He gestures to a pair of shears lying in a pool of blood. A trail of crimson liquid leads to the back of the salon, starting off as wet droplets and dribbles before turning to smeared blood as though something or someone was dragged through it.

"Who called this in?" I ask.

"An employee from the café next door. They noticed the smashed window when they passed by on their way to work."

"Do we have an idea as to who this blood belongs to?"

"My guess would be the owner, Carissa Brooks. Her purse and cell phone are in the office, and a Kia Sorento registered to her is parked out back."

I survey the scene, taking in every detail, attempting to string them all together to re-create the story of what could have happened here. I follow the trail of blood until it becomes smeared and suddenly stops at the back door. Pushing it open, I canvass the lot. The Kia Sorento is parked in front of a sign that reads *Cuts by Carissa Employee*, and there's a security camera fastened to the outside wall, aimed at the exit door.

"What about this camera?" I say, pointing up at it.

"That was the first thing I checked. It's not connected to anything. Just a dummy cam to scare off would-be thieves."

I shake my head. That's the problem with a small town. No one thinks anything bad can happen to them, so they go with security that's meant to deter but doesn't actually work. I follow the blood back inside, double-checking if I missed anything unusual—well, more unusual than a trail of blood.

"What's your take, Sheriff?"

"Most obvious and simple explanation would be that someone came in to rob it, not expecting anyone to still be here. There was a struggle, chaos ensued, someone got hurt, maybe she stabbed the perp with a pair of scissors . . ." I walk around the overturned chair, careful not to track through any of the blood. Set on top of the cabinet beneath the smashed mirror is a straight razor. The blade is stained red. "Or a razor. Then whoever was hurt fled out the back." I continue scanning the salon, not fully believing my own explanation.

"That's what I figured," Nagel says.

I scratch my chin. "This wasn't a burglary gone wrong though."

"You think?"

"I know. If it were, Carissa would be here—or at least her body would."

"Maybe whoever did this took her," Nagel posits.

"Burglary to abduction is a big leap, and they didn't even take her purse or cell phone."

"So, you're thinking it was an abduction?"

"Possibly. What do we know about Carissa?"

Lieutenant Nagel doesn't reply right away, so it's clear we know nothing yet. "Put out an APB on her and pull a background check. Assign a couple patrol deputies to talk to her friends, coworkers, and any family she has. See if there're any working security cameras in this shopping strip, and if there are, have a deputy start reviewing the footage. And I want lab results from the scene expedited, so we can figure out exactly what we're dealing with here."

"Yes, sir," Nagel says. "Want me to pull in BCI?"

I let out a sigh. "Yeah, may as well."

"What'd I miss?" Olson calls out. I turn to find her sidestepping over broken glass and snapping on a pair of latex gloves as she surveys the scene.

"Possible abduction."

Her brows shove together. "Another one? Think they're related?"

"Who knows? It's just one thing after another," I say, shaking my head.

Stevens is dead, murdered by God knows who. Stacy Howard is missing by possible abduction. And now, we have another missing woman. Plus, I've got the Kelly Summers case being jammed down my throat by the public and the media.

Something catches my eye at the check-in desk. The entire place is turned upside down, but on the counter sits the appointment ledger, untouched, in its rightful place. I walk to it, skimming over the list of appointments from the past week until I reach the very last one from yesterday evening at eight p.m.

"Well, I'll be damned," I say.

"What? What is it?" Olson asks.

"You're never going to believe who had the last appointment yesterday."

Nagel and Olson exchange a confused look and then meet my gaze.

"Bob Miller."

32

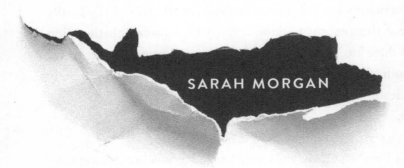

SARAH MORGAN

The knife slices through the meat like butter, blood pooling from the middle of it. I stab my fork into the severed hunk and bring the piece of steak to my mouth, chewing it slowly to savor the flavor.

Bob sits across from me, sawing his steak into several smaller bites. He spikes his fork into a piece of meat and dunks it into his mashed potatoes before shoving it into his gullet. A heaping bowl of mac and cheese is positioned in front of Summer, who sits to my left. I made it especially for her because it's her favorite. Steak and mashed potatoes are Bob's favorite. And the Paso Robles Cabernet heavily poured in my and Bob's glasses is my favorite. I figured since the topic of conversation wouldn't be enjoyable for any of us, at least the food and drink would be. It's a last supper of sorts for our family because Bob and I are finally going to tell Summer about our divorce—before things get any worse than they already are.

"How was your day at school, sweetie?" I ask.

"Good . . . but not as good as this mac and cheese," she says with a mouth full of food. I'd tell her to mind her manners but now isn't the time.

I smile and look at Bob. "And how was your day at work?"

He lifts his head and forces a smile back, his lips quivering in every direction. "Just dandy, and how was yours, sweetheart?" His tone is nothing short of sarcastic.

"Wonderful as always," I say, picking up my glass of wine and bringing it to my lips.

I gulp it, readying myself to tell Summer because I just can't put it off any longer. I wasn't much older than her when my mother had to sit me down for a similar conversation. The only difference is I'm telling Summer that her dad and I are separating, whereas my mom told me my dad was dead. The news I received was far worse, and I got through it, and so will she.

I set my glass down and dab the corners of my mouth with a napkin. "Summer," I say. "Your dad and I have something we want to talk to you about."

Her eyes veer to him and then back to me. Bob drops his silverware on his plate and places his elbows on the table, clasping his hands in front of his face. Red creeps up his neck like a curtain of anger is being drawn. I didn't tell him that this conversation was happening tonight—because I knew if I did, he'd either argue against it or just not show up. And I felt it was important for him to be here for Summer's sake.

My daughter crinkles her brow but doesn't say anything.

"Your father and I are getting a divorce. Do you know what that means?"

Her eyes instantly develop a sheen and her lip trembles.

"Summer?" I ask.

"Yeah." She pushes the word out. "Courtney's parents are divorced, and she says it sucks."

"It does, and it's not going to be easy at first, sweetheart, but eventually, it'll be the norm, and you won't think anything of it."

"I don't want you to get divorced," she says, tears streaming down her face.

"I know. But it's best for all of us."

"No, it's not," Summer yells. "Why are you doing this?"

Bob remains silent, his chin still resting on his clasped hands. It's clear I'm not going to get any help from him, even though he's the one responsible for the separation. But somehow, he made himself the victim in all this. I'm not surprised though. A narcissist can be either right or wronged. There is no in-between.

"Sometimes marriages don't work out, Summer, and I want you to know our decision to separate doesn't have anything to do with you. You did nothing wrong." I extend my hand to take hers, but she jerks it away, hiding it beneath the table.

"Why can't you just make it work?" she cries.

"We tried, but we couldn't."

I catch Bob rolling his eyes from my peripheral view. I glare at him and then return my attention to my weepy daughter. "I'm sorry this is hard for you, sweetie. It's hard for us too."

Summer shoots up from her chair. "It's not hard for you. If it were, you'd stay together. I hate you," she screams at me. "And I hate you too," she says to her dad before sprinting out of the room. "I wish I could divorce both of you," Summer yells before her bedroom door slams closed. A moment later, a Taylor Swift song blares.

I take a long sip of red wine, briefly holding it in my mouth to feel the sharp tannins and taste the rich notes of ripe black cherry and smoky cacao.

"Are you happy now?" Bob asks as he stabs his fork into a piece of steak. A smug look is plastered across his face.

"No, I'm not, but we had to tell her sooner or later."

"Oh, and it had to be now? You know, before you frame me for Stacy's disappearance?" His eyes flash with anger as he stuffs the food into his mouth, chewing obnoxiously. He might be chewing normally, but I find everything about him obnoxious.

I give him a pointed look and sip my wine, refusing to acknowledge his question. It doesn't matter what I say anyway because he won't believe me—just like I won't believe him. Once you lose someone's trust, you never really get it back. Even if you think you do, there will always be that little niggling thought lodged in your mind, forever wondering, *Are they lying to me . . . again?*

When I don't respond, he says, "I would have appreciated a heads-up that you were telling her tonight."

"And I would have appreciated you not cheating on me. We all can't get what we want, now can we, Bob?"

See? The resentment I feel toward him and that little niggling thought are permanent fixtures in my brain now.

"I've already apologized countless times, but it doesn't matter what I say because you'll never forgive me. That's just who you are."

"You're wrong about that. I have forgiven you; I've just chosen to forget you too." I peer at him over the rim of my glass as I slowly sip, my dinner forgotten.

He sits stone-faced and motionless. "I think you're going to have a hard time forgetting me, Sarah."

I stifle a laugh. "Oh yeah. Why's that? What makes you so unforgettable?"

Bob's always had a God complex. Most narcissists do. He thinks he's more important, more memorable, more charming, more interesting, more of everything than he actually is.

"Did Adam ever forget about you?" he says, cocking his head. "He didn't, did he? He thought about you every single day for eleven years while he was locked up in a six-by-nine cell, a cell, unbeknownst to him, you put him in. And he thought about you in his final moments when the little bit of life he had left was ripped out of him, one decompressed needle at a time. So, yeah, Sarah, I think you're going to have a very hard time forgetting about me." He seals his thinly veiled threat with a small menacing smile.

"I'm not your Adam, Bob, and you're definitely not my Sarah."

"You sure about that? Do you think I didn't know back then that I needed to have an insurance policy with you? Something to guarantee you couldn't do to me what you did to Adam."

I squint, taking in every inch of his face, searching for a tell, something to tip off that he's lying. But he's stoic. "You're bluffing," I say.

My fists become balls beneath the table, and my heart hammers in my chest so fast and frenzied, it feels like it could smash through my rib cage and leap right onto my plate. I'm sure if it did, Bob wouldn't hesitate to eat it. I take several short, deep breaths—trying to keep my cool. I don't know what he has on me. My brain acts like a Rolodex now, going over our memories together, moments when I may have left myself vulnerable. But nothing stands out. I've always been careful, but maybe I wasn't careful enough.

"Then call my bluff," Bob says. "I've been patient with you, Sarah, and I've been beyond nice. But we're past that now. If Stacy Howard doesn't make a sudden reappearance, my insurance policy goes straight to the police." He raises his chin, deepening the fire in his eyes.

"I don't know what you're talking about." I drain the rest of my wine.

"Sure, you don't." He grins, chewing slowly on a piece of steak. "Don't say I didn't warn you."

I fiddle with the stem of the glass, rotating it, while my eyes remain on Bob. He shovels the food I bought, prepared, and cooked into his gluttonous mouth—and all I can think now is, *I should have killed him when I had the chance.*

33

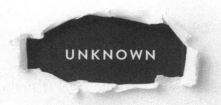

UNKNOWN

The sound of whimpering stirs me awake. It takes a moment for me to open my eyes and pull myself into a seated position. Even then, I'm foggy, almost in a daze, like coming to after going on a multiday bender. The whimpering is emanating from the other side of the room, or what I think is the other side of the room. It's the first noise I've heard besides boots clomping across the floor above me, the sound of a bottle of water or plastic-wrapped sandwich hitting the pavement, or the door at the top of the stairs closing. I can't see the stairs, but I know they're there.

"Hello?" I call out.

The whimpering stops as though they've sucked in a breath, and the room falls silent.

"Is someone there?" I ask.

"Hello?" a shaky, faint voice answers back.

"Oh, thank God. You have to help me. My leg is . . ."

The familiar sound of a chain dragging on concrete fills the basement. The woman shrieks in a panic. "Why are you doing this to me?" Her voice cracks, and a sob erupts.

"I didn't do anything to . . ."

"Let me go!" she screams. At me or at the room, I'm not sure.

"I can't," I say. "I'm chained up too."

I think back to when I first woke up down here. I was completely panicked, disoriented, terrified. I don't even know how long ago that was. But if I were her, I'd be suspicious of me too.

"Did you see him?"

The woman doesn't respond right away, but when she finally does, she says, "Who?"

"The man that put us down here."

"No . . ." she cries. "Did you?"

I shake my head but realize she can't see me in the darkness. "No. I haven't seen him. He tosses food and water from the top of the steps, always when I'm asleep. But he's never come down."

"How long have you been here?" she asks.

"I don't know. No light gets through, so I have no idea how many times the sun has risen and set while I've been chained to this fucking pole." I shake my chain, and it rattles against the floor as I let out a long, frustrated scream. When I'm done, all I can hear is my own labored breathing, and I worry I've scared her more than she already is.

"Sorry," I say, letting out a deep sigh. "Are you hurt?"

It takes her a moment to answer. "My head hurts, and I feel dizzy and nauseous and like I'm not real. I don't know if that makes sense."

"It does. That's how I felt when I woke up down here," I say, trying to comfort her, but there's nothing comforting about our shared experience other than me still being alive.

She sniffles. "Why is he doing this to us?"

"I don't know."

It's clear she doesn't like that answer because she starts screaming again. Her chain slams against the concrete over and over as she tugs, pulls, and shakes it.

"Shhh. Shhh. No one can hear us," I say. "Save your energy."

"I don't wanna die." She weeps through her words.

"I don't either, but we're not gonna let that happen, okay?" She might be nodding her head in the dark, but I hear nothing except her continuous crying. "I'm Stacy, by the way. What's your name?"

She hesitates before she speaks. "Carissa . . . My name's Carissa."

34

BOB MILLER

Brad isn't at the station when I arrive the next morning, so I sit in an interrogation room alone, refusing to speak to anyone without my lawyer present. Once again, I don't know why I'm here, but I'm not going to give them the chance to twist any of my words, so I'll wait silently until he arrives. Hudson and Olson didn't handcuff me to the metal table, which is good because it means this chat is voluntary and they don't have anything to hold me for . . . at least not yet.

I can't see what's beyond the two-way mirror off to the left, but I can guess that they're watching me, seeing how I react. Am I panicking? Do I look nervous? Am I sweating? Are my eyes bouncing back and forth at a hundred miles per hour while I try to twist the skin off my hands, wrenching them over and over in fear? No. I sit calmly, staring forward, biding my time. They think they've caged me, that they have the upper hand on their home turf. But they're wrong. This isn't my first rodeo, and I'm sure it won't be my last.

The door creaks open and Brad enters.

"Have you said anything?" he asks, getting straight to business before he's even taken a seat. He's dressed in a sharp navy suit, a freshly starched bright-white shirt, and a red tie with whimsical patterns dancing all over it in a way that signals it could only be from one brand. He looks the part of a high-powered defense attorney, which is exactly what I need right now.

"No," I say, shaking my head.

A moment later, Chief Deputy Olson enters the room, closely followed by Sheriff Hudson. He closes the door behind him, and they take their seats across from me and Brad.

"Would you care to tell me why you've requested my client to your station for questioning twice in one week?" Brad pulls a legal pad and pen from his designer briefcase.

Sheriff Hudson eyes Brad. "We'll get to that," he says and then turns his focus to me. "Bob, do you know a Carissa Brooks?"

My brows shove together, and I look to Brad for guidance. He nods, indicating I can answer if I choose to. I know all the things I would tell my own client to do, but I'm paying Brad for a reason. Because sometimes you can't see what's right in front of you.

I have no idea where they're going with this or why Hudson is asking me about a hairstylist. I figured I was summoned here to be reinterviewed about the Kelly Summers case or that they would follow up with more questions related to Stacy Howard's disappearance.

"Yes, I know Carissa. She cuts my hair."

"When was the last time you saw her?" Olson asks.

"Sunday night."

"About what time?"

"My appointment was at eight, but I was running a few minutes behind."

Hudson nods. "And what time did you leave?"

"Nine fifteen, maybe nine thirty. Not sure on the exact time," I say.

"How was she when you left?" Hudson asks.

I look to Brad so he'll know to interject. "My client can't give you an assessment of Ms. Brooks's state of mind."

"Let me rephrase that then. Did she seem okay when you left?"

"Define 'okay,'" Brad says.

Hudson lets out an exasperated sigh, and Olson cuts in, "Did anything odd or out of the ordinary occur during your appointment?"

"No," I say, just wanting to get this over with . . . whatever *this* is.

"Did you and Carissa argue at all?"

I answer no again.

"Have you ever argued?"

"No," I say pointedly.

"Have you and Carissa ever been intimate?" Hudson asks.

"What! No, absolutely not," I say, incredulous.

Sheriff Hudson twists up his lips. "How did the salon look when you left?"

"The same as when I arrived."

Brad clears his throat. "My client is a highly respected attorney, and he's here voluntarily, so with all due respect, Sheriff Hudson and Chief Deputy Olson, can you please get to the point?"

"We're getting there, Mr. Watson," Hudson says to Brad and then looks to me. "Mr. Miller, we received a call for a B&E at Cuts by Carissa yesterday morning, and when we arrived, we found that the place had been ransacked. Nothing was taken but there was blood everywhere. Ms. Brooks's purse, cell phone, and car were all left behind. According to the salon's appointment schedule, you were Carissa's last client on Sunday night and presumably the last person to see her."

My eyes go wide. This can't be happening. Everything was fine when I left . . . well, besides Carissa seeming a bit off. Did she know something was coming? Was she expecting someone?

Hudson leans forward in his chair, placing his elbows on the table. "Given your connection to the Stacy Howard disappearance, it seems a bit odd, don't you think? Two women going missing in the same week and Bob Miller is the last person to see either of them."

"That is speculative at best. There is no way to prove my client was the last person to see either of those women before they went missing,"

Brad argues. He's animated, sitting forward in his chair and waving off the implication.

"There's always a way to prove anything, Mr. Watson," Hudson says coolly.

"My client has already stated that he hadn't had any communication with Ms. Howard in weeks. If you can prove otherwise, then I'd like to hear it. In terms of Ms. Brooks, having a hair appointment isn't evidence of anything other than my client having been a customer at the salon, which he already said he was, and you can tell by his hair, he recently had it cut." Brad motions to me.

The sheriff leans back, places his hands behind his head, and looks to Chief Deputy Olson.

"We found Stacy's abandoned car," she says, staring into my eyes. "And inside her car, we found your business card and her cell phone. There were text messages exchanged to a contact labeled *Bob Miller*. Do you know anything about that?"

"What number is connected to that contact in her phone? Is it registered to my client?" Brad lifts his chin.

Hudson deflates slightly and drops his hands. "We're still looking into that."

"Exactly," Brad says. "You've got nothing."

The room quiets while the sheriff and his chief deputy share what appears to be a smug look. *Fuck.* I know what's coming. My stomach drops, and my throat dries, making it nearly impossible to swallow.

"But Stacy did text a phone number registered to your client a few weeks ago. Isn't that right, Bob?" Hudson cocks his head.

Before I can explain, Olson is already pulling out a piece of paper and sliding it across the table. *Shit!*

"This is a text conversation we pulled from Stacy's cell phone. It's from three weeks before Stacy went missing, and it's between her and your client's *registered* phone number," Olson says. "Do you remember this exchange, Bob?"

Brad forces a puff of air out of his nose, clearly frustrated that I failed to mention this to him.

STACY HOWARD

Hey Bob, I have a proposition for you.

BOB MILLER

Who is this?

STACY HOWARD

Stacy, your favorite one-night stand 😉

BOB MILLER

How'd you get my number?

STACY HOWARD

I knew we had future business to settle, so I snagged one of your business cards on my way out.

BOB MILLER

Yeah, along with my Rolex and all the cash in my wallet. You're lucky I didn't file a police report.

STACY HOWARD

I knew you wouldn't because you wouldn't want your wife to find out about us, now, would you?

BOB MILLER

What is it you want from me?

STACY HOWARD

What everyone wants. Money.

BOB MILLER

How much?

STACY HOWARD

You tell me. How much is your marriage worth?

BOB MILLER

Don't you fucking play with me. You're a goddamn thief and a whore. You meant nothing, and if I hadn't been wasted, it would have never happened. You know that just as well as I do.

STACY HOWARD

The only thing I know is that you cheated on your wife, Bob. Now, how much is my silence worth to you?

BOB MILLER

It was a mistake. You took advantage of me.

STACY HOWARD

Lol I think I got the short end of the stick, literally. 😂

BOB MILLER

Fuck you, bitch!

STACY HOWARD

You already did.

"You must have been livid, Bob," Hudson says, arching a brow. "I mean, Stacy was trying to extort you, even made fun of your manhood. That had to have made your blood boil."

"Don't say anything," Brad instructs, pursing his lips firmly together.

Hudson's trying to corner me, but I've done nothing wrong . . . well, at least nothing that he's aware of. I know I didn't send a text to Stacy after that, despite her continuing to message me. I stopped responding to her for a bit because I was due in court, and by the time I was going to reply, Sarah had already found out.

"This evidence is damning," Olson notes, gesturing to the piece of paper.

"It's circumstantial at best," Brad says. "Where's the rest of the conversation, or is this all you got? The only thing this proves is that Stacy's an extortionist."

"There was also blood found on the steering wheel of Stacy's vehicle. We have forensics examining the DNA from both scenes as we speak. Is there something you want to get off your chest before those results come back, Bob?" Hudson asks.

"No," is all I say because I know it's important to always say as little as possible when dealing with the police. The more words you give them, the more they can twist them into a whole new story, particularly in court.

The sheriff squints his eyes as he studies me. "That cut on your neck looks pretty fresh. How'd you get that?" he says, pointing to my throat.

I reflexively reach up and feel the long thin scab on my neck. *Shit.* I forgot about that. I should have mentioned it right away. They're going to find my blood at the salon. "Carissa nicked my skin when she was shaving me."

Brad gives me a strained look. He's pissed I'm just bringing it up now.

"That must have been painful. Did that make you angry, Bob?" Olson asks.

"No, it was just an accident."

"I'd be pretty mad if someone cut me," Hudson says.

They're clearly trying to lead me down a path of speculation where I'm this enraged lunatic who lashed out in a spurt of anger, but I'm not falling for it. I just have to keep my cool and give him the complete opposite of what he thinks I am.

"I wasn't. Carissa's usually a very good stylist. She was just off on Sunday night."

Olson gives me a pointed look. "What do you mean by 'off'?"

"Not her normal self. She seemed almost paranoid, like she was watching for something or someone. The door was locked when I arrived too, which it never is. And she relocked it as soon as she let me in. I think that's why she accidentally cut me. She was distracted, worried even."

I can tell Olson is starting to believe my story, but Hudson is still hell-bent on not believing a single word that comes out of my mouth.

"Maybe *you* worried her, Bob?" he says.

"No, she was already anxious before I got there."

"But no one can verify that except you . . ." Hudson tightens his eyes.

"My client has already told you everything he knows," Brad interjects.

"Do you own a burner phone, Bob?" Sheriff Hudson stands from his chair.

"A what?"

"A burner. A disposable phone. Whatever you wanna call it. Those prepaid flip phones you can purchase from shitty convenience stores. Do you own one?" He's moved to the side of the table, resting one hip on it as he positions himself right in front of me.

"No. I have a regular phone with a wireless plan through Verizon. I'm sure you can check that for yourself," I say, pushing my chair back to create some distance between myself and the sheriff.

"Yeah, of course we can look up that one. But not a burner phone. That's the exact reason why they appeal to criminals. You're a lawyer, Bob. I'm sure you know all about burner phones, don't you?"

It's a gotcha question, so I don't answer it. Something in Hudson's eyes flickers.

"We're done here," Brad says. He stows his legal pad back into his briefcase and stands.

"We're not finished yet, Mr. Watson." Chief Deputy Olson rises.

"Oh, I think we are, and I'll make this very simple. Are you charging my client with anything?"

"Not yet, but he's admitted that his DNA is all over a crime scene," Hudson says.

"You mean the hair on the floor from a haircut he received at the salon?" Brad belts out a single staccato laugh.

Hudson points a finger directly at my neck. "Let's not forget the blood too."

Brad shakes his head and addresses me. "Let's go, Bob," he says, walking toward the door.

The blood is a problem. Brad knows it and so do I. That's why he ignored Hudson's comment.

I stand from my chair, making eye contact with Hudson and Olson. They clearly think I'm the main suspect in the disappearance of not one, but two women.

"I told you everything I know. I get that the circumstances seem . . . suspicious, but that's all it is, optics . . . and it's exactly what Sarah wants." I don't mean to say that last part aloud, but I do; it just comes out quieter.

Brad snaps his head in my direction.

Hudson and Olson exchange a look of pure confusion. "What was that?" she asks.

"Yeah, what do you mean it's 'exactly what Sarah wants.' Why would your wife want any of this?" Hudson tilts his head.

Before I can say anything else or clue them in to what is really going on, Brad cuts me off—and that's probably for the best.

"That's enough!" he yells, herding me toward the exit. "My client is under a lot of pressure and stress right now, both personally and professionally. If you have any further questions, you can contact my office." He guides me to the door, opens it, and pushes me to the other side.

I keep walking down the hall, through the lobby, and out the front entrance. The fresh air feels nice, like a piece of life is being pumped back into my body. I close my eyes and look up to the blue sky, inhaling through my nose and exhaling slowly through my mouth, letting the tension in my shoulders ease away. Suddenly, a hand presses against those same shoulders and shoves me forward.

"What the hell was that in there?" I turn around to see Brad squaring up to me, his face red and his eyes darting back and forth quickly between mine, searching for answers.

"I've already tried telling you this. Sarah is setting me up."

He huffs. "Even if that were true, you don't tell *them* that, especially since you have zero proof. You're in the midst of a divorce, and you're in there blabbing to the cops about your wife setting you up for abducting women? My God, Bob, that's insane, and you know it." Brad pauses and rubs his forehead, letting out a sigh of frustration. "The reason I'm here is so you don't have to answer anything, but you're just freely offering ludicrous theories to the police who are pegging *you* as the bad guy."

"I'm telling you. This is all her. It has to be." I turn from him, looking away at nothing in particular. I know this is Sarah, but how is she doing it? How can I prove it? How do the pieces fit? I could see her paying off Stacy to skip town. But the salon break-in doesn't make any sense.

"What is it that you think she's doing, Bob? Help me understand."

"I don't know, exactly."

Brad steps forward and places his hand on my shoulder. "I'm sorry, man, but I think you're paranoid."

I shrug his hand off. "I'm not paranoid. You just have to trust me."

"Fine. I do trust you, okay? But me trusting you doesn't change anything. If you really think Sarah's behind *all* of this, then you need something concrete, something definitive. Because right now you look like a deranged, paranoid asshole who's unable to deal with the consequences of his own actions."

"None of that's true."

"I didn't say it was, but those are the optics right now. And what about those text messages with Stacy? Why didn't you mention those before?"

"It slipped my mind," I say with a heavy sigh.

"Jesus, Bob. My best legal advice for you right now is to lay low, leave your wife alone, and stay far away from this investigation."

"No, I'm going to prove Sarah's behind this. I've got eyes on her, and she'll eventually slip up," I say, pressing my lips firmly together.

"Hold up." Brad lifts his hand. "What do you mean you have eyes on Sarah?"

"Exactly what it sounds like. I put a tracker on her car too. So, I've got all my bases covered, and if she goes anywhere out of the ordinary—"

"Bob!" he interrupts, gritting his teeth. "What the hell do you think you're doing? If she finds out about any of that, you'll be even more screwed than you already are!"

"How could it get any worse than it already is?"

Brad pans his hand across the air in front of him like he's reading the marquee of a theater. "*After wife of cheating husband files for divorce, she finds GPS tracker on her car placed there by said cheating husband.* How does that sound? Do you think you'll have a shot in hell of getting any custody rights for Summer?"

"I just need to figure out one thing, that's all, and then it's over, for good."

Brad scrunches his face at me. "Whatever you're cooking up, you need to do it quickly and quietly. As your friend, I understand why you're not doing your best right now, but as your lawyer"—Brad steps toward me and pats the side of my arm—"you need to get your shit together or a divorce is going to be the least of your worries."

I nod in reply. I know he's right; I know I must seem like the crazy, desperate, spiraling husband, but he doesn't know what I know. He doesn't know what lengths Sarah will go to to get what she wants. I just need to beat her at her own game, and the only way I'm going to do that is if I accelerate my pace and do what she thinks I'm incapable of. Because if anyone can best Sarah, it's me.

Brad turns to head toward his car. "Hey, remember that thing you told me about?" He stops and snaps his fingers. "The one you said that would ensure you get full custody of Summer. What is it?"

"It's a smoking gun with the trail wisping right back to Sarah. But . . ." I pause, deciding whether or not I should bring Brad in on this.

"But what?"

"It has far more implications than just helping me get custody of Summer," I say.

"Okay, but what exactly is it?"

I let out a heavy sigh, staring at the ground for a moment before I meet Brad's gaze. "It's better if I show you."

35

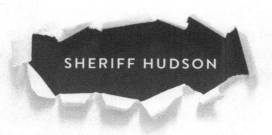

SHERIFF HUDSON

Chief Deputy Olson finishes tacking photos of the two missing women onto the corkboard in the briefing room. Stacy Howard and Carissa Brooks stare back at me, smiling, both with at least fifty years of life still ahead of them . . . hopefully. Their pictures now hang in a place no one ever wants their photo to end up. The evidence we have on their disappearances so far is minimal—a busted-up salon; two abandoned cars, one empty, the other containing a cell phone; Bob Miller's business card; and blood we're still waiting on the results for. It's a shame we didn't have a tail on Bob the night Carissa went missing. That would have really helped, but we're short-staffed and we've got too many fires to put out.

My on-duty deputies slowly trickle into the room, and I wait for them to get seated and settled.

"All right, everyone, busy Tuesday; we have a ton of groundwork to do and we're running out of time, so let's get started."

I walk over to the corkboard and point at the photos of Stacy and Carissa hanging in suspension, much like their well-being.

"Stacy Howard and Carissa Brooks. These two names should be very familiar to you. Missing person cases are some of the most time sensitive we deal with, and I don't need to tell you all that every second counts. What do we have so far? Unfortunately, very little. There have been no updates on the Howard case since the last briefing, and we're still waiting on the forensics results from the crime scene at the salon." I clear my throat. "Like the Howard case, BCI has facilitated putting out a critically missing adult alert for Carissa Brooks as well as a media release and social media posts. We're hoping we'll get a solid tip from the public."

I grab a photograph from the table in front of me and pin it up on the corkboard beside the two missing women. "Bob Miller," I say, pointing to the professional headshot we pulled from the Williamson, Miller & Associates website, "is a person of interest in both cases. According to our findings, he's the last person to have had contact with either woman prior to their disappearances."

"Why isn't he in custody then?" Sergeant Lantz asks. As usual, he's leaned up against the back wall with his arms folded over his chest.

"We don't have enough to charge him yet. At this point, everything is circumstantial. Olson and I brought him in for questioning this morning, but his lawyer stonewalled much of it, and Mr. Miller didn't offer up anything of substance. He did admit that we *would* find his blood in the salon, but he had a somewhat plausible story for why it ended up there. However, we still have to wait on lab results from the scene anyway."

A deputy raises a hand before speaking. "What do we know about Carissa Brooks? Aside from being Bob's hairstylist, how else is she connected to him?"

"That's actually a perfect segue." I step aside and hold an arm open. "Olson, could you fill us in on the background check you pulled on Carissa Brooks?"

"Sure thing, Sheriff." She steps forward and opens the folder in her hand. "Ms. Brooks had a permanent protective order in place against her ex, George Carrigan. That PPO expired less than two years ago, but an extension was granted. However, it came too late because George attacked Carissa in the interim and ended up putting her in the hospital. He was sent to prison for battery but served only a third of his sentence. He received early release due to good behavior three weeks ago."

"When's the extended PPO set to expire?" I ask.

Olson flips a page. "Next month."

"Do we know if Carissa filed a motion requesting to extend the order?" I furrow my brow.

She shakes her head. "I couldn't find anything filed with the court."

"Has Carissa's ex had any recent contact with her?" Lantz asks.

Olson and I exchange a look but neither of us has an answer.

"I feel like that guy is suspect numero uno," Lantz adds.

The door of the briefing room opens, and Nagel slips in wearing a pleased look on his face, like he's got something good to share.

"You're right, Sergeant Lantz. Given his history with Ms. Brooks, George Carrigan is a person of interest, so we'll need to bring him in for questioning."

"Already ahead of ya, boss." Nagel steps forward. "Several of Carissa's employees and friends mentioned her ex, so I contacted his parole officer and informed her of the situation. George is sitting in Interrogation Room One as we speak."

"Excellent work. Before we adjourn, any updates on the Stevens case?" I ask.

"No, sir, unfortunately not," he says. "We're still conducting interviews with those who made death threats toward Ryan online, and we're in the process of reviewing traffic cams in the area surrounding the hospital. But with Stevens's murder, Howard's disappearance, the reopening of the Summers case, and now the Carissa Brooks investigation, we're stretched really thin."

There are nods all around, and I take in the faces of my officers. Most of them sport dark circles and heavy bags around or under their eyes. They all have cups of coffee or energy drinks set out in front of them.

"I know you're all exhausted. Believe me, I am too, but we've got people's lives depending on us. So, try to push through, just for a little longer. BCI is assisting on the Stevens, Howard, and Brooks investigations, but we are the lead on them. I'll see if I can get us more support. I appreciate all your hard work. Keep it up. Let's get these cases solved, and let's bring Howard and Brooks home."

The entire room erupts, and much of the energy we've lost due to exhaustion and lack of progress is back, at least for now. Chairs scrape across the floor as my team gets to their feet. There are cheers and chants of *let's do this* and *we got this*, along with high fives and pats on the back. It's exactly what we need right now.

I turn to Olson. She smiles, pleased with my little motivational speech. "Wanna come with me and have a chat with George?"

"I think I'd like to do more than just chat with him," she says, narrowing her eyes.

I feel the same way. Men who lay their hands on women are the scum of the earth, and it's going to take everything in me not to do to him what he did to Carissa.

Through the two-way mirror, we can see George Carrigan sitting at the table in Interrogation Room One, dressed in a white tee, ripped jeans, and a pair of combat boots. A black leather jacket is hung on the back of his chair, and his blond hair is pulled into a tight ponytail.

"Someone here fancies themselves a big tough biker," I say to Olson.

"Nah. Check out the ponytail, wouldn't fit under a helmet." She smirks.

We enter the room, and I let Chief Deputy Olson take a seat across from the man while I stand in the corner. He has a history of abusing women, so I want to see how he handles being interrogated by one.

"Morning, George. Thanks for coming in to talk with us," Olson says.

"Part of my parole requirements are that I cooperate with you people anytime you ask, so I didn't have much of a choice." He glares at her.

"Well, we appreciate it all the same." She's keeping the tone light . . . for now. "When was the last time you had contact with Carissa Brooks?"

George leans back in his chair, squinting his left eye and curling his lip. "I'm not allowed to talk to her or be near her, otherwise they'll throw me right back in jail."

"Yes, we're aware of the restrictions concerning the protective order against you. Care to tell us more about that?"

"No."

Olson turns and briefly looks over her shoulder at me. There's always a point in an interrogation where you can tell if the person you're questioning is going to be helpful or not, and we just got our answer.

"Have you spoken to or seen Carissa recently?" Olson asks again.

"I just told you I'm not allowed to."

"Right, but *not allowed to* and *not doing* are two different things, aren't they?"

George juts his chin forward, and the early signs of a scowl form across his face. "Are you accusing me of something?"

"Why? Did you do something worth being accused of?" She angles her head to the side.

George points a finger at her. "Don't you start with your bullshit cop games. I didn't do anything, all right?" He holds his finger steady in the air as if the longer he points, the better chance he has of ending all of this.

"Then just answer the question," she says. "When was the last time you had any contact with Carissa?"

"A few weeks ago. But she's the one who texted me, okay? I didn't break the rules." George's voice cracks in a panic, the tough-guy act fading like the leather of his jacket.

"Why did she text you?" I ask, my arms crossed in front of me as I lean my back against the wall.

He snaps his head in my direction, surprised, as though he forgot I was still in the room. "She asked if I was really out."

"Now, why would she go and do something like that? Especially after you put her in the hospital, and then she went through all the effort to get a protective order against you, not once but twice?" I ask.

"I don't know." He shrugs. "Maybe she still cares about me."

"Right. And what else was said?" Olson asks.

"Nothing. I answered her question. I told her I got early release, that I was sorry, and that I wasn't the same man that went into prison. I told her I loved her and that I always would." George glances down at his lap.

"Came on a little strong, don't ya think?" Olson says.

He doesn't respond.

"And did Carissa reply to your text?" she adds.

"No, she didn't."

"Must have made you real mad to get rejected again? Especially after pouring your heart out and making all those changes while spending months behind bars. You must have been enraged."

George's finger is back in the air, pointing at Olson. "I know what you're fucking doing. Shut your mouth . . ."

I step forward out of instinct.

"Or what? You'll hit me?" Olson cocks her head.

"No! I'm not gonna . . . ugghh . . . See, this is what you cops do. You get people to—"

"Lose their temper? Show their true selves?" she says.

"I'm not losing my temper!" George slams his fist against the table, the ring of metal reverberating in the room.

The sound dies out into an air of total silence, save for George's labored breathing. His eyes dart between me and Olson, the look on his face changing from rage to shock to embarrassment.

"I'm sorry," he says, hanging his head and rubbing the underside of his fist with his other hand.

Olson leans forward, placing both of her hands on the table. "Where were you Sunday night, between the hours of nine p.m. and two a.m.?"

"At home."

"Can anyone verify that?" I ask.

"Yeah, I can." George lifts his head, meeting my gaze.

"Anyone else?"

"No. Does someone need another person in their house for them to be able to just relax?" he challenges.

"To relax? No," I say. "But to verify someone's whereabouts? Yeah, it would help."

"I don't know what to tell you. I was at home with a frozen pizza and a six-pack."

Olson takes out her notepad and jots down a few lines. "You didn't leave your house at all between nine p.m. and two a.m. on Sunday night?"

He shakes his head.

"What's this about anyway?" George's voice becomes angry again, his patience wearing thin. "I'm not answering any more questions until you tell me why the hell I'm here."

Olson looks back at me, lifting her brows to ask, *Should we?* I nod, giving her the go-ahead.

"We received a call yesterday morning reporting a break-in at Carissa's salon. But when we got on scene, it appeared to be more than just a standard burglary."

A wave of red flushes across his neck and face. "What do you mean? Is she all right?"

"We're not sure, because she's missing."

His gaze intensifies, flipping between Olson and me. "Why are you here talking to me then? You should be out there looking for her!"

"You said it yourself, Mr. Carrigan, you would never stop loving her. When she didn't reply, did you take matters into your own hands? Ensure that if you couldn't have her, no one else could?" I slowly walk toward the table.

He pulls his head back. "You think *I* did something to Carissa?"

"I don't know, did you?"

George narrows his eyes and stands quickly from his chair. "Are you detaining me?"

"No. We're just talking," I say.

"Am I being charged with anything?"

"Not yet," Olson replies.

"Then, I either want a lawyer or I'm leaving."

Olson and I exchange a frustrated look. He knows his shit because he's been through this several times before.

"You're free to go, Mr. Carrigan. But we'll be in touch," I say, stepping aside.

George stomps toward the door and grabs the handle, pulling it down but with no success. He struggles with it for a few seconds before I intervene.

"You need a card for that," I say, retracting mine from my utility belt as I cross the small room. "It's a safety measure." I scan the card and the lock clicks.

George wears a look of annoyance mixed with fear. He pushes the door open and bolts out of the room without another word.

I turn to Olson as she stands. "So, what do you think?"

"I think he's an asshole, but other than that, I don't know."

I sigh and shake my head. "At least we're on the same page."

36

SARAH MORGAN

It's true what they say. You can get used to anything—like reporters swarming and shouting out questions or comments nearly every time I pull up to the office. Luckily, they're only around in the morning, and they leave shortly after I enter the building. But they'll be here as long as there's a story, and I know our story isn't finished yet. I exit my vehicle and hold my head high because I have nothing to be ashamed of. My stilettos clack against the pavement while cameras flash incessantly and microphones clutched in the hands of overzealous reporters are thrust into my face.

Ms. Morgan, do you have any thoughts on Ryan Stevens's death? Are you glad he's dead? Did you want him dead after what he did to you and your husband? Were you involved? Do you think Ryan killed Kelly Summers? What does your current husband think of all of this?

The sheriff's office released a statement on Ryan's murder last night—along with a grainy still of a man dressed in scrubs and a surgeon's cap and mask—and a plea to the public to come forward with any information that would help them identify the suspect. I don't answer or acknowledge any of their questions, even the loud ones. Any lawyer worth their salt knows sometimes the best thing to say is nothing at all, and the second-best thing to say is a lie.

"Goddamn," Roger grumbles as I arrive in the lobby. The media knows not to enter, but that doesn't stop them from pounding on the glass doors. Roger gets to his feet and shuffles around the front desk. His hand hovers a foot or so from the gun nestled in his holster. It's supposed to make me feel safe, but I think I feel less safe with him having it.

"Get. Get," Roger yells, waving them off. He turns to me. "You all right, Sarah?"

I nod. "Yeah, I'm fine. They're mosquitoes," I say, flicking my wrist. "Just a nuisance, nothing serious."

Roger makes a *humph* sound. "Mosquitoes kill more people a year than any other animal, including humans." His eyes go to the screaming reporters and then back to me. "So, I'd say that's an accurate description." He smirks.

"I'm not worried about them." I tightly smile as I continue through the lobby and call for the elevator. "Have a good one, Roger," I say, stepping into it.

"You too, Sarah."

Natalie stands from behind the reception desk as soon as I push open the door to the Morgan Foundation. "Good morning, Sarah."

"Morning, Natalie."

"Here's your coffee," she says, extending a to-go cup from a local café to me.

I take it and thank her.

Anne appears from around the corner. "There you are," she says, breathing a sigh of relief. She's dressed in a pencil skirt and matching blazer with a folder tucked under her arm.

"Yep, here I am." I gesture with my coffee cup before bringing it to my lips and taking a quick sip.

Anne falls into step with me, and we walk through the office. I smile and acknowledge my employees as I pass by them.

"I heard the police were here yesterday," Anne whispers.

"You heard right," I say, unlocking my office door and flicking on the lights. "Sheriff Hudson and his chief deputy had some questions for me about the Kelly Summers case," I add as I drop my bag beside my desk and take a seat. "Where were you yesterday?" I ask, looking to Anne, realizing I didn't see her at all. I just assumed she was here because she's always here.

"I took a sick day," Anne says, having a seat. "I wasn't feeling well."

"Are you feeling better now?"

She nods. "Yeah, it was just a migraine. Did you see the news about Ryan Stevens?"

"Briefly," I say, unpacking my bag. "But Hudson had already filled me in on it yesterday before the news broke."

"I can't believe he's dead." Anne chews on her thumbnail, looking off in the corner as though she's deep in thought. "Who would even want to kill Stevens?"

"A lot of people in this town wanted Stevens dead." I place a stack of folders on my desk.

She draws her brows together. "So, he stopped by to talk to you about the Summers case but then brought up Stevens's murder. Does he think they're related?" Anne's asking a lot of questions right now, and I'm not sure I like that.

"He didn't say. What's the status on the appeal?" I say, changing the subject.

"Oh, sorry. That's why I ran to find you. We just got word: The court granted the appeal."

I force my mouth to curve at the corners. It's good news . . . I mean if I wanted the case to be reopened, which I don't. But I knew it would be.

"Good," I say. "Are they reversing it and sending it back to the circuit court for a new trial or dismissing it entirely?"

"Still being determined. I think they granted the appeal quickly due to the media blitz and pressure from the public. Plus, some of the strings the foundation was able to pull. What do you think they'll decide on?"

"Reversed and sent back to court for a new trial. Dismissals are extremely rare."

She nods and stares at me, quiet for a moment. "How are things going with the separation? Is Bob still giving you grief?"

"Always. Plus, he's completely unreliable. I let him take Summer to DC for one night this past weekend, and he left her alone for hours."

"What!?!" Anne's voice rises. "Why? What the hell was he doing?"

"I don't know. When I asked him, he said, quote, 'That's none of your business.'"

"That's ridiculous. That's your daughter. It *is* your business."

"That's what I said, but Bob's too thickheaded to understand that."

Anne shakes her head in dismay. "Too bad whoever offed Stevens couldn't take out Bob too." She laughs.

"Divorce is making him suffer far worse than death would." I faintly smile.

Anne extinguishes her laugh, her face turning serious again. "And how's Summer through all this?"

"Not great. We told her about the separation last night, and she didn't take it well, and now she's refusing to talk to me." I sigh.

"She'll come around. My parents divorced when I was thirteen, and I remember hating them at first until I realized how much better it was to live in a house without constant fighting and screaming." Anne pulls her lips in.

"I hope so because I can't stand her hating me. Everything I do is for her. She just doesn't realize it."

"No kids do, but she will someday."

My phone vibrates against my desk, and *Unknown* is splayed across the screen.

"I should take this."

Anne nods, stands from her seat, and walks to the door. Before she exits my office, she turns back. "If you need anything, anything at all, just let me know."

I know she means it.

"I will," I say.

She closes the door behind her as I hit *Accept*.

"Sarah Morgan."

"Sarah, it's Sheriff Hudson. Do you have a moment?"

"You had more than a moment of my time yesterday."

"This isn't about Kelly Summers or Stacy Howard," he says.

"Then what's it about?"

"Carissa Brooks. Now, I understand your company did some pro bono legal work for her, is that correct?"

"Yes," I say. "But there is attorney-client privilege here, Sheriff."

"I know, Sarah."

I hear him let out a long sigh, maybe out of frustration, maybe out of exhaustion. I'm not sure. But it rattles the speaker, forcing me to pull the phone from my ear for a moment. He sounds desperate, and I'm not surprised based on everything he's dealing with—or attempting to deal with. I take a short, deep breath, deciding that I'll throw him a bone.

"What do you need, Sheriff?" My tone changes from defensive to agreeable, so he knows I'm willing to go out on a limb for him just this one time, regardless of attorney-client privilege.

"Do you know if Carissa had any family out of state she could turn to?" he asks.

"Not that I can recall. All I know is she had an ex who treated her like a punching bag." My free hand balls up into a fist at the thought of that poor excuse of a man. And I'm aware that's ripe coming from someone like me. But we all have a moral code. Some are just more lax than others.

"And your foundation helped Carissa get a protective order against her ex, George Carrigan?"

"Yes, twice actually," I say, spinning in my chair.

"And it was set to expire next month, is that correct?" Sheriff Hudson asks.

"That sounds about right. They're good for two years, so yes. I'm not sure on the exact date though . . . Actually, I'm surprised I haven't heard from her. I assume she'd want to file a motion to extend it again."

"When's the last time you heard from her?"

"Around the time we filed the last one. I mean, I've seen her around town since then and waved and said hi, but I haven't had a conversation with her regarding the protective order . . . Why? Is she okay?"

He lets out another heavy sigh. "I don't know, but she's missing."

"Missing!? Have you talked to her ex? If something happened to her, he had something to do with it."

"We have talked to him. He doesn't have a solid alibi, but we've got nothing tying him to it yet."

"Tying him to what?"

Sheriff Hudson is quiet, and for a second, I think the call has disconnected. I pull the phone from my ear, checking the screen. The timer for the call length is ticking up. "You still there, Hudson?"

"Yeah," he says. "I probably shouldn't be telling you this since it's an active investigation, but you were her attorney, so you know more about the relationship between her and her ex than anyone else."

"What is it?"

"Carissa's salon was ransacked late Sunday night. Nothing was stolen. Her car, purse, and cell phone were left behind, and . . . there was blood everywhere."

"Jesus! You've gotta go after that fuckface ex of hers."

"I'm with ya, but here's the thing though: We don't know if the blood we found in the salon even belongs to her because she's not in the system and we've got no family to compare it to."

"At the very least, you know she's missing."

"Yeah, we do, and if her ex had anything to do with her disappearance, we'll find out."

"Good. You better."

"I appreciate your cooperation, Sarah."

"I'd say anytime, Sheriff, but you know that's not the case."

"Oh, I know," he says, and I can practically hear him smile on the other end of the line. "Take care."

"You too."

Before I can even set my phone down, there's a knock at my office door.

"Come in," I call out.

It opens slowly, revealing Alejandro on the other side, dressed in a button-down and a pair of jeans.

"You never showed yesterday, so I figured I'd come to you." He meekly smiles.

"Ugh, I'm sorry. I got swamped with some stuff and then it just slipped my mind. Come in," I say, beckoning him with my hand.

Alejandro closes the door behind him and takes a couple steps toward me, his eyes scanning the room.

"Nice office. It serves you well."

"It does." I gesture to a chair. "Have a seat."

He sits and crosses his legs, resting his ankle on his knee. "Did you purposefully forget to stop by?"

"Not at all," I say, pulling my checkbook from a drawer. Plucking a pen from a cup, I click it and place the tip on the amount line. "Think I'd skip out on a bill?" I look to him.

Alejandro stares back at me. "No, I just figured you didn't want to see me again."

"Like I said, I got swamped and it slipped my mind." The pen glides across the paper.

"I could charge you interest, you know?" The corner of his lip perks up. "For being late with payment."

"You could," I say. "But how about dinner instead?"

His smile grows. "I suppose I could accept those terms. When?"

"Tomorrow night at seven."

I tear the check from the booklet, extending it to him. It's a couple hundred more than we discussed, not for interest, just because I know he needs it more than I do—and he's earned it . . . or at least, he will. He takes it from me and gets to his feet. Folding the check in half, Alejandro slides it in his back pocket without even looking at it.

"And how do I know you won't stand me up again?" he asks.

"You don't. But we can have dinner at my house, so I won't have the opportunity to stand you up."

"And what if you're not home?"

"I will be," I say. "Promise."

37

BOB MILLER

I stand beside Brad, watching his reaction as he rolls the object over in his gloved hands. He's seated at his desk, and his eyes are wide as he slowly shakes his head.

"What exactly am I looking at?" Brad asks.

"It's the knife that was used to murder Kelly Summers."

He stares up at me in disbelief. "How do you know that, and why would you have this?"

"Because Sarah gave it to me eleven years ago. She told me to get rid of it, make sure no one ever found it."

"But you didn't."

"No." I smirk. "I needed an insurance policy with her, in case she ever tried doing the same thing to me."

"The same what?" Brad asks, but I don't respond. I let the gravity of what I've just implied sink into him, and his look goes from one of curiosity to horror. "Let me get this straight. Are you telling me that Sarah killed Kelly Summers . . . and you knew about it?"

"Yes."

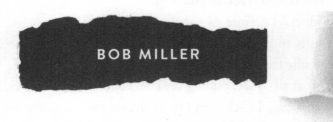

"But . . . why? Why did you . . ." He stops himself when he realizes he already has the answer. "Because Kelly or Jenna, or whatever her name was, killed your brother."

I nod and say, "An eye for an eye."

Brad sets the knife down and stands from his chair, pacing his office. "Jesus, Bob, do you realize what you've just told me? Do you understand the implications?"

"Of course, I do. I've been living with them for over a decade."

I can see the cogs turning in his mind. Maybe this is all too much for him. "What are you thinking, man? You wanna jump ship?" I ask.

"No . . . no, no. I get it. She killed your brother . . . and I didn't even know the girl. So what do I care? But fuck. Now it all makes sense. The shit you were saying about Sarah and how paranoid you've been." He sits at his desk again, rubbing his temples as he leans back in his chair. "How?"

"How what?" I take a seat across from him.

"How can you prove that Sarah used that knife in the murder?"

"Well, there's dried blood on it. A DNA analysis will match it to Kelly Summers, and I have an airtight alibi the night she was murdered."

"Okay, that helps prove you weren't the one that killed Kelly. The blood on the knife solidifies it as the murder weapon, but how do either of those things put this knife in Sarah's hands on that night?"

"They don't. And unless that thing"—I gesture to the knife resting on top of the bag on Brad's desk—"is covered in her fingerprints, which I doubt it is, then all we can do is use it to put some heat on Sarah. Maybe that knife magically finds its way to the Prince William County Sheriff's Office with an anonymous note attached." I raise my eyebrows in quick succession while fluttering my fingers.

Brad begins stroking his chin with his thumb and index finger. "The case *is* reopened, and they'll be reexamining every piece of evidence, so the timing would be rather . . . advantageous."

"Quite."

He leans forward and gestures to the knife. "This isn't enough to convict her, even if the blood on here is Kelly's."

"I know that, but I don't need a conviction. I just need the spotlight on Sarah. Her every move would be examined under a microscope, so whatever she's currently scheming will be ten times as hard for her to pull off. She might even slip up and ruin her whole plan with that kind of pressure."

"What plan?" he asks.

"I'm not sure yet, but I know it involves taking me down, so I've gotta take her down first."

"She's gonna know it was you who turned this in," Brad says, eyeing the weapon.

"Good. I want her to." And I mean that. I want Sarah to learn to fear what she rightfully should . . . me.

He raps his knuckles on the desk, sucks his lips in, and breathes a short burst of air out of his nose, like a bull ready to charge. "Well, I hate to tell you this right now, but . . ."

"What?" I say, panic in my voice. "What is it?"

"I got wind from one of the clerks down at the county judge's office. Sarah . . ." Brad pauses. "She filed a protective order against you."

"On what grounds?"

"She's made a claim that you threatened and physically assaulted her."

"That's bullshit!" I seethe.

This is a low blow, even for Sarah. Not only is she trying to set me up for whatever's going on with Stacy, but now she's painting me as an abusive husband, someone she doesn't feel safe around. For God's sake, I'm the one that shouldn't feel safe around her.

"Sarah submitted text messages that you sent her and also provided photographs of injuries she's claiming you gave her when you grabbed her arm at your daughter's swim meet."

"I barely touched her. Look what she did to me!" I hold up my hand, showing the two-inch scab across the palm of it.

"I thought you said you did that on accident."

"I lied. I was just trying to downplay what happened, but she slashed me with a fucking knife."

"On purpose?"

"Sarah never does anything by accident."

Brad lets out a heavy sigh. "Look, I don't know all the details, but I just wanted to give you a heads-up. It hasn't been granted yet, and a hearing still has to be scheduled, but don't be surprised when it comes."

"Does this mean I can't go near Summer?"

"Technically, no. The protective order would only apply to Sarah but . . ."

"But what?"

"If Summer is with Sarah, then you . . . have to avoid them both."

"My own daughter, Brad. My own goddamn daughter. Do you not see what she's doing?" I stand from the chair and pace, my hands becoming fists at my sides. She must be getting real desperate to pull a move like this. But why? Maybe I scared her with the threat of my *insurance policy*. I probably should have kept that to myself, Sun Tzu and all, but I did enjoy watching her squirm. It was the first time I've ever actually seen her nervous, on edge, worried—it was almost like she was human, just for a moment. I stop pacing and look to Brad.

"What should I do now?" I ask, already knowing what I'm going to do, what I have to do. I didn't want it to come to this, but Sarah's left me with no other choice.

"As your lawyer, I would advise you to avoid her, even though the protective order hasn't been granted. Act like it has. Don't give her any more ammo than she's already got." He looks at the knife. "What are you going to do with that?"

"Me? Nothing. But you're going to get that knife into Sheriff Hudson's hands. I trust you can do that discreetly."

"You know I can," Brad says. "And you want it to point to Sarah?"

I'd love to stab it right through her heart . . . but I don't say that part out loud, even with attorney-client privilege. "Yes, tie it to her, however you can."

Brad nods, and I leave his office, heading for my car. Once inside, I scan the parking garage to ensure no one is watching. There are several vehicles spread out, sitting empty. I reach down, pulling a flip phone from beneath my seat. There's a small recess under there where two metal support bars cross, just big enough to fit the unassuming object.

I flip the phone open and turn it on, the screen illuminating back to life. My fingers tap against the keypad as I type out a message. When I'm finished, I send the text to the only contact I have saved in the phone.

Plans have changed. Meet tomorrow at that boutique hotel off 28, near Sudley. 11 a.m. Room 518.

Immediately, I receive a message back. It's short and straight to the point.

Noted.

I power the phone down and let out a deep exhale.

'Til death do us part, Sarah. Yours . . . not mine.

38

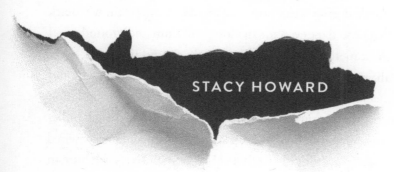

STACY HOWARD

"Hey, Carissa, are you awake?" I whisper in the dark.

She sleeps most of the time, and I don't blame her. That's all I did when I first got here—well, aside from screaming and trying to escape. But it's hard to find a way out when you're trapped in the darkness with nothing to ground or guide you. Carissa screamed and cried for a long time until she wore herself out, the little bit of energy she had completely sapped. For a while there, she was so quiet I thought she was dead. I waited, listening for breathing, a whimper, any sign of life. When I finally heard a soft purr, I was relieved to know she was still alive because at least there was someone else down here with me.

After she fell asleep, I ate the sandwich and water that were thrown down the stairs. I was going to offer her some, but she was asleep, and I've been down here longer, so I needed it more. Plus, I'm sure she'll receive her own food and water. I passed out not long after I ate. The food always makes me sleepy, my digestive system needing more energy to process the nutrients than I have to offer it.

"Carissa," I whisper again.

Her chain scrapes against the pavement. I hear her yawn, and then

I yawn too. Even in the pitch-black, without me being able to see her, it's still contagious.

"Are you okay?" I ask.

Her voice croaks. "No. Where am I?"

I'm the same way every time I wake up in this basement, having to remind myself of where I am and how I got here. I wonder how long it'll take me to get used to it. I'm sure I will eventually. One day, my eyes will open, and I'll inhale deeply, welcoming the moldy, damp scent. My black environment that's too dark even for shadows will calm and ground me. I won't feel the thick metal shackle fastened tightly around my ankle, and I may forget it's there altogether. The squeaks from the critters that come and go from the outside, seeking warmth, and the creaking of the foundation won't scare or surprise me anymore. I'll take comfort from their familiar sounds. And when all of that happens, I'll know that my brain has rewired itself and successfully convinced me that this is home. That's the human spirit for you. We can endure the worst in the physical world and still persist because only our body lives here. And that's why, when we perish, we leave only our body behind. I wonder if anyone will ever find mine.

Carissa's panicked breathing brings me back to reality.

"You're fine, Carissa," I say. It's a lie but it's what she needs to hear. "We're going to get out of here." Another lie, because I don't know if I'll leave by walking up those stairs or if I'll be carried up them, my lifeless limbs dangling over someone's shoulder.

"Where *is* here?" she asks.

"I don't know."

Her breathing slows as the panic from waking up in an unfamiliar place finally settles.

"I think I remember something," she whispers in the darkness.

I scooch closer to where her voice is coming from, but I'm only able to move a couple feet before the chain is pulled taut, and the cuff scrapes against my tender skin. My brain immediately sends pain signals throughout my body. I wince and absorb the agony in silence. There's no sense in crying. It's just wasted energy, and I need to retain as much of it as I can if I'm going to have a chance in hell of getting out of here.

"What do you remember, Carissa?"

Personally, I still remember nothing . . . well, almost nothing. I was sitting in my car, reading a text message on my phone. My driver's-side door was flung open and then something soft and damp covered my face. It smelled sweet, pleasant actually—however, the harsh pressure against my mouth and nose was anything but. I tried to scream but it came out muffled like I was yelling into a pillow. I felt a pinch in the side of my arm too. I flailed for only a moment before my world went black. And when I woke up, my world was still black.

"I was at work," she says.

"Where . . . where do you work?"

"At a salon. My last client of the day came in, and then there was blood."

"Did they hurt you?"

"No . . . I hurt him. It was an accident though. I was shaving his neck, and I slipped."

"What happened after that?"

"I cleaned him up, finished cutting his hair, and then . . . I don't know."

"Did he leave? Did someone else come in? Did you leave the salon?" My questions are rapid, one after another.

"I don't think he left."

"Who is he?"

"Bob. His name is Bob."

The name strikes something deep inside me, like a puzzle piece has just fallen into my lap but I'm not sure where to place it yet.

"Miller?" The word comes out slow and shaky.

Carissa's quiet for a moment. The damp, still air muffles all sounds until she asks, "How do you know his name?"

If she could see me, she'd see the whites of my eyes as my lids crawl back on themselves. My heart races, pounding fast and hard. I wouldn't be surprised if she could hear it echoing off the concrete and the piping. Maybe she can even feel its vibration through the floor. The shock wave after a nuclear explosion.

"I was seeing him—well . . . I had an affair with him, just one time though."

Carissa gasps.

"What? What is it?"

"I remember something else. It's fuzzy though, almost feels like a dream, but I think it was real. I was in the back of a vehicle, tied up, or maybe I wasn't restrained at all. I don't know. I only know I couldn't move."

"What else do you remember?"

"He was talking to someone, or maybe he was talking to himself. Something about not letting someone get away with something. He wasn't going to let her get away with it . . . his wife or *a* wife. And that he'd take her down first . . ." Carissa trails off.

"Did you see him?"

"Not in the car. I couldn't move. Couldn't even lift my head . . . but earlier at the salon, I did. I only heard his voice in the car."

"Are you sure it was Bob Miller?"

"It sounded like him. I just don't understand why he would do this to me," she cries.

I hang my head, knowing he had a reason to do this to me. I threatened to tell his wife about us. He told me it was a mistake, a onetime thing, that he was drunk, that I took advantage of him, that I was a whore and a thief. He wasn't wrong. I did steal from him. I did take advantage of his inebriated state. I targeted him because I knew he had money and a wife. That's my type. Being an event model doesn't pay the bills, but fucking over other people sure does. It's a risky business, and it's landed me in legal trouble before, but I never thought it could land me six feet under—and at this point, that's only if I'm lucky.

"I threatened to tell his wife about the affair if he didn't pay me," I confess.

"Like blackmail?"

"Yeah, exactly like blackmail," I say.

"Did you tell her?" Carissa's voice has a little bit of hope in it, like that could be our way out.

"No, I didn't tell her."

"So, he paid you?"

"No, he didn't do that either. I never actually tell the wife."

"What . . . ? What are you talking about?"

"Bob's not the first guy I threatened with the truth. He's just the first guy that took matters into his own hands."

I can hear Carissa's panic set in again. Her breaths turn rapid and short as she tries to suck in huge gulps of air.

"Carissa."

Her breathing becomes more labored as dread mixes together with uncontrollable sobs.

"We're gonna be okay. Calm down," I say, trying to relax her before she has a full-on panic attack or worse.

"No," she cries out. "We're not okay. We're gonna die down here, and it's all your fault, you fucking whore."

I open my mouth to yell at her, to argue with her, to convince her we'll be fine . . . but then I snap it closed. Because I think she might be right.

39

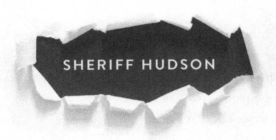

SHERIFF HUDSON

I rub my eyes to alleviate some of the strain that's built up from staring at the computer screen while sitting in the dark. Lifting my arm to check the time, the face of my G-Shock reads 2:28 a.m. I can't lie in bed, curled up under the blankets, getting a comfortable night's sleep, when I know two women are missing and that there's a killer on the loose.

I've been studying the footage from the hospital security cameras for over an hour now. I had our tech team splice together all the shots where the suspect appears on camera into one continuous video to save me time from jumping between camera files. Even with the more cohesive footage and the quality of it slightly amplified, the video tells me nothing. But there has to be at least one clue. In my gut, I know I'm missing something.

I'm about to start the footage over from the beginning again when I hear the door of my office creak open. Turning in my swivel chair, I find Pam standing in the doorframe dressed in a pair of my boxers and a white tee, rubbing the sleep from her eyes.

"It's like three in the morning. What are you doing up?" she says. The second part she pushes through a yawn.

"Can't sleep. So, I figured I'd review the footage from the hospital."

"We already had half a dozen deputies review the tape nearly a hundred times. They found nothing."

"I know. But maybe they missed something," I say as I extend a hand to her, inviting her to join me.

Pam slowly shuffles across the room and takes my hand, letting me pull her into my lap. I rotate the two of us back in front of the monitor.

She moves the mouse and clicks *Play*. The video starts again. "We're never going to ID that guy. He's in a surgeon's gown, cap, and mask." She points at the computer monitor, a tinge of whining mixed with frustration in her voice. "This isn't some average Joe. This guy's a professional. Maybe ex-military or police or even a hit man. But this definitely isn't his first time killing someone and leaving without a trace."

Finding the target in question for the tech team to splice together footage was easy, at least at first. All we had to do was look at the large gap in security, the time when Deputy Morrow vacated his post, and track it backward. A man in surgical gear entered Stevens's room and then left less than a minute later—blood covering his gloves and gown. He dipped into a supply closet and changed into clean gear so no one would pay him any mind, and they didn't. Once he looked like a regular doctor again, it became difficult to track him as not all of the hospital cameras overlap into another feed. This isn't a bank or a casino floor after all. The one odd piece, at least to me, was that he entered the hospital already dressed for surgery. Even though there weren't that many people walking the halls at that time of night, he just looked so . . . ordinary.

"It won't be easy, but everyone makes mistakes," I say, staring at the footage, watching the man on his exit path out of the hospital. He never changes his pace. Even when he can see the exit, he doesn't rush. He's cool, calm, and collected—like he belongs there. Something does feel familiar about his gait, but it's not enough to place him. One of the tricky things about being a cop as long as I have is that so many people have blurred together over the years. Sure, we have our high-frequency repeat offenders, the guys with multiple DUIs, the guys who can't seem to stop beating their wives, the petty drug dealers who go right back to dealing the minute they get out of jail. But even they blur together, seeing as they are all really cut from the same sleazy, grease-covered cloth.

Once outside the building, the man removes his surgical gloves and tosses them into a trash can. His hand flicks into the air as he lets go of the gloves and watches them drop into the black hole. The light from a streetlamp illuminates his now-exposed hand.

"Wait! Pause it there," I say to Pam. She clicks the mouse. "Can you zoom in on his hand?"

"Sure, but it'll get blurry."

"That's fine. Just do it, please." I squint as the picture tightens in, more and more until it takes up the entire screen. "Holy shit."

"What?"

"I know who it is."

A memory takes hold. It's so strong, it's like it's playing out on the monitor before me.

Bang! Bang! Bang! Bang!

Gunshots echo off the walls of the shooting range and casings clatter to the ground as I watch him fire at a paper sheet. Some rip through the target, others don't hit it at all, instead smashing into the back wall. He's supposed to be aiming between the eyes and down to the throat. This area is known as the fatal triangle, the zone where a shot is most effective at hitting the cerebellum, the brain stem, or the cervical parts of the spinal cord. Cops aren't taught to "shoot to kill," but we are taught to "shoot to stop." The difference is subtle, but the result is the same. On a paper target that isn't moving, with no threat of danger, he should be hitting his mark every single time, but he's not.

"You need more physical therapy, bro. You can't shoot for dick," I yell.

"What!?" he shouts back. With his hearing protection on, my words must be muffled to a whisper. He removes the earmuffs. "What did you say?"

"I said you can't shoot for dick."

"I know that. That's why I'm practicing, so I can get cleared and get off

of fucking desk duty. It's killing me." He shakes out his hand, flexing and clenching it, grimacing as he does.

It was an unfortunate situation for him. During a routine traffic stop, while he was instructing the driver of the vehicle to step out on a suspected DUI, they instead sped off. And as a result, his hand got crunched in the door, fracturing it in the process. He had surgery, went through months of physical therapy, but now he's gotta pass firearms training again in order to go back into the field.

"Didn't you complete PT three weeks ago?" I ask.

"Yeah, and I don't know why it's taking so long to get my aim back," he says, shaking his hand out again, harder this time.

"It's probably 'cause of your weird-ass fingers," I tease.

"What the hell is wrong with my fingers?" He looks down at his hand as he keeps flipping it back and forth.

"Your pointer finger is longer than your middle finger. You're probably pulling on the trigger weird compared to your grip."

"Shut up. My marksmanship was better than yours before this injury, thanks to this finger," he says, making a finger gun.

"Well, not anymore. Maybe you should go to a doctor and ask if they'll shave your pointer finger down. Or, better yet, just take a bolt cutter and trim a little off the top." I chuckle as I mime chopping it.

"Hard pass on both, asshole. I'll just keep practicing, and eventually, it'll come back to me. Hopefully, sooner than later. Like I said, man, I can't take desk duty anymore."

"You better, because you'll be a liability if I need backup."

"I'm not a goddamn liability." He puffs up his chest and flips me the bird. "Sit on it and spin, bitch."

"Sit on what? I can't really see anything behind that alien finger. You tryin' to phone home?"

We both start laughing again as he does an ET impression, waddling around the shooting range with his pointer finger raised. "Me phone home. Me phone home."

"Marcus," Pam says, pulling me out of the memory I fell into. "Who is it?"

I stare at the hand on the screen again. The pointer finger is significantly longer than the middle one, and suddenly, the familiar gait makes sense. I recognized him in the crowd too, the day I gave my statement to the media. The beard threw me off because I've never seen him with one, but it was him. He must have shaved it off before he decided to kill Stevens, but now I can see him as if he were wearing no disguise at all, walking around with his face clear for all the cameras to see.

"It's Scott Summers," I say. "He's back."

40

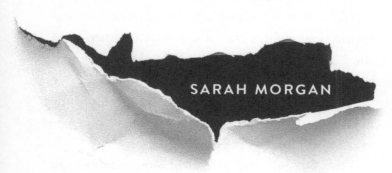

SARAH MORGAN

"Will you please put your feet down, Summer?" I say, gripping the steering wheel as I drive down a back road, heading into town. It's a bright sunny day without a cloud in sight, and I'd probably enjoy it much more if it weren't for my angry passenger. She's continuing to give me the cold shoulder. But today, her attitude is much snarkier—slamming doors, stomping her feet, random huffs and puffs, refusing to eat breakfast, and anything else she can do to annoy or frustrate me.

Summer huffs. *See?* Like I said, random huffs and puffs. She begrudgingly removes her feet from my dashboard and places them on the floor.

"Thank you," I say, glancing over at her and forcing a smile.

Her blond hair hangs in front of her face like a curtain, so I can't see her expression, but I'm sure she's wearing a scowl, especially for me.

"Why'd you pack my stuff up in a suitcase?" Her tone is harsh, almost accusatory. But at least she's talking to me. Summer crosses her arms over her chest, sinking deeper into the passenger seat.

"You're gonna be staying with Aunt Anne for a few days."

"Why?" she snarls.

"Because you said you wanted a divorce from me too."

She huffs again, blowing a piece of hair out of her face.

"Anne will pick you up from school and take you to her house. It'll be good for you to have some space and time to process these new changes."

It's only a half truth. Yes, I'd like her to cool down, and I think it will be beneficial for her to talk to someone who grew up with divorced parents. Anne can resonate with Summer in ways I can't. But I also have no idea what Bob's up to, and I'm sure as soon as he hears about the protective order, he's going to blow a gasket. I can't have Summer around if or when that happens. Last night, I dreamt Bob took Summer, and I never saw her again. I know it was a dream, but I wouldn't put it past him to do something like that. He wants to hurt me, and that's the way to do it. So, at the very least, having her stay with Anne will put my mind somewhat at ease.

"Why can't you and Dad just stay together?" she pouts.

"We've been over this, Summer, and no matter how many times you ask, the answer isn't going to change. Why don't you look at the bright side? You'll have two Christmases, two birthdays, two of every holiday, and two bedrooms." I slow the vehicle down, stopping at a red light, and smile at her again.

Summer's neck is craned toward the passenger window, and I can see the reflection of her face in the glass, all scrunched up and angry. "I don't want any of that. I want you and Dad together."

"Well, I don't want to be with your father," I nearly yell as I press the toe of my shoe on the gas pedal, accelerating through the intersection.

Summer swivels her head, staring at me. "Why?"

"Because I don't trust him. He broke our trust," I say, turning the vehicle onto her school's street, located just a few blocks down.

"Can't you just . . . trust him again?" Her tone has changed from cutting and full of disdain to one of understanding, or at least trying to understand.

"I wish I could. But the damage's already been done, and there are some things you just can't salvage."

"What did Dad do?" she asks.

I pull up to the school and throw the vehicle in Park. Other kids hop out of their parents' cars, smiling and waving before they sprint toward their friends.

Taking a short, deep breath, I turn partially in my seat to face my daughter. Her green eyes have a sheen to them like she's scared or already upset at what I'm going to say.

"That's between me and your father, Summer. Your dad may have broken my trust, but he still has yours. And although he hasn't been the best to me, he's been that to you. We both love you more than anything, and whether your dad and I are together or not, that'll never change." I reach for her hand, fearing she'll pull away, but she doesn't. Instead, she squeezes mine, and I squeeze back. "I'm sorry you're unhappy, sweetie, and I know none of this is easy. But one day, you'll understand that everything I've ever done is because I only want the best for you."

A tear rolls down her cheek, and I quickly swipe it away. She outstretches her arms and leans into me. I wrap mine around her small body and hug her tight, running a hand through her soft hair.

"You're the only thing that matters to me in this world," I whisper. A tear falls from the corner of my eye, splashing onto the top of her head. She hugs me even tighter.

"I'm sorry Dad hurt you." Her words come out muffled.

I catch a glimpse of my reflection in the rearview mirror. Sometimes I don't recognize the woman staring back at me. But today, I do.

"I'm sorry too," I say.

Summer tells me she loves me, and I tell her I love her more. We break our embrace, and I wipe her wet eyes. She tries to return the favor, dabbing at mine, but I tell her it's okay. Sometimes it's good to see the tears.

The school bell rings. "Go on," I say.

Summer nods and exits the vehicle, closing the door behind her before sprinting up the sidewalk. She turns and waves, and I wave back, smiling. Children are resilient. They go through change every day—their bodies growing, their brains developing—so they can accept it and adapt to it much faster than adults. She'll be okay, just like I was.

My phone rings through the car, startling me. The name *Bob Miller* flashes across the dashboard screen. I put my SUV in Drive and pull away from the school, accepting the call.

I don't even get a chance to say hello before his voice is roaring through the speakers. "You miserable bitch," he spits.

"Good morning to you too, Bob."

"You requested a protective order against me. Are you out of your goddamn mind?"

I pause briefly at a four-way stop sign.

"No, but I think *you* might be, which is why I filed it."

He chuckles. It's forced, more of a manic laugh. "You messed with the wrong person, Sarah."

"No, Bob, you're exactly who I wanted to mess with. Fuck around and find out, as the kids say."

He's quiet for a moment. "I hope you're ready for what's coming next." His tone is sinister, and the call immediately disconnects.

41

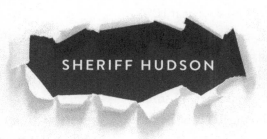

SHERIFF HUDSON

Olson walks through the open door of my office carrying a package in her hands. She sets it down on my desk and takes a seat, staring at me without saying a word.

I eye the box, wrapped in craft paper and a single piece of twine tied into a bow at the top. "What's this? Did you get me a present? Is it a cut of Wagyu!?"

"Sorry to disappoint, but no. It was slipped into the station's drop box. Front desk handed it to me on my way in." She lets out a sigh and asks, "Have we heard anything back on Scott Summers?"

"BCI is taking it over from here," I say, studying the box on all sides, now wondering what its contents could be. The station has an anonymous drop box for people to leave any illicit drugs and prescriptions they find and want to turn in, but they're never packaged like this.

"Well, is there anything else we can do?"

"Not really at this point. They've put out an APB on Summers, and his photo has been circulated to all police stations in the surrounding states. I'll continue to be in contact with them, in case there's anything we can help with. But right now, we've got our hands full as it is."

There's no address on the package, just the words *Attn: Sheriff Hudson* scrawled across the top in black Sharpie.

"Should I be worried about opening this?" I arch my brow. My cop brain goes into overdrive with the possibilities of all the nasty things that could be in it. Anthrax, a pipe bomb, something worse.

"I had the guys run it through the X-ray scanner. I know what it is, but I don't know *what* it is."

"Huh?" A look of confusion takes over my face. "You know what it is, but you don't know what it is?"

"I know what the object is, but I don't know why it's in there, what makes it special, or why it's been sent to you."

"Well, now I'm intrigued, Olson. Would you like to do the honors?" I push the box toward her, all smiles.

"Nope." She pushes it back. "I brought it to you for a reason."

I nod, snap on a pair of gloves, and pull at the twine. The bow unravels easily. I slip my knife from my utility belt, flick it open, and carefully cut into the package. Inside the box is a cloth bag with a note tied around it. I unfold it and read the words out loud.

"'This belongs to Sarah Morgan. Test the blood, and you'll find out what it was last used for.'"

Olson and I exchange a confused look as I reach my hand into the bag and slowly pull out the object inside of it. It's a knife with a six-inch blade, covered in what appears to be dried blood.

"What the hell?" Olson gets to her feet, taking a closer look.

I slip it back into the bag and put the bag in the box, sliding it to her. "Get this knife to the lab ASAP."

She nods, collects the box, and heads for the door.

No matter what I do, the past seems to keep haunting me, chasing me into a corner I can't get out of.

Before Olson exits my office, she pauses and looks back at me. "What do you think this means?"

"It could mean nothing. It could mean everything."

42

BOB MILLER

Three soft knocks rap against the wooden door of my hotel room. I press mute on the TV remote, swing my legs out of bed, and plant my feet on the floor. Lining my eye up with the peephole, I steal a quick glance before unlocking the door and pulling it open. The man I've been expecting stands there, shoulders held high and hands clasped in front of him.

"Come in," I say, stepping aside to let him enter.

He surveys the room, and I'm not sure if he's just assessing the amenities of the hotel or checking to make sure we're truly alone.

I close the door and double-lock it before checking my watch. He's exactly on time, not a second late, a true professional.

"Thanks for meeting me here, Alejandro."

He sits in the sofa chair set in the corner, crossing his ankle over his knee. "Nice digs."

I can't tell if he's being sarcastic or not, but then again, I'm used to a life much more comfortable than his.

"It's just a place to rest my head tonight."

"Why are you staying in a hotel anyway?" Alejandro asks. "Don't you have multiple homes?"

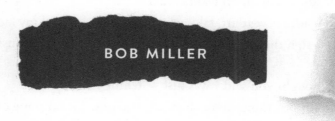

"Because I'll need an alibi for what you"—I point my index finger at him—"are about to do."

Confusion fills his face as he cranes his neck toward me and twists his lips. "What is it that *you* think I'm going to do?"

I grab the TV remote and crank the volume up before taking a seat on the edge of the bed, only a few feet from Alejandro. "You need to take her out," I say in a quiet voice, just barely audible over the loud commercial playing on the television. I can never be too careful, and I already know I'm on Hudson's radar.

Alejandro's eyes dart, taking in every square inch of my face, searching for a sign that what I'm saying is a joke. "Are you serious?"

"Very."

"I thought you said I was just watching her."

"I did. But things have changed, and now I need some of your . . . other . . . services."

Alejandro slowly shakes his head as he rises from the chair and walks toward the door. I think he's about to leave, but he pauses in front of the full-length mirror and studies the man before him. After a few seconds, he turns to me. I stand and stare back.

"Is that really what you want?" His face is stoic, and I can't tell what he's thinking. Either he hides his emotions well, or he doesn't have any.

"It's not what I want. It's just what needs to be done."

"And you're sure?"

"Yes. You don't know what Sarah's capable of, so I need it done fast," I say.

"How fast?"

"Tonight."

He tapers his eyes. "And you've thought this through?"

"Yeah, I have. Now, what's with all the fucking questions?" I scoff. "Maybe you're not the right guy for the job. You already spent too much time around her, and she has a way of drawing people in. She's probably already ensnared you." I cross my arms over my chest and forcefully exhale through my nose.

"You're asking me to take someone's life, so yeah, I'm gonna have some questions, Bob. If you're not sure, and I go through with this, that's a problem. Because if, all of a sudden, you grow a conscience, then my life's on the line." Alejandro lifts his chin, squaring up with me. "And I don't like my life anywhere near the line. So you will answer my questions, or you'll do it your fucking self, which we both know you're not capable of."

He never raises his voice when he speaks, but he doesn't need to to strike a sense of fear in me. I remind myself of who he is and what he's done. He's not the type of man I can push around. I put my hands in front of me, palms facing him, signaling that I mean no disrespect. "Fine," I say. "What other questions do you have?"

Alejandro opens his mouth but closes it, clenching his jaw and staring at me intensely as though there's a rage building inside of him. Guys like him don't like to be disrespected, even though they live a disrespectful life. Maybe he wants to tell me to go fuck myself, tell me he's out and that I'm on my own, or maybe he wants to punch me square in the face, retribution for questioning him. But he doesn't do any of that.

Instead, he says, "I'll need half up front."

"No," I say adamantly. "Not after what happened last time. You'll get all of it once the job is done."

His eyes become slits, and his mouth moves side to side. I can see him thinking back to the events that occurred well over a decade ago, how things turned out versus how they were supposed to—all because he was too late.

"I never asked for that money back either," I remind him, "even though you didn't hold up your end of the deal."

His face relaxes, and he simply nods in agreement. "How do you want it done?"

"I don't care. You're the expert. When I take my car to the mechanic, I don't tell him how to fix it. Just figure it out and do it quickly."

Alejandro stuffs his hands into his front pockets, squinting at me. "I thought you said you had other stuff in the works, things in place that would get you what you wanted without having to take it this far."

"I do. But Sarah being alive isn't a prerequisite for any of them. In fact, they actually work better if she's dead. Then I don't have to worry about her weaseling out of it, or what she'll do to me."

"You're scared of her, aren't you?" he says with a laugh.

"I'd be an idiot to say I wasn't." I close the space between us, walking toward him with a raised chin. I stop when we're standing face-to-face and lightly slap a hand on his shoulder, giving it a squeeze. "Don't underestimate her, Alejandro. Because I guarantee if you do . . ." I narrow my eyes. "It'll be the last thing you ever do."

The smirk on his face fades, and he clears his throat.

I remove my hand from his shoulder and step back, putting distance between us again. "Text me with confirmation once it's done."

"And when can I expect the money?"

"As soon as I have confirmation." I reach into my pocket, retrieving a folded slip of paper that I hand to him. "The money will be wired to this account."

"Won't that leave a trail?" he says, taking it from me.

"Not one that any person could track in a lifetime. It's all very complicated, but it'll be there . . . waiting for you."

"My rate is much higher than it was fourteen years ago." He slips the piece of paper into the front pocket of his jeans. "Inflation and whatnot," he adds.

"How much more?"

"Double."

"Perfect, because I'd question your capabilities if your price hadn't gone up. The last thing I want is a bargain hit man. Now, no mistakes this time."

Alejandro nods and leaves my hotel room without another word. There's not much left to do now, except hope that Sarah is one step behind me for once.

43

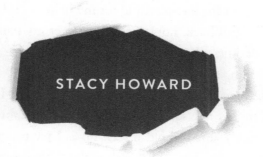

STACY HOWARD

I don't wake naturally, and it's not the squeaking critters or the shifting foundation that pulls me into consciousness. It's a bloodcurdling scream, the kind you only produce when your life is in danger.

I sit up, my heart pounding at top speed, the abnormal rhythm echoing in my ears. My skin perspires despite the cool, damp air. Another scream pierces the darkness, followed by loud noises, banging, things toppling over, thuds against the floor above me. Glass shatters. Another loud boom. More screams. Heavy footsteps or maybe feet kicking against the ground.

"Carissa," I whisper in the dark. "Wake up. There's someone here."

She doesn't answer. She doesn't stir.

I pull on my chain so hard, it rips away the skin on my palms. I wince in pain, but I keep tugging. There's no give.

A woman shrieks. Something hits a wall upstairs. It shatters, the pieces rattling against the floor above.

He must have brought another person here . . . or maybe someone found us.

"Carissa," I exclaim, trying to get her to wake up. She doesn't respond.

With no other options, I yell, "We're down here! Please help us!"

A woman screams again. It sounds like pure terror, and I realize quickly that she's in no position to help us, at least not yet.

There's more commotion. Kicking and screaming and scrambling, a continued struggle.

"Stacy!" the voice from upstairs cries out. "Help me!"

My mouth falls open and tears spring to my eyes as I realize the woman calling out for me, pleading for my help . . . is Carissa.

"Carissa!" I yell back, hoping she'll whisper my name from somewhere in the darkness. But she's not down here with me anymore. She's upstairs with him.

When did he come down and take her? How did I sleep through that? Or did she get free somehow and make a break for it? I get to my feet shakily, barely able to hold myself up as I try to scramble toward where I think the steps are. The length of the chain doesn't let me move very far.

"Help me!" she screams again. There's quick pounding against the ceiling like she's running . . . or maybe she's flailing and kicking, which means he has her.

"Carissa!" I yell, shaking the chain, hoping there's a weak link that will break and set me free so I can get to her. "I'm coming," I lie. "Keep fighting," I shout.

I don't know what to say, but all I can do is try to help her find the strength to live. I'm screaming and crying and hollering things I'm not even sure she can hear or understand. The pounds against the ceiling are still resounding, but there are fewer of them, like he has her pinned to the ground or maybe she's losing the will to fight.

"Please!" she yells, but it comes out strained and breathy.

"Hold on, Carissa," I shout, ripping at the chain again, but all it does is shred more of my skin. I scream in agony and frustration.

How did I not hear him come down and take her? I don't understand. And why her and not me? My foot skids against something on the floor, causing me to lose my balance and fall, my knee cracking against the pavement. I cry out in pain, holding my throbbing knee for a moment before I feel around in search of what I slipped on. It's the wrapper from the last sandwich that was tossed down. Actually, there were two, one for me and one for Carissa. We compared the taste—well, described it to each other—and figured they were the exact same, ham and cheese. I fell asleep after I ate mine. I always pass out after I eat . . . My eyes widen. He's drugging us. He has to be. That's why I didn't hear him bring Carissa down in the first place. That's why I didn't wake up when he took her. It must be in the food. I think of the other times he fed me before Carissa arrived. Every time, I was out cold for who knows how long. Did he come down then? And if so, what did he do? What has he been doing to me?

I scream Carissa's name again, telling her to fight, to be strong, to live, and to not let him win. It's much quieter upstairs now, but there's still turmoil. It just sounds far away. Suddenly, there's a bright light illuminating the darkness. It's too much for me to take in. My eyes burn, and I squeeze them shut as I instinctively shield them with my hands, looking away from the source. There's a buzzing sound nearby. The sound of worn light bulbs that haven't been flicked on in a long time.

I think I hear her gasping . . . but maybe I'm imagining it. I bring my fingers to my eyes and pry open my lids. It hurts but I have to keep them open, force them to adjust to the light I haven't seen in days, maybe even a week.

Something thuds against the ceiling, directly above me. It feels final, like I won't hear another. Then it's silent. After what feels like an eternity, something thumps against the ceiling once, twice. The floorboards creak and moan; then there's silence again.

I blink over and over and over until my eyes are able to stay open on their own and I can see more than just a bright light. My surroundings start to come into view. The heavy boots clomp slowly above me, followed by one continuous swooshing sound across the ceiling. Tears pour from my eyes and stream down my face. I know what that sound is. It's Carissa's body being dragged from one room to another. A door near the back of the house creaks open. Another thud. Then it slams closed, and there's silence again—at least upstairs.

Down here, I'm in a state of panic, or maybe it's shock. I can't breathe. I gulp for air, puffing and panting, struggling to catch my breath. My throat feels like it's in a vise. I cry out, but I barely make a sound. I'm fine, I remind myself. I mean I'm not, but I am—because I'm still alive. I'm the lucky one. I close my eyes and inhale deeply through my nose, hold for four seconds, and then exhale out my mouth. I focus only on my breath, not on anything else. I do this until my breathing is steady and my mind is clear. Panic won't get me out of here, so I have to stay calm.

Opening my eyes again, I take in my surroundings. There's a staircase right where I thought it was. It's made of old wood, rotted in some places. I crouch and look up to get a glimpse of what's at the top of the steps. A door. I get to my feet and look at where I thought Carissa was. She's not there anymore, but I know she was. Because there's a thin, old mattress lying on the floor next to a support beam where a thick, metal chain is connected to it. The ankle cuff lies open on the concrete. Beside it are an empty water bottle, a sandwich wrapper, and a large crimson bloodstain. My hands fly to my mouth. *What did he do to her?*

I turn away before panic takes over again, and I focus, trying to take in everything. I'm standing in a large decrepit basement that continues past the stairs for I don't know how long. There are stacks of boxes and random furniture strewn about in piles, all decaying and rotten and moldy. I turn slightly, and that's when I spot it, lying on the cracked concrete in all its glory. It's off to the right, a little behind where he had Carissa chained up. Has it always been there? And if so, how did I miss it? Maybe it fell out during his struggle with Carissa. It seems too good to be true. My heart pounds, but I don't want to get my hopes up. It could be nothing at all, or it could be my ticket out of here. The metal chain scrapes against the pavement as I stagger toward it. It sounds like nails on a chalkboard, but I like the sound because I know when I can't hear it anymore, that means I'm at the end of my leash.

I extend my arm, stretching my hand out as far as I can, the pads of my fingers barely touching the cold metal. It's not quite within my grasp, but it's close, and I think I can reach it. I place my unchained foot a step or two in front of me and lunge forward. The cuff digs into my skin, grinding against my ankle bone as I stretch. A cry escapes me as the metal cuts deeper into the skin, but I don't stop, no matter how much it hurts—because I know what's coming is far worse. My fingertips graze, not enough to grasp it. I groan and crawl back to my mattress, grabbing the sleeping bag from it. When I whip the bag, it lands on top of it, and I pull slowly, hoping it'll drag the item closer to me, but it doesn't. I try again and nothing. This time, I scoop up pieces of cracked pavement and toss them in the zipped-up sleeping bag. I fling it again and again, pulling it back, until finally the weight from the pavement catches the item. It scrapes against the concrete as it's dragged toward me. I lift the sleeping bag, revealing that it's now within reaching distance.

I can't believe my eyes when I see it. I blink several times just to make sure I'm not imagining it. When I open them, it's still there. Cautiously, I pick it up. It's cold against my skin and heavier than it looks. The light catches the silver metal, making it glint. When I bring it to my line of sight, the cylinder ejects. I sigh with relief as two of the six holes have no light passing through them, the bullets nestled snugly in their escape pods, waiting to be ejected into orbit. Two is a gift—because all I need is one.

44

SARAH MORGAN

Alejandro sits across from me at the dining room table, a seat previously reserved for Bob, but he occupies it better. He's dressed in a white button-down shirt and a pair of dark jeans. I know they're the nicest clothes he owns, so I appreciate the effort. He didn't show up empty-handed either. The bouquet of wildflowers set in the vase on the counter is from him. They're unusual, clusters of tiny blue petals with yellow centers, but they're pretty. The deep-crimson wine, poured heavily into two Château Baccarat glasses, is also from him. I almost canceled on Alejandro, given everything that's been going on, but I decided a distraction would be nice. Plus, I figured it was in my best interest not to stand him up again—and my best interest is the thing I'm most interested in.

"This is incredible," he says as he lifts a fork of seared salmon and mashed potatoes to his mouth. The potatoes alone take hours, if you want to do them correctly in the French tradition, so I'm pleased they are getting the praise they deserve.

"I'm glad you like it." My hand cradles the wineglass, and I sip slowly, peering over the rim at him.

Unlike the breakfast he consumed the other day, he eats tonight's dinner at a much more relaxed pace. I'm not sure if it's deliberate.

"Where's your daughter?" he asks.

I softly smile and place the wineglass on the table. "She's staying at a friend's house."

At the mention of us being alone, I notice a flicker in his eye—it's brief, but I still catch it. I have no real intentions for tonight, but I think he might. Pressing the side of my fork against the seared salmon, I lop off a flaky piece. It has the perfect balance of flavor: rich and oily with notes of citrus and a touch of sweetness.

"I was relieved you answered the door tonight," Alejandro says. His face is serious, and his stare is intense. This isn't banter, not yet anyway. He's all business right now, but banter is what I want. I'd like a fun distraction, not another heavy conversation mired with expectations.

"I'm sure you were." I tuck my chin in and bite my bottom lip, wetting it with my tongue. His gaze falls a few inches to my mouth as his fingers clutch the stem of the oversized wineglass set in front of him.

"How's the job search going?" I ask, flicking my eyes up at him, letting my lashes bat once more than is necessary.

"Good." He nods. "I actually just got some work today." He lifts the glass, bringing it to his mouth, and sips, never taking his eyes off me.

"That's great. What's the job?"

Alejandro sets the glass down and picks up his fork, the metal tines scraping against the porcelain plate.

"Waste management," he says. "It's just temporary, but it pays well." He looks down as though he's embarrassed.

"Nothing wrong with that. That's a good job," I say, smiling wide enough to hopefully convince him to feel the same way.

He lifts his head and smirks back at me. I'm not sure if it means he agrees or if he's playing off something unspoken.

We eat in silence for a few minutes, exchanging glances and polite smiles. We don't have to speak to know at least one of the thoughts running through our heads. I can tell by the look in his eyes that he wants to tear into me—and I think I might let him.

"I almost didn't take the job," he says, shoving the last forkful of food into his mouth. He chews slowly, watching me.

"And why's that?"

Alejandro wipes his mouth with the cloth napkin, then folds it and places it on top of his cleared plate, signaling that he's finished.

"I wasn't sure if it was the right job for me." He brings the rim of the glass to his lips and tips it back, making all the red liquid disappear. The last legs dance down the side of the crystal.

I stand and pluck the decanter from the center of the table, walking to him slowly. My hip brushes against his arm as I lean over him, refilling his glass.

"What changed your mind?" I ask.

He looks up at me, his gaze skimming over my bust, my neck, my lips, and then locking onto my eyes. I notice the corner of his mouth twitches. "In a way . . . you did."

I set the decanter down and turn my body, leaning against the table to partially sit on it. My leg presses against his arm, but he doesn't move it.

"How so?"

Alejandro takes a moment to respond. His eyes search mine as though he's looking for something. Maybe he's already found it, and he's unsatisfied with his discovery.

"Your foundation's program doesn't work unless I do."

"That's true." I tilt my head. "But if the job's not right, the job's not right."

"I'm the only one that can do it," he says, mirroring my movement.

"You're quite sure of yourself, Alejandro."

"Is that a question?"

I give him a teasing smile. "It's whatever you want it to be."

His large hand reaches up, grazing my cheek before it moves into my hair, pulling me into him. Our mouths crash together, and he nearly steals my breath. It's fluid and happens so fast, as though he was envisioning it ever since he took a seat at this table. I wonder what other scenarios he's played out in his mind.

45

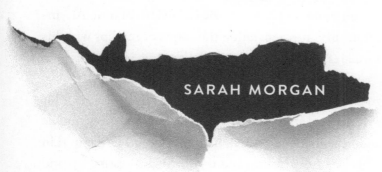

SARAH MORGAN

Alejandro is inside of me, and I'm inside of him—tangled up in the honey-colored Egyptian cotton sheets Bob picked out. I remember his hand gliding across them after he'd put them on the bed. His smile was a mix of pride and passion, pleased that he was able to provide this luscious gift for us. He described them as pure perfection. I wonder if he would still describe them that way.

Alejandro leaves a trail of wetness down my neck as he licks and kisses every inch of my skin. We haven't said a word since he picked me up off the kitchen table and carried me in here. By the time we reached the bedroom, we were both magically undressed. But he's been undressed for me long before. He just didn't know it. I was right about his tattoos. They continue everywhere, covering his hard pecs, abs, shoulders, and the sum of his wide, muscular back. I've learned things about him through the ink that's been sewn into his skin. He's religious . . . or at least he likes the iconography. One tattoo that claims he has no fears contradicts another, because it's death that he's afraid of, and that's why images of skulls and crosses are prevalent throughout his colorful skin.

His lips find mine, and his kiss becomes aggressive, so I give it right back. My teeth sink into his flesh, and he moans, thrusting harder into me as though he wants to share the pain he feels. I gasp, releasing his lip. He squeezes my breast and flicks his finger against my erect nipple. It's like he wants to ensure every part of me is paying attention to him. My hands go to his back, nails raking across it. His skin is wet, so I know I've drawn blood, but he doesn't react. Maybe because he's felt far worse in his life. He thrusts deeper and faster. I wrap my legs around his hips, drawing him in even more, so I can take the full length of him. Alejandro smiles and leans into me, separating the seams of my lips with his tongue. Mine ensnares his like barbed wire, slithering and coiling in a double helix of passion.

His body goes rigid, tensing up as he pants and grunts. I mirror his breathing, so he feels good about it too. When he finishes, every muscle of his relaxes, and he collapses on top of me, breathless. His damp skin sticks to mine, his lungs expanding and contracting, pressing up and down in unison with my own. His heart races, pulsating throughout his body. I can feel every beat. Does it beat for this moment or the next? Alejandro lifts his head and stares at me. That little black dot pressed into his iris is unmoved. He's tired, maybe from the sex or maybe from life itself. But he wears no expression. Then I see something else. It's fleeting, a sadness in his eyes before he rolls off, untethering our bodies.

Beside me he lies on his back, gazing up at the ceiling. Neither of us says a word; only our slow, decreasing pants of breath fill the silence. What's there to say? How great it was? We both know that. How good it felt? We both know that too. I stretch my arms out over my head as Alejandro starts to peel himself from the mattress. Then I feel it, something hard and cold pressed into the side of my abdomen.

My gaze goes to him. The sadness in his eyes has returned, but it's mixed with something else . . . shame . . . or maybe it's grit. It looks the same when you're doing the wrong thing for what you think is the right reason.

"I'm sorry, Sarah," he says, pulling back the hammer of the gun.

46

BOB MILLER

My phone vibrates. I mute the television and sit up in my hotel bed, staring at it. My heart rate immediately accelerates to a level I hadn't anticipated. A light flashes on the side of it, indicating I have a message. I know what this text is supposed to be, what it's supposed to say. Right now, I can live in limbo because I haven't looked into the box yet to see if the cat is still breathing, but once I flip open that phone . . .

Alejandro's questions race through my head: *Is that really what you want? And you're sure?* The problem with Sarah is that there's no stopping her, no changing her mind. Once you are in her crosshairs, you are as good as dead unless you intervene with drastic measures. I didn't have a choice because she never gave me one. I just had the chance to strike first.

I flip the phone open and read the message on the screen.

It's done.

I tap my fingers over the keys using T9 wording.

Send proof.

And then I wait. The seconds seem like hours, and I fear that I'll pass out due to a buildup of anxiety from too much anticipation. Finally, an image slowly loads down the screen, row after row of pixels revealing the gory details of the act I put into motion. First, the pillows on our bed, then the hair, weaving its way down to the head. And then she appears. Sarah. Her lifeless face looking off to the side, blood smeared across it, still bright and fresh.

Tears begin to well in my eyes, pooling to a level the lids can no longer contain. I'm relieved she's dead because the horror she was going to put me through would have been far more unbearable than what I'm feeling right now. What I've done doesn't change the fact that I loved her. I'm staring at the image of my wife and the mother of my child dead—and I'm both elated and heartbroken. It's like an old dog that's gone senile and starts biting people out of confusion. Putting it down is the right thing to do, but still, it rips your heart out. Sarah needed to be put down.

I grab a tissue from the box on the nightstand and wipe the tears from my eyes. My phone vibrates again. Another message. I click it and another image loads. This time it's not just her face, it's her whole body, lying naked in our bed. Her limbs are twisted and splayed out. A large pool of blood has settled under and around her hips. My brow furrows. Why did she have to be naked for this? Then it hits me, and a rage starts to take over. I exit the message and call the only number in this phone.

It rings once before Alejandro answers with a "What?"

"Did you fuck my wife before you killed her?" I begin with a yell but quickly quiet down to an aggressively loud whisper, remembering that I have neighbors on either wall of my hotel room. I unmute the TV to cover the volume of my voice.

"I believe your direct quote was, 'I don't tell the mechanic how to fix my car.' So don't worry about it."

"I am worried about it. That's my wife and fucking her wasn't a part of the deal."

"You just wanted her dead, and that's what she is. Plus, she's not your wife anymore. She's . . . not anything anymore." The voice comes through the phone cold, toying.

I deeply sigh and rub my temple. "What about Summer? Where is she?" I ask, worried about what his answer could be.

"She's staying at that Anne woman's house. The one who works at the foundation."

"I know who Anne is." It's not the ideal spot for Summer to be, since Anne will be resistant to me taking her without confirming with Sarah first, but there's nothing I can do about that at this moment.

"Now what?" Alejandro asks.

"Clean up the scene and then leave town. Put as much distance between yourself and here as you possibly can. Go to California. I don't care. But disappear."

"And my money?"

"It'll be wired to you first thing in the morning."

"No, I want it tonight, and that's not negotiable. Unless, of course, you want me to expand my list."

"That wasn't the deal, and you know I'm good for it, so it'll be wired in the a.m. You don't need to threaten me to ensure you get it."

He's silent for a moment, like he's thinking it over.

"Fine." Alejandro caves, for now. I know what he's capable of, so I have no intention of not paying the man.

"Did Sarah say anything about Stacy Howard before you . . ." I trail off. I don't need to say what we both already know.

"No."

"Shit." A dead end—literally. I need to find something that can remove the thorn of Stacy from my side . . . and maybe Carissa too. "I know she was planning something."

"If she was, she isn't anymore," he says matter-of-factly.

Alejandro doesn't get it. Even a half-baked plan that Sarah's not around to finish could still blow up in my face. The only thing that's changed is her not being able to interfere with me anymore.

"I still have to find Stacy. I can't have that looming over me."

"Well, you had me put that tracker on Sarah's car. Just use that."

"I've tried. It's pointless. All she does is go to the foundation, the grocery store, and Summer's school. It's all routine and boring, nothing out of place."

"Sounds like it's nothing then."

It's possible he's right. Sarah was amazing at contingency planning, but she probably never anticipated this. Maybe her plans will just fizzle out and die, but I can't count on that.

"Just get out of there and make sure you remove the tracker from Sarah's car before you go. And don't contact me at this number again. It won't work anyway."

"And what if there's an issue with the money?" Alejandro asks, a sense of anxiousness and annoyance in his voice.

"There won't be. After I wire you the funds, I'll reach out to you from another number once everything is clear."

I press the red phone icon on the touch pad and end the call. There's no sense in going back and forth anymore. He's gotta get out of town, and he's gotta do it fast. I pull up the picture of Sarah, taking her in one last time, knowing that once I delete this message, I'll never see her again, not really.

After a few minutes of tricking my mind to ignore the blood and the lifeless face, I finally clear the call log, delete Alejandro's number and all of our messages, and then snap the phone in half. Wrapping the two pieces in a towel, I stomp on it, smashing it into tiny fragments, most of which I flush down the toilet.

In the bathroom, I toss water on my face and find my reflection in the mirror. I stare at the man looking back. Tears stream down my face, and I begin to chuckle. "I did it. I finally did it."

Someone bested the great Sarah Morgan. She thought she could keep this up and keep getting away with it. Playing with people like they were nothing, mere puppets attached to a string of lies and deceit and corruption, all clumped and tangled into a web of shit with Sarah smiling at the other end. Not anymore.

I look down at my watch and the reality of something as concrete as the time snaps me back to the plan at hand. As good as modern forensics are, the time-of-death proclamation still has a window in which it could have occurred, and we are within that window right now. So I need to be seen by as many people as possible, somewhere public.

I change into something a little more formal and eye-catching before making my way down to the hotel bar.

"Good evening, sir," the bartender says as I take a seat at the counter. "What can I get for you?"

He looks young, in his early thirties maybe, sporting a man-bun and a black leather butcher's apron with tan straps.

"What do you recommend?" I ask.

I know exactly what I want, but I need to make conversation so he remembers me and, if questioned, can tell the police I was calm, conversational, and courteous.

"Depends, what are we thinking for base alcohol? Gin? Bourbon? Scotch? Vodka?"

"Bourbon."

"Something sweet? Strong? Smoky? A mix?"

"Dealer's choice, but not too sweet."

"You got it," he says with a small grin. He quickly drums his hands on the bar and turns away, off to mix up his concoction.

I turn and scan the hotel bar, which features a chandelier, moody lighting, oak-colored fixtures, and a dark-green-and-burgundy color palette. It's meant to look elegant and refined, but a discerning eye will pick up that the chandelier is made of plastic, not crystal, and the oak color is merely a laminate over cheap particleboard. Many things in life can fool you into thinking they're better than they actually are, if one doesn't take the time to really look at things.

Unsurprisingly, the bar is fairly empty. It's a weekday in a town that's not known to draw tourists or businessmen. However, between the bartender, the few other heads in the restaurant, and the front desk staff that saw me walk in—not to mention the security camera in the lobby—my alibi will be airtight. I'm sure there's a security camera somewhere in here too.

I pull out my personal phone and stare at the black screen, unable to turn it on. Letting out a deep sigh, I set it down on the bar. I know I need to delete some things on this phone as well, like the app I was using to track Sarah's car, but my mind can't stop thinking about that picture of her. I know I've done the right thing . . . for me. But it doesn't make it any easier, and I wish my love for Sarah would have died along with her.

"Here you are," the bartender says, placing before me a wooden board with a drink set on top and a glass dome enclosing it. Smoke dances around inside, masking the cocktail within. The bartender waits for me to give him my full attention. He wants to complete his show, so I'll allow that indulgence. With a grand gesture, he removes the dome and invites me to waft in the smoke. It smells of rich applewood and hickory.

"I call it the Bull Run Mists," he says with a grin.

I pick up the cocktail glass and bring it to my mouth, sipping it. The flavors explode, and my taste buds are taken on a sweet and smoky roller coaster.

"What do you think?" he asks, tossing a rag over his shoulder.

"It's incredible."

"Enjoy, and let me know if I can get you anything else."

I smile, and I'm finally able to focus again, the alcohol coating the lining of my stomach, pulling me out of my daze. I pluck my phone from the counter and unlock it, going right to the tracking app I used to monitor Sarah. It's the last thing remaining of my wife—her life, displayed as a web of routine in blue lines covering the screen. Work, school, store, home. Work, school, store, home. Repeat, repeat. It's actually kind of pathetic when you see it like this.

I put my thumb on the bottom of the screen, ready to swipe up, close the app, and delete it—but then the map disappears, replaced by a spinning wheel with the word *Loading* underneath it. I stopped checking the app sometime yesterday, so I suppose it hadn't refreshed. When it reloads, it's no different than what was just on-screen, except for one line. I take my thumb and index finger and touch it, spreading them to zoom in on the route. It runs south from our lake house, past Greenwich and the golf course, into the middle of nowhere. I click on it and the details pop up—noting it was traveled to earlier this afternoon.

"No way," I say out loud, unable to contain my surprise.

"Pretty out-of-this-world drink, huh." The bartender looks over to me, smirking as he polishes a glass.

"Yeah, unbelievable," I reply, thankful that he provided me an excuse for my outburst.

Where were you going, Sarah? I pull my wallet out of my pocket, ready to throw my card down on the bar and go investigate the location she visited. But then I remember, I still can't leave yet. The time-of-death window. I check my watch. I need to wait at least an hour.

"Actually, as soon as I'm done with this one, I'll have another," I call down the bar.

"You got it."

47

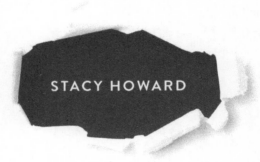

STACY HOWARD

My hands and fingers ache from gripping the gun. It's outstretched, pointed at the stairs. The muscles in my arms have grown tired, quivering. I'm not sure how long I've been sitting here with my back against the pole I'm chained to, legs spread out in front of me, looking down the sight of the revolver. Beads of sweat have gathered at my hairline, slithering down my forehead and the nape of my neck. I hear footsteps above me, heavy, like always. Tears instantly cascade from my eyes. My heart races as the adrenaline kicks in, slowing the whole world down.

The door at the top of the stairs creaks all the way open, and I finally see them—the shoes I have heard so many times before. They descend, methodically, calmly, one by one. More of the figure comes into view, his shins, his knees, the tips of his fingers hanging at his sides, his waist, his chest, his neck, and then his face.

"Stacy," he says, wide-eyed as though shocked to find me down here.

I recognize him immediately. He puts his hands up and takes a small step toward me.

His mouth parts as he's about to speak, but nothing comes out because I don't give him the chance to talk. I pull the trigger and scream out in unison with the two deafening bangs. Squeezing my eyes shut, I hear the hammer of the revolver click over and over but there're no more bullets left. All I can hear is a high-pitched ringing and the sound of my own cries.

48

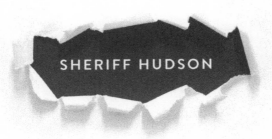

SHERIFF HUDSON

Lieutenant Nagel's name lights up across my phone screen. I swiftly answer it, thinking maybe we got word from another police station that Scott's been spotted.

"Nagel, what's up?"

"We followed Bob to an abandoned farmhouse south of Greenwich off of 603. We're parked a little down the road to ensure our cover wasn't blown, but we just heard shots fired. What do you want us to do?"

I bolt from my chair, grabbing my utility belt off the rack. "Stay there. Wait for backup. I'm on my way now."

I hang up the phone and race to Olson's office. "Shots fired. Come on."

Without saying a word, she's on her feet and running right behind me.

I press the button on my radio, calling for all available units.

In my squad car, I flick on the sirens and press down the gas pedal, the engine being pushed to its limit as the RPM needle goes deep into the red.

"What's going on?" Olson yells over the screaming siren.

"Nagel and his team followed Bob to an abandoned farmhouse. Shots were fired a few minutes after he entered. They're standing by for backup in case we have a hostage situation on our hands." She nods in response and draws her gun from her holster, looking it over, pulling back the slide and ejecting the clip to check that it's full.

We're on the scene in under twelve minutes. The SWAT team beat us there, and they're prepping at the back of their van as Olson and I exit the vehicle. The SWAT commander is animated, giving them directions, his arms flailing and pointing wildly to different entrance points of the building. Portable lighting has already been set up, illuminating the area surrounding the front of the house. The structure before us is rotten. Slats of wood are completely missing, and the foundation looks as though it's ready to collapse in on itself.

Nagel jogs over to greet us.

"What's going on?" I ask, surveying the scene.

Lieutenant Nagel quickly rattles off the few available details. "Same as before. Bob Miller entered, and a few minutes later we heard two gunshots. We had property records checked and no owner is listed, so we have no idea who all could be inside."

"Is it a hostage situation?" Olson asks.

"SWAT isn't sure, and there's been no response from anyone inside, which usually isn't the case in a—"

A piercing scream rips through the air, originating from the abandoned house. Everyone freezes in an instant, all looking to where the sound came from. A person can bleed out from a gunshot wound in minutes and we already spent all of those on the drive over. *Screw it.*

"I'm going in," I say, sprinting toward the house.

"Sheriff, wait! Let my team clear it first," the SWAT commander shouts as I run past him. I can't wait. I took an oath to protect and serve my community, and I'm not going to let someone suffer or die while we formulate the best plan of action. Putting my own life at risk is what I signed up for.

"Damn it! Squad, move out now," I hear the commander yell behind me as I breach the entrance.

My Glock enters the house first, my arms extended out in front of me. A damp cloud of mildew hangs in the air. I flick a switch, but nothing turns on, so I grab my flashlight and click on the beam, panning it across the room. A table is flipped over, and the floor is littered with debris, shattered glass, and toppled chairs. There are dark smears and droplets of what I presume is blood on the furniture and floor. Insects scurry through thick dust, leaving trails behind them.

"This is the police! Is anyone in here?" I call out.

"Help!" a woman screams, but it comes from below me.

I frantically search the house, trying not to trip over any of the objects spread across the rotting floor. Blood splatter stipples cracked drywall that appears to have had something or someone thrown into it. Past a swinging door, I enter a kitchen set at the back of the house. Cockroaches scatter when the beam from my flashlight sweeps across them. At the far end of the room, off to the right, a doorframe ablaze with a yellow glow catches my eye. My boots crunch over broken glass as I move toward the open door. A set of stairs descends into a cellar, and at the bottom of the steps, I can see the pant legs and shoes of someone on the ground. There's commotion from the other end of the house now. Officers enter, calling out, "Clear," as they check each room.

I hear Olson yell my name.

"Marcus."

She never uses my first name on the job . . . so I know she's scared, but I don't answer because my eyes are fixated on the motionless person lying in the cellar.

"Prince William County Sheriff's Office!" I call down.

"Please, you have to help me!" a woman yells back.

I start to descend the stairs, gun drawn in front of me, taking them slowly. They creak beneath my boots, and I notice drops of blood leading all the way down them. Pam is now at my back, but she's quiet. She rests her hand on my shoulder and squeezes once, letting me know she has my six covered. I crouch slightly as I move down the stairs, so I'm able to see beneath the ceiling line into the basement before I reach the bottom of the steps. The first thing I notice is Bob Miller, lying face down on the concrete, his head craned to the side, eyes still open, lifeless. I don't have to check his pulse to know he's already gone. Descending another step and looking to the right, I can see an old, stained mattress, a chain tethered to a support beam, and a pool of dried blood. One more step, and I can finally see the woman a little off to the left, her ankle chained to a pole and her arms outstretched in front of her with a revolver clutched in her hands.

"Ma'am! Put the gun down," I say calmly.

"He killed her, and he was going to kill me too," she cries out.

"I hear you and I believe you, but you have to put the gun down," I say, planting my boots firmly on the concrete floor, so we're in full view of each other. I hold up one hand while the other grips my gun at my side. I don't want her to feel any more in danger than she already does, but if I have to draw up again to protect myself and Pam, I will. Her red hair is matted, going in all directions, and tears streak her face, which is covered in dirt and grime. I recognize her immediately. How could I not? Her photo has hung on the wall of the briefing room for the past week.

Stacy Howard blinks several times like she can't believe her own eyes, as though she's trying to convince herself that I'm real and she truly is safe now. She looks at the gun clasped in her hands, then at the body on the floor, and then back to the gun. The firearm shakes, and with a quick movement, she finally pitches it toward me, sending it skidding across the floor.

I holster my weapon and bend down, placing two fingers on Bob's neck. No pulse, just as I suspected. I glance back at Olson and shake my head, signaling that he's dead.

I move toward Stacy, not too fast. "You're going to be okay now."

She holds her face in her hands, rocking back and forth, trembling, and I don't blame her. From what I can make of this cellar, it's the stuff of nightmares.

"I had to do it. I had to do it," Stacy says, weeping uncontrollably.

49

SHERIFF HUDSON

Stacy Howard is lying in a hospital bed, tucked snugly under the scratchy, sterile sheets. The beeping from the vital monitoring system punctuates a healthy, normal heart rate—hopefully she'll be ready to speak with us now. She's hooked up to an IV, providing her with the fluids and nutrients needed to restore her strength. Other than dehydration and the wounds on her hands and ankle from the chain, she was mostly unharmed. But not all injuries are borne on the body. Doctors also found she had trace amounts of scopolamine in her system, a powerful anticholinergic drug that, if taken in large doses, can render a person unconscious for twenty-four hours or more.

Olson and I take a seat in the guest chairs beside her bed. "Stacy, can you tell us how long you were down in that basement?" I ask.

Her voice is weak, and she strains to talk. "It was hard to tell without any light, but I would guess at least a week, maybe. What day is it?"

"Thursday, June 8," Olson says.

"Were you taken to another location before the basement?" I ask.

"I don't know. Sorry," she says, tears rolling out of her eyes. "I just woke up down there."

"Don't apologize. Every little piece of information you can give us is helpful, and don't worry about the parts you can't remember." Olson reaches out her hand, touching Stacy's.

We know, given the drug that showed up in her blood analysis, she probably won't remember much.

"There was someone else down there with me, not the whole time though. She said her name was Carissa. But . . ." Stacy stops as pain twists her face, a sob threatening to pour out of her. "I think he killed her. She was screaming, calling out my name, begging me for help, but I couldn't. And then . . . then . . . I didn't hear her anymore." Stacy meets Olson's gaze and begins to weep, her shoulders shaking uncontrollably.

Pam brushes away the hair caught in her tears. "Shh, shh, shh, it's okay. You're safe. No one is going to hurt you anymore. You can just rest." Olson looks back at me and shakes her head.

Now isn't the time for questioning, despite how badly we need information in relation to Carissa's whereabouts. But the last thing we want to do is push a tortured woman back into the recesses of the hell she just crawled out of.

Olson and I say our goodbyes and tell Stacy not to worry. We leave the room and continue through the hospital, stopping off at a vending machine area to grab what will surely be a horrendous cup of fifty-cent coffee.

"Forensics came back with the results from the blood on that knife that was dropped off at the station," Olson says as the machine dispenses the hot, brown liquid into a matching brown paper cup.

"That fast?" I ask, shocked at the turnaround.

She nods.

"And?"

"It's pig's blood." She snaps a lid onto the coffee cup and hands it to me. She inserts two more coins and presses a button to start the brewing process again; another cup drops down the chute and falls into place.

"Pig's blood?" I reply, snarling my lip in disbelief.

"I was just as surprised as you are. So, unless what the person wanted to tell us is that the last thing Sarah Morgan did with that knife was butcher a pig, then I think we've got a prankster on our hands."

"What about fingerprints?" I ask.

"Wiped clean."

I sip the coffee. It's scalding and flavorless, just as I predicted. "Why would somebody send us that, and why point it to Sarah?"

"I don't know, but you were right," she says, retrieving her cup and placing a lid on it.

"About what?"

"You said it could be everything or it could be nothing. Turns out it's nothing." She shrugs, bringing the coffee to her lips.

"Speaking of Sarah, someone has to inform her about Bob."

Olson shakes her head. "That's two dead husbands now. I feel bad for her."

"They were in the middle of a separation," I say.

"Still. They have a kid together."

I sigh, feeling sorry for their daughter. She's going to be the one that takes this the hardest. "We should go tell Sarah," I say. As we begin walking toward the exit, something still nags at me. "We know Bob took Stacy, and the motive as to why is pretty clear, given their history. But the part I don't get is, why Carissa?"

"I don't know," Olson says. "It's not like we can ask him anymore."

If Bob did murder Carissa as Stacy indicated, we might never find her body. Right now, we're waiting on forensics to compare the blood found in the basement near the other mattress and all over the abandoned house to the blood found at the salon. If they're a match, then at least we'll know Carissa was down there.

I knock three times on the front door of Sarah's home and take a step back, waiting for her to appear. It's Thursday, just before eight in the morning. The birds are chirping, and the sun is ablaze. Notifying the next of kin that a loved one has passed is the worst part of this job, even if they were a criminal or got what was coming to them. The person receiving the news often has no idea of the scope of their loved one's misdeeds, and instead, they're simply in shock at the news that the person they hold dear is gone forever.

Thirty seconds pass, and no one comes to the door—so I knock again, this time with more vigor.

"Maybe she's not here," Olson says.

"Her car's here." I point to the white Range Rover parked in the driveway before I knock on the door again. I walk along the front of the house, trying to peer into the windows for any signs of movement, but the curtains are all drawn. I return to the door, pounding loudly again.

"Do you think we should go in?"

"I don't know," I say. The number of circumstances that allow us to break down a door and enter someone's private residence is a small list, but someone being in danger of great bodily harm is one of them. Would Bob have done something to his own wife?

A sense of dread starts to slowly build in the pit of my stomach. What if that farmhouse wasn't the only place Bob went last night?

Frantically, I continue pounding on the door and yell, "Sheriff's office. Open up!" My heart rate is accelerating with each passing second, and Olson begins to shake her head, our two minds likely thinking the same thing. I step back and hoist my pant leg up, readying to kick down the heavy wooden door.

A lock clicks.

A dead bolt slides.

The door opens, and on the other side stands Sarah Morgan. Her head is tilted at an angle as she dries her wet hair with a towel. She's dressed in a white waffle robe and a pair of matching slippers. A few droplets of water slither down her neck, disappearing into the material as they're absorbed by it.

Her eyes dart back and forth between the two of us. "Sheriff Hudson. Chief Deputy Olson," she says with a slight nod. "To what do I owe the pleasure?"

50

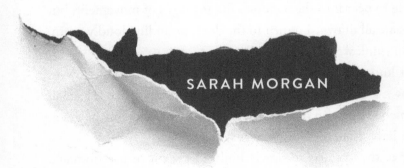

SARAH MORGAN

TEN HOURS EARLIER

The gun pressed into my abdomen isn't as deadly as the gun I have pressed to the side of Alejandro's head. But if he pulled the trigger, I'd most likely die a slow and painful death, while his would be quick, instantaneous. His brain would shut off before it even had time to send signals to the body, letting it know it was in pain.

"No, *I'm* sorry," I say. "Now, tell me who the fuck you really are."

His eyes go wide as they flick to his gun, then in the direction where he knows mine is. Finally, he meets my gaze and sees the grave look on my face—it's a warning: If he makes any movement, I won't hesitate to pull the trigger. He's lucky I haven't already. I could have done it as soon as I answered the door, but I didn't. I wanted him to make the first move . . . or at least *think* he was making the first move. The moment I laid eyes on Alejandro, seated in my conference room, waiting for me to welcome him into the program, I knew he wasn't who he said he was.

"How'd you know?" he asks.

"Bob's never recommended a candidate for the program, not once, and I knew it wasn't because he had some soft spot for you." I narrow my eyes. "And that bullshit background check he compiled didn't check out either, so tell me who you really are." I press the muzzle against the side of his head with a little more force.

He winces and swallows hard, his Adam's apple rocking up and down. I can practically see his brain churning, trying to decide whether he should answer the question or attempt to get the upper hand on me.

"I won't ask you again," I say calmly.

"He hired me to kill you."

"Seriously?" I scoff, disappointed that it wasn't something more clever than him just not wanting to get his hands dirty. "He's such a pussy."

The corner of Alejandro's mouth perks up. He must think the same of my husband. He stays still, waiting for my next move; his hands are calm, unshaking, like this isn't the first time he's been in this position. His gun is still pointed at my abdomen. My gun remains firmly pressed against his temple.

I'm surprised how far Bob was willing to take this. I really didn't think he had it in him. Well, clearly he didn't—because he couldn't do it himself. But I wonder what pushed him over the edge . . . or had he planned this from the very beginning, the moment I told him I was divorcing him? Was his coup de grâce always me being buried in the ground somewhere as he rode off into the sunset with our daughter's hand reluctantly in his?

"When did he hire you?" I ask.

It takes Alejandro a moment to respond, like he's trying to make sure he answers correctly. One wrong move, one lie, and he won't have the chance to answer any more of my questions.

"A few weeks ago."

Called it. He went on the offensive as soon as he knew we were over, but why all the groveling and begging for me to take him back then?

"I was originally hired just to keep an eye on you though," he adds.

"What changed?"

"I don't know exactly. He texted me yesterday, asking to meet this morning. That's when he told me the new arrangement. Said something about having other plans, and how they'd work much better if you were dead."

"What 'other plans'?"

"He didn't say."

I search his eyes, looking for a twitch, something to tell me he's lying. But there's nothing. He's stoic as he stares back at me, his gaze never faltering.

"How long have you and my husband known each other?"

"A long time."

"And has he ever used your services before?"

Alejandro lets out the smallest sigh and says, "Yes."

I remember it was Bob who suggested we hire someone to kill Kelly, but I was against it—because if you want something done right, you do it yourself. He clearly didn't learn anything from me.

"It didn't go as planned though," Alejandro adds. I think he's just offering up information, stalling in hopes that I won't pull the trigger.

"I guess you're oh for two on that." I smirk. "If you fucked up the first time, I'm surprised he'd hire you again."

"Bob never knew how badly it went sideways."

"What do you mean?"

He clenches his jaw. "I'll tell you if you stop pointing that gun at my head."

I respond to his request by driving the muzzle a little deeper into his temple, making him wince. "You're not in a bargaining position. So, you'll tell me, and then maybe, I'll let you live."

Beads of sweat start to form at his hairline. His eyes bounce again from the gun he's holding against my naked body to my face and then to his peripheral view, where my pistol hasn't moved. My pointer finger rests on the trigger with the smallest amount of pressure. A milligram more of added weight would cause the firing pin to strike and the bullet to surge through the barrel, plunging right into his brain. He'd be dead before he even had time to blink. My wall would get a new coat of red paint. And he knows that . . .

"Nearly fifteen years ago, Bob hired me to kill a woman named Jenna Way."

"Well, I know you didn't kill her," I say.

"How?"

"Because I did, twelve years ago, in this very room."

Alejandro's eyes go wide. Maybe it's shock or the realization that I'm more deadly than he is. Then they flicker with something else . . . passion, lust, desire. If I weren't already undressed, he'd be undressing me with those eyes right now.

"Don't act so surprised," I say.

"I'm not. I'm impressed."

"Bob clearly knew you failed at taking out Jenna, so what is it that he doesn't know?"

"He'll kill me if he finds out."

"No, he won't. That's why he hires you." I narrow my eyes. "But I *will* kill you if you don't start talking."

Alejandro sighs heavily, realizing he doesn't have a choice. "I had breached Jenna's house, and I was waiting for her to return home like she did at the same time every night. But she didn't, not that night. She'd apparently gotten a flat tire, which set her back forty-five minutes. Instead, her husband arrived home first—Greg, Bob's brother, earlier than usual too. Thinking it was Jenna, I pulled the trigger the second the front door opened, but the gun jammed. Greg heard it, and he came flying at me. He had seen my face, so I knew what I had to do. He fought hard, but I fought harder. I got the upper hand and plunged a kitchen knife right into his gut. I was going to make it look like a break-in gone wrong but decided I could stage it as a crime of passion instead, so I stabbed him over and over, and then I left the knife in his chest. I wiped down the handle, cleaned up evidence that anyone else had been there, and took off just as Jenna arrived home. He was taking his final breaths, still coughing on his own blood when I slipped out of there. Lucky for me, she panicked and pulled the knife from his chest, thinking she was helping him. But really, she accelerated his death and added evidence that would point to her as the murderer."

I burst out in a manic laugh. "So, Bob killed his own brother?" I can barely get the question out because I find it far too comical.

"In a way, yeah. I told him I hadn't gotten the opportunity to kill

Jenna. So, when he found out his brother was dead, he thought she did it. Plus, all the evidence pointed to her."

"But why'd he hire you to kill her in the first place?"

"Something about Jenna finding out what kind of shady shit he was up to. She threatened to tell the authorities if Bob didn't fess up himself. Apparently, whatever she knew, it was enough to land him in prison, so Bob figured the only way to stop her from talking was to make sure she could never speak again," he says.

I shake my head. "That's pathetic."

"It is." Alejandro nods.

"Out of curiosity, how much did Bob offer to pay you to kill me?"

"Two hundred and fifty K."

"I'll pay you the same not to kill me."

He raises a brow, staring into my eyes, determining whether I'm serious or not. He doesn't really have a choice either way. He goes along with me, or he doesn't go along at all. I'm sure he's wondering why I'd offer him any money to begin with. I could just kill him for free. But that's a far bigger mess than I want to deal with. Plus . . . my eyes skim over his chiseled body; he's probably 220 pounds of solid muscle. And I don't feel like spending my whole night trying to get rid of it.

Alejandro removes the gun from my abdomen and flips it around, extending it to me, handle first. "Deal."

"Wise choice. But I'll need a few other things from you as well."

"Whatever you want," he says with a small smile. "And by the way, Bob had me put a tracker on your car. He's been following your every move for weeks."

It's an olive branch, Alejandro's way of showing that his loyalty has instantly shifted.

"I already know." I smile back as I pull the gun from his temple. It leaves behind a nasty red bruise, the imprint of the muzzle marked on his skin.

We lock eyes, an intensity burning between us. I wrap my hand around his head and jerk him toward me. Our lips and teeth smash against one another as I slide on top of his body, taking the length of him inside of me. This time, I'm going to fuck him.

51

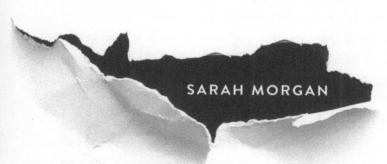

SARAH MORGAN

TEN HOURS AND SIX MINUTES LATER

They just told me my husband is dead. My face is frozen, mouth partially open, eyes wide. Hudson and Olson are seated at the kitchen table, directly across from me. They said it was better if I was sitting before they delivered the news. It's hard to make my face sad for Bob. That asshole was going to kill me—well, hired someone to kill me. If his plan had worked out, he'd be the one sitting here receiving the news from two uniforms. Had he truly learned nothing from me? Too many loose ends, and the only person you can count on is yourself. But then again, Bob doesn't know that, and now, he never will. He'll never know that I'm still alive, and he'll never know that he was the one responsible for his own brother's death. I kind of wish he had learned those things before his untimely death. I bite my tongue to stop myself from laughing again.

"Sarah," Sheriff Hudson says, pulling me from my thoughts.

I blink, making it look like I'm in shock, still reeling from the news. But now it's time to turn on the waterworks. Not too heavy though, as we were going through a divorce, but just enough to show that I cared for him as my husband and as the father of my child. My eyes instantly develop a sheen. A few tears escape, running down my cheeks. My face crumples, not all the way, just enough. And my lip quivers. That's the hardest part to get right. It appears like it's involuntary, a reaction to deep grief—but with practice comes perfection.

Chief Deputy Olson folds her lips in and looks down at her hands. I know it's working because she feels awkward to be witnessing this grief. She doesn't know what to do or what to say. Hudson takes a deep breath, slowly exhaling through his nose. It's working on him too.

"How?" I ask. My voice cracks on the single word.

"We're not exactly sure yet. But we found his body in the basement of an abandoned farmhouse just outside of town. He had been shot twice," Hudson explains.

"By who?"

The two of them exchange a look.

"There was a woman chained to a pole in that basement. She shot Bob, and she claims he kidnapped her and another woman," he says.

My hands fly to my mouth, and I shake my head slightly in mock disbelief. "No, that . . . that can't be true."

"We're still verifying her story, but we do have a few questions for you, if that's okay?" Olson asks.

I nod, removing my hands from my mouth. The tears keep falling intermittently. "Of course. Of course. Anything to help."

She pulls a Kleenex from her pocket, extending it to me. I take it and thank her, dabbing lightly at my eyes. Don't want to dab all the tears away though. They're like camouflage for how I'm really feeling. She retrieves a pad of paper and a pen from the front pocket of her shirt. Flipping it open, Olson presses the tip against the empty page, ready to write down all the lies I'm about to tell.

"Was Bob living here with you?"

"Not for the past month. We're in, I mean, we were in the middle of a separation." I force my lip to quiver again.

"The woman we found chained up in the basement was Stacy Howard," Hudson says. "You remember who she is?"

I nod and push out more tears. "I can't believe it," I lie.

I *can* believe it because I'm the one who put her there. In truth, I really had nothing to do with Bob sleeping with Stacy, as much as he wanted to blame that on me. He fell into her web of deceit and blackmail all on his own. But that mistake landed them both in my web, and there can be only one queen. Stacy's lucky she wasn't a casualty in this war.

"I know it's difficult to wrap your head around," Olson says, attempting to comfort me. "Sometimes you think you know a person, but you never really know everything."

She's right about that.

"Is Stacy sure Bob did this?" I ask. "He couldn't have. I mean, he had his flaws, but this is something else entirely. I just . . . I can't believe it. Is she really sure?" I'm piling it on a bit thick.

This question is more for me than them. I was careful. Extremely careful, ensuring she never saw me, not even a glimpse. After Stacy was unconscious from that chloroform-soaked rag I shoved into her face and that Propofol injection I jabbed in her arm, I hauled her out to the abandoned farmhouse. This was much earlier in the day. I returned to Stacy's place on my way home from work and texted her roommate from her phone, which I had left there. I said she was going to meet up with Bob. This made the time of her disappearance Monday evening rather than Monday afternoon, when she really went missing. Then, I sent a few texts to a contact labeled *Bob Miller*, a number I had stored in her phone that connected to a burner. Even if they ask her about those texts, her memory is so fuzzy she won't remember whether or not she actually sent them.

"She is," Hudson says.

I take a deep breath, in through my nose and out through my mouth, as though I'm having a hard time digesting this information. But really, it's a sigh of relief.

"Stacy reported that another woman in the basement with her was Carissa Brooks," Hudson explains.

My expression is a mix of sadness and shock. I add in a lip quiver. "Was? What do you mean 'was'? Is she okay?"

They exchange another look. "We can't locate her at this time," he says.

And they never will, I think to myself as I conjure up more tears, pushing them out as fast as I can produce them.

"We found blood in the basement where Stacy reported Carissa was chained up, as well as on the stairs and first level of the house. It looks like there was a struggle. Forensics is comparing it to the blood found at the salon to see if it's a match."

It'll be a match. I don't need to wait for forensics on that.

"We talked previously about Carissa Brooks and the legal work you did for her in relation to a protective order she had against her ex, George Carrigan," Hudson says.

I simply nod.

"I know you were sure it had to have been George who was involved in her disappearance, and we were too. But given the circumstances, that's changed. Do you have any idea what kind of relationship Bob and Carissa had?"

"As far as I know, they were friendly. He was a client of hers." Appearing saddened, I shake my head. "I'm the reason they were even introduced in the first place. If I hadn't accepted her as a foundation client, Bob would have never met her and maybe she'd be . . ." I trail off, overcome with contemplation and anguish.

"You can't blame yourself for that." Olson delivers a sympathetic look.

"How can I not?"

"So, Bob became a client of Carissa's after you represented her?" Hudson asks, trying to steer the conversation back to the facts.

"Yeah, I thought he switched salons to help her out and to keep a close eye on her, given her situation—or at least that's how he framed it."

"This is a difficult question to ask, but do you think Carissa and Bob might have been having an affair?" Sheriff Hudson pulls his chin in.

I force more tears out because that seems cry-worthy, the thought of my husband cheating on me with more than one woman. "I don't know," I say. "Months ago, I would have said no, but now . . ."

I do know, actually, and the answer *is* no.

"Do you think Carissa is okay?" I add.

"Given the amount of blood found at the salon and in the abandoned house, it doesn't look good—I mean, if they're a match. But we are hopeful we'll find her regardless," Hudson says.

I lower my head and sniffle. "I hope so too."

They won't find her though. She's long gone. Carissa came to me seven weeks ago, asking for my help. She had heard her ex was up for early release, and she knew he'd come around again. The protective order she had against him was almost up. I told her we could get it extended, but she said it wasn't enough. She said he would kill her this time, and a stupid piece of paper wasn't going to stop him. She said the only way he'd ever let her go was if she were dead, and she basically felt like she already was. She said she couldn't live this way anymore, always in fear, looking over her shoulder every other second, scared of what was around every corner. She begged for my help, begged me to help her escape, to get away from him for good. And I agreed, as long as she did exactly as she was told. If she did, she'd be free of him forever.

I gave her the supplies to start drawing her own blood and told her how to properly store it. One pint every ten days so she'd collect nearly five pints, enough for the police to determine she was dead without a body. I told her what vitamins to take to lessen her blood loss symptoms: iron, B12, folic acid, and a few others. She'd be weak during this process, disoriented too—but she'd live, and she'd finally be free of her ex for good.

I didn't tell Bob what I was doing, and when I found out he had cheated on me, I was glad I hadn't told him. Because he'd now be an unknowing participant in freeing Carissa. I informed her of the slight change of plans nearly four weeks ago. I picked the day she would disappear. Conveniently, it fell on a day Bob had his standing appointment, every third Sunday like clockwork. I instructed her to accidentally nick the last customer. She asked why. I told her not to ask any questions and to speak to no one about any of this because there was a reason for everything. Unbeknownst to her, my reason was just to set up Bob. I'm sure she must have thought he was in on it too since he was my husband.

After her last customer left for the day, I told her to dye and cut her hair, get rid of all evidence of her new hairstyle, and remove her piercings. Then she was to stage the salon to make it look like it had been ransacked. Three of the five pints of blood she drew from her own body were to be spread throughout the salon—a pool near a tipped-over chair, smears and droplets here and there, and then a trail leading to the back of the salon. I've seen many crime scenes throughout my work as a lawyer, so I knew exactly how to make one look real, and I made sure Carissa knew it too.

While she was taking care of the physical evidence that was needed for this plan to work, I was setting her up with a new identity—because once it all went down, she couldn't be Carissa anymore. There was a car waiting for her in the back of the lot, keys tucked in the visor, and a bag sitting on the passenger seat filled with extra clothes, cash, a wig, and a baseball cap to help her travel in disguise, at least until she was out of the state. Then, inside a purse were her new documents: passport, driver's license, Social Security card, a credit card opened in her new name, and a plane ticket leaving the next morning out of Atlanta, headed for Ecuador. All she had to do was drive.

"There was another thing," Hudson says, squinting. "Stacy stated Carissa told her she had overheard Bob—or at least someone that sounded like him—when she was first abducted. Allegedly, he was talking about you, about how he wasn't going to let you get away with it and that he'd take you down first. Do you have any idea what he would mean by that? Specifically, the part about getting away with it?"

It's strange having someone recite the words I said back to me and attribute them to someone else. Carissa was never in that basement. I was. I fed Stacy everything I needed her to know, and everything I needed her to relay to the police when they inevitably found her. It was easy to slip in and out of that basement. I'd go to work and take one of the foundation's many vehicles out to Stacy. If I couldn't find a way to visit her during the day, I'd do so late at night but not before taking Bob's stupid tracker off my vehicle. Then, upon arrival, I'd throw on a pair of men's steel-toed work boots, stomp around above her, and toss down a sandwich and a bottle of water—both of which were drugged with scopolamine, or as the kids call it, "Devil's Breath." The drugs could have a very long-lasting effect, depending on the dosage, so I'd stop back when I knew they were wearing off, and I'd slip in through the cellar door at the far end of the basement, hidden in a storage room. Another drink and sandwich would be delivered, and then, I'd position myself twenty or so feet from Stacy, waiting for her to wake up. Whenever Stacy didn't hear Carissa, she just assumed Carissa was passed out. Stacy was easy to manipulate because she was drugged nearly the entire time.

Even the night I made it seem like Bob killed Carissa was easier than I thought it'd be. On that evening, it was just me up there, causing a ruckus. Screaming and flailing, breaking and smashing things, crying out for Stacy's help. Then I slid on those work boots and dragged a sleeping bag full of bricks out of that house. It was all very convincing. I made sure to use the rest of Carissa's blood to stage the scene before I fake killed her. There was a puddle where she was chained up, more on the mattress, then droplets up the staircase and throughout the house with smears and splatters on the floors and walls.

"Sarah," Hudson says.

"Bob didn't take the news of our separation well," I say, lowering my head and shaking it slightly, giving myself time to create more tears to go along with these lies. I lift my head and stare back at the sheriff. "He changed for the worse after I filed for divorce, becoming abusive and rather unhinged. I had never seen him act like that. He even threatened my life . . . more than once, and I was terrified for my own safety and for my daughter's, so I filed a protective order against him—well, my divorce attorney did. Bob went even more ballistic after he found out. So, no, I don't know exactly what he meant by that, because he had become a person I didn't even recognize anymore. All I do know is he was dead set on getting full custody of Summer," I say, planting the seed, waiting for it to grow in their heads.

Olson raises a brow. "Do you think Bob would try to frame you for a crime in order to get full custody?"

There it is . . . the seed, cultivating in her mind. Thank you, Chief Deputy Olson, for nurturing it, giving it the sustenance it needs to grow.

"I would hope not, but I really don't know."

I can't come on too strong with that theory of mine because it's theirs now, or at least they think it is. Such clever cops.

There are a few beats of silence before Hudson rises from his chair. I've given them enough. Now, they've got to make sure all these pieces fit together into a narrative they can sell to the public, the media, and the justice system. I know it all will go together perfectly, and it will tell an unbelievable story everyone will eventually come to believe. After all, truth is stranger than fiction, or at least that's what people will say when they hear it.

"Well, we'll get out of your hair now, Sarah. I'm very sorry for your loss," Hudson says with a nod. "We'll be in touch with any further questions."

Olson pockets her notepad and gets to her feet too, echoing the sheriff's sentiment.

"Thanks," I say, standing from my chair.

"Also," Hudson adds, "we'll be executing a search warrant for Bob's apartment in the city as well as his office at the firm, and hopefully, that will help us better understand everything."

I say, "Okay," and walk them to the front door.

That's good police work. They'll find the knife I stashed in Bob's safe, hidden in the wall, behind a piece of gaudy artwork. It'll have Kelly's blood on the blade and Bob's fingerprints on the handle. I remember the night I gave it to him. He held it in his hands, admiring the blood-streaked blade. Then I asked him to get rid of it and told him to get a rag so he could wipe down the handle. He left the room, and I switched them out—replacing the real murder weapon with one covered in pig's blood. I knew he would keep it. I could see it in his eyes. He loved me, but he was terrified of me too, and rightfully so. Bob needed something that could protect himself in the future, just in case he ever ended up on my bad side. It was a test, and he failed it miserably.

"Please let me know if I can be of any help," I say as they step onto the porch.

"We will, and again, I'm very sorry." Sheriff Hudson nods and the two of them head to their vehicle.

Closing the door, I smile so wide, it feels like my top lip has split. There will be more questions. More inquiries. An array of theories as to what really happened. Some will even speculate that I had something to do with it. But all the evidence will point to Bob and only Bob. Tears spring to my eyes . . . but this time, they're real.

52

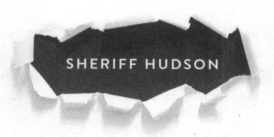

SHERIFF HUDSON

I throw the report down on my desk. "It was Bob," I say to Olson, who sits across from me. "Fingerprints on the knife found in his safe match his, and the blood is a match to Kelly Summers."

"Wow, that's . . . incredible." She picks up the report, reading it over.

"I guess that solves that case."

"It sure is convenient." Olson shakes her head, still flipping through the report.

"It is, isn't it?" I say, moving my mouth side to side. "Bob winds up dead, killed by the woman he kidnapped, and when we search his apartment, the murder weapon in the Kelly Summers case, after all these years, was in his safe, like it had a bow tied around it." I bump my fist against my knee a few times softly, a reflexive habit I have when thinking.

Sometimes evidence in a case is convenient because . . . well, that's what evidence does; it helps solve a crime, tells the story of what really happened. But it isn't usually just gift wrapped in a place we would have never thought to look.

"And the other pool of blood in the basement?" she asks.

"It's a match to the blood found at the salon, so we can assume it was Carissa's."

"Wow" is all Olson can say.

"Forensics said they estimated that between the two scenes, there were approximately five pints of it."

"So, we can presume Carissa Brooks is dead?"

I nod and let out a deep sigh.

"Do you really think Bob did this all alone?"

"What do you mean?" I ask.

"Well, Bob and Sarah married shortly after Adam was executed. And you're telling me Bob framed Adam for murder and then went off and married Sarah." She cocks her head and tosses the report on my desk.

"But Sarah didn't know any of that yet."

"Or did she?"

I stand from the desk and pace my office. Why though? Why would Sarah marry and have a child with the man who framed her husband for murder? Unless, of course, she was in on it. Adam was having an affair with Kelly Summers. But Bob turned out to be worse than Adam. He cheated and then abducted his mistress and Carissa in order to frame Sarah. Maybe it wasn't about their daughter, Summer, after all. Maybe it was about him ensuring he wouldn't go down for Kelly's murder.

I squint and look to Olson. "It just seems too far-fetched. Sarah and Bob kill her first husband's mistress and frame her husband for it? They never get caught, and they just start a life together living happily ever after until they decide to turn on each other? I feel like that leaves a lot of things to chance, especially framing Adam."

"Not if you're also the husband's defense attorney," Olson quips, crossing her arms in front of her chest.

That is true. It was such an unusual circumstance. But I was in that courtroom every day. Sarah did a phenomenal job. It was some of the best work I've ever seen by a defense attorney.

"I think we're stretching a bit far here. What's more likely? That Sarah worked with Bob to cook up some evil genius master plan spanning over a decade, or that Bob was just a sick individual that used Sarah?"

Olson shrugs, still not convinced.

"Plus . . ." I sit back down in my chair. "Even if your theory was true, we've got no evidence tying Sarah to this case, not a single shred."

"Except that knife that showed up on our doorstep."

"Except that."

"And it looked identical to the real knife." Olson leans forward to punctuate her point.

"That *was* bizarre, but that's all it is right now. Bizarre. Bob was most likely behind that though, and he would know what the real knife used in the murder looked like. It was probably another scheme of his to frame Sarah."

We sit in silence for a few minutes before I check my watch, noting the time. "I've gotta go fill the press in on everything. They're going to have a field day with this."

"What about Scott Summers?"

"What about him?"

"He's a murderer on the loose. We can't just do nothing."

"Olson, you already know the feds took it over, so it's not BCI's case anymore, and it's not ours either."

She shakes her head. "I just wish we could do something more to help."

"I do too, but my hands are tied. And look at what we just did. We solved three cases."

She sighs. "I know, but Scott's still out there."

"If it makes you feel any better, I don't think Scott's a danger to society, not unless he thinks there's another person involved with his wife's death."

"It doesn't, but I'll leave you to it so you can write up your statement for the press." Olson stands and walks to the door.

"Chief Deputy Olson," I call out.

She glances over her shoulder at me. "Yeah?"

"I love you."

A smile cracks across her face. "I love you too," she says, leaving my office.

I turn to my computer and start typing, "Good evening, everyone. They say truth is stranger than fiction, and if you didn't believe that phrase before, you'll believe it by the time I'm done explaining how the events occurring over the past week and a half connect to a murder that happened more than twelve years ago."

53

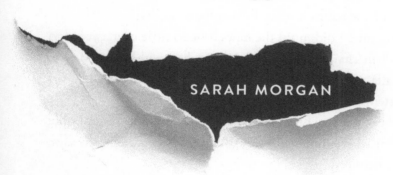

SARAH MORGAN

ONE YEAR LATER

I'm seated across from Caroline Wood of *60 Minutes* on a cozy set that resembles a sitting area one would have in their own home. She's an elegant woman, fifteen years my senior, dressed in a pair of expensive slacks, a silk blouse, and a smart blazer. Her hair is a shiny gray, stopping right at her shoulders in a perfectly cut bob. She looks down at her note cards, reviewing them before the cameras start rolling. I know there's a teleprompter set up for her behind me, but she's old-school, and she likes the feel of paper in her hands.

A young woman readjusts my hair so it falls symmetrically to either side of my chest. She powders my face and delivers a soft smile before scurrying behind the crew.

A man yells out, "Quiet on set," and then asks us if we're ready. Caroline and I nod.

She offers a tight smile. It disappears just as quick as she readies herself to begin. I don't hear the introduction for my interview, as it was previously recorded—but I know what was said, and I know how I'll be introduced. This is the first interview I've agreed to. I've had dozens of offers, many attached to large amounts of cash. But I don't need or want the money. I just want to tell a story.

"Did you always believe your husband Adam Morgan was innocent?" she asks, getting right into it.

"No, I *knew* he was, which is why I chose to stand by his side as his wife and as his lawyer."

"Did you blame yourself when he was found guilty?"

"For a long time I did, until the news broke a little over a year ago that the sheriff in charge of the investigation had withheld evidence, including an affair he had been having with the victim. Then, I blamed the justice system."

"It must have been awful to learn that your husband was not only wrongfully accused of murder, but was also wrongly executed," she says, slightly tilting her head.

I take a short, deep breath. "It was devastating. Adam was the love of my life, and the commonwealth of Virginia murdered him right in front of my eyes."

She pauses for a moment, allowing me the time to gather myself. There's nothing to gather though.

"Tell me about Robert Miller," Caroline says.

"Bob?" I correct. Robert was too distinguished of a name for him. "He wasn't who I thought he was."

"But you married him. He was your second husband."

"Unfortunately," I say.

"Did you ever suspect that Bob murdered Kelly Summers and then framed Adam for his crime?"

It's a stupid question, but I answer it anyway.

"No, not even in the slightest."

"And how do you think he got away with it?" she asks.

"He didn't."

"But he did for a long time. How do you think that was possible?" She maintains eye contact with me, rarely blinking. It's unnerving, but I mirror her.

"The Prince William County Sheriff's Office made that possible. They were essentially an accomplice to Bob's crimes," I say, lifting my chin.

"What about you, Sarah? How was he able to get so close to you?"

I clear my throat before I speak. "I was vulnerable, and he knew that. I lost my husband the day he was found guilty and put on death row. The world thought he was a monster, so I wasn't able to even grieve him properly. It's a horrible feeling to lose someone and for no one else to care because they don't deem it as a loss. Bob took advantage of my grief and my vulnerability. The whole situation was beyond complicated for me to process. But Bob was there when no one else was, and that made it easy for him to get close to me."

"Do you regret marrying him?"

I shake my head. "No, he gave me two things I wouldn't have had otherwise. My daughter, Summer, and closure."

"What do you mean by 'closure'?"

"I know what really happened to Kelly Summers now, and the world does too. If I hadn't married Bob, I'm not sure I would have ever discovered the truth," I say with a bit of conviction.

"How has all of this affected your daughter?"

"Her grief is complicated, like mine was with Adam when the world thought he was a monster. She understands her father's actions were immoral, vile, and unforgivable, but he was still her dad. It's been really hard for her, but she's doing much better now."

I did feel awful telling Summer what had happened to her father and what he had done. It took her a while to wrap her head around it. She didn't believe it—for good reason, because it wasn't true. But eventually, she came to terms with the narrative. We're much better off now, just like I knew we would be. And she's taken a liking to Alejandro too. He's nice to have around; my relationship with him isn't anything serious, mostly just sex. Plus, he's a little bit of a loose end, and the only way to ensure loose ends don't unravel is to keep them close. And I say *little* because who would ever believe the word of a felon? I mean, a person with felon status. Alejandro and I both have skeletons in our closets, and we know exactly who they are.

"Do you think you were a part of Bob's master plan or merely a bonus?"

"I don't know what I was to him, and I don't care to know."

"Understandable," she says with a nod. "Adam's mother, Eleanor Rumple, passed away before the conviction of her son was overturned. How do you think she would have felt had she been alive to see her son's name finally cleared?"

"She would have been thrilled, and it's a tragedy she didn't get to witness that."

"It certainly is," Caroline says. "A federal jury in Virginia awarded you thirty-two million dollars for the wrongful conviction and execution of your husband Adam Morgan. Are you happy with that settlement?"

"Not really. How could that make me happy? It doesn't undo what they did. It doesn't bring Adam back."

She pulls her lips in and nods before moving on with the interview. "Do you have any plans for the money?"

It's an insensitive question, but people want to know.

"A portion of it will be set aside in a trust for Summer. I plan to reinvest the rest of it into the Morgan Foundation, intending to use the funds to continue to provide pro bono legal work to those who can't afford it, as well as expand our Second Chance program, which helps previously incarcerated individuals reenter society in a positive and productive manner."

"That's very admirable, Sarah. Most people would take a vacation or retire early."

"I'm not most people."

She tightly smiles. "No, you are not. You have an incredible story, one that many have called stranger than fiction. You've lost so much, endured more than most could ever imagine, and yet you continue to persevere. You've made it your life's mission to help others, despite the fact that there was no one there to help you and your husband Adam when you needed it. Do you feel any sort of resentment?"

"I'd be lying if I said no."

"Then how is it you choose to lead with generosity and compassion?"

It's the last question. I know this because I had them sent over beforehand so I could prepare my answers. This one I practiced more than all the others to ensure I hit the right tone and message. It's short and sweet, rather ridiculous too. But America will eat it up. Good versus evil is mankind's oldest fight. It's clichéd and overly simplified because people aren't inherently good or evil. They're a little of both, maybe more of one than the other, but that's too complicated for most to digest. So, I'll give them simple. The light on set brightens just a little before I answer. How poetic.

"I don't have a choice, Caroline. It's just who I am," I say with a soft, angelic smile.

ACKNOWLEDGMENTS

Greetings! Some of you are here because you're curious as to who I'll be acknowledging. Most of you are here because you're looking for the deep, dark secret I promised you in my previous acknowledgments. And the vast majority of you aren't here at all because you stopped reading when the book ended. That is a mistake because I will in fact be sharing a deep, dark secret within this text . . . so keep reading.

Back in 2017, when I was drafting what would later become *The ~~Perfect~~ Marriage*, I never in a million years thought I would be writing the acknowledgments for its sequel one day. But here I am, and it's all because of my readers, so that's who I want to thank first and foremost. I get to do what I love for a living because of all of you. That is truly a gift, and it's the best one I've ever received. So, thank you! Special shout-out to my gaggle of silly geese, a.k.a. the members of my Facebook reader group, "Jeneva Rose's Convention of Readers," a.k.a. the people I dedicated this book to. Thank you for being a part of my flock and a positive little spot on the internet.

Every time I write a book, I have a select few people read an early draft to give me constructive criticism and, most importantly, compliments and praise. It's a delicate balance because sometimes I have the skin of a rhino and other times it's more like a moth's wing. Thank you to Cristina Montero, Bri Becker, and Delaney Starr for reading an early draft of *The ~~Perfect~~ Divorce.*

Thank you to April Gooding for doing what you always do. You made this book so much better.

Thank you to the team at Blackstone Publishing for championing my work. Special shout-out to Sarah Riedlinger and Stephanie Stanton for the beautiful cover and interior design; John Lawton for making sure my books are in stores; Kathryn Zentgraf and Josie Woodbridge for editorial; Tatiana Radujkovic, Rachel Sanders, and Kathleen Carter for PR and marketing; and Stephanie Koven for wheeling and dealing around the world.

Thank you to all the people who make the book world a better place. I'm looking at you, librarians, booksellers, booktokers, bookstagrammers, bloggers, and teachers.

Thank you to my husband, Drew, for your endless support, constantly pushing me to be the best writer I can be, and for not freaking out when you read an early draft of this. I promise this is fiction . . . mostly.

Now, for a deep, dark secret since I know you're skimming through here looking for it. It's not a juicy one. It's not even dark. It's barely a secret. But if you ever see this punctuation mark → : in my novels, I'll tell you right now, I didn't put it there, and that's because I don't know how to use it. Where does it go:? What: is its purpose? Whew! Felt good to get that off my chest. That's all from me. Apologies that my deep, dark secret lacks depth and darkness and secrecy. I'll have a real one for you in my next set of acknowledgments. So, stay tuned.

Oh, wait, here's a little secret: Sarah Morgan's story isn't over yet.

Xoxo:

: Jeneva : Rose :